Elegies
for the
Brokenhearted

Elegies

for the

Brokenhearted

A NOVEL

Christie Hodgen

W. W. NORTON & COMPANY

NEW YORK · LONDON

For information about permission to reproduce selections from this book,
write to Permissions, W. W. Norton & Company, Inc.,
500 Fifth Avenue, New York, NY 10110

For information about special discounts for bulk purchases, please contact
W. W. Norton Special Sales at specialsales@wwnorton.com or 800-233-4830

Manufacturing by Courier Westford
Book design by Chris Welch Design
Production manager: Anna Oler

Library of Congress Cataloging-in-Publication Data

Hodgen, Christie, 1974–
Elegies for the brokenhearted : a novel / Christie Hodgen. — 1st ed.
p. cm.
ISBN 978-0-393-06140-6 (hardcover)
I. Title.
PS3608.O47E54 2010
813'.6—dc22

2010011149

W. W. Norton & Company, Inc.
500 Fifth Avenue, New York, N.Y. 10110
www.wwnorton.com

W. W. Norton & Company Ltd.
Castle House, 75/76 Wells Street, London W1T 3QT

1 2 3 4 5 6 7 8 9 0

for my family

&

for Michael,

who works in pessimism . . .

"In fact, the conviction that the world and man is something
that had better not have been, is of a kind to fill us with
indulgence towards one another. Nay, from this point of
view, we might well consider the proper form of address to
be, not *Monsieur, Sir, mein Herr,* but *my fellow sufferer, Socî
malorum, compagnon de misères.* This may perhaps sound
strange, but it is in keeping with the facts; it puts others in
a right light; and it reminds us of that which is after all the
most necessary thing in life—the tolerance, patience, regard,
and love of neighbor, of which everyone stands in need, and
which, therefore, every man owes to his fellow."

—Arthur Schopenhauer

Elegies

for the

Brokenhearted

Elegy for

Mike Beaudry

(1952–1989)

Every family had one and you were ours: the chump, the slouch, the drunk, the bum, the forever-newly-employed (garbageman, fry cook, orderly, delivery truck driver) and the forever-newly-unemployed (*I didn't need that shit,* you'd say), the chain-smoking fuckup with the muscle car, an acorn-brown 442 Cutlass Supreme named Michelle, the love of your life (*Let's see what this baby can do,* you'd say, all six of us cousins piled in the back, and how we screamed when you rolled down the windows and *put Michelle's pedal to the metal* on Route 20, how we flew past those strip joints, those 24-hour diners, those squalid motels and scrap metal yards, behind which, in a sunken valley, our neighborhood of two-bedroom cinder-block houses sulked and cowered), the bachelor uncle with the bloodshot eyes and five-day beard come late to holiday dinners, rumpled shirt and jeans, breath like gasoline—Michael Timothy Beaudry, for a time you were ours.

The seventies: Nixon and Carter, culture and counterculture, two roads diverged in a wood. You were twenty, then twenty-five, then thirty, and all that time it always seemed you were fresh out of boyhood, it seemed your proper life—as a schoolteacher or a fireman, as a husband and father, as an upstanding, tax-paying citizen—would begin directly. Although, what was the point? You had a bad heart, a weak valve that threatened to kill you at any moment, as it had your mother when you were only three. Off-limits to you was a host of activities (including, conveniently, service in the armed forces) and you made a sport of engaging in them in front of your sisters. With their hands on their hips they watched you chase us around the backyard, toss us high in the air and catch us, watched you play football with their husbands and boyfriends, watched you drink and smoke and smoke and drink. All that was wrong with you they blamed on your heart. Your drinking, your drugs, your debts and your gambling, your sleeping around (the way you'd take a girl out for a week or so, fuck her in Michelle's backseat and then break her heart . . . You'd get yours, though, your sisters always told you, one of these days a girl would get to you and the grief of losing her would kill you, just you wait, they said, those three long-haired witches, those bitches, and how they were right), the way you could never keep an apartment for long, how you always came knocking at ungodly hours, standing on the front steps with your whole life stuffed in a duffel bag, how you went in an endless circle between Lily, Ellen, Margaret, from couch to couch to couch—all of this they blamed on that weak valve. "His heart, his heart, his heart!" they said, meaning much more than that, meaning you might have been better in ten thousand ways, meaning, if only.

In later years, though, after you'd left home for good without word of your whereabouts, your sisters spent their holidays sitting on those Mike-grooved couches, eating their slices of pie, drinking their coffee, smoking their Virginia Slims, reading aloud to each other their horoscopes from the newspaper just as they had done every night at the dinner table as kids— Pisces, Aries, Cancer, and then, for the hell of it, your Capricorn (TODAY YOU MAY WANT TO TAKE SOME TIME AWAY FROM YOUR BUSY WORK SCHEDULE TO SPEND WITH YOUR FAMILY!)—in later years on every one of those dreary holiday afternoons they sat turning you over in their minds, they craned their heads toward the window whenever a car passed, and they decided they weren't quite sure it was your heart, after all, that had ruined you, decided you would have turned out the same regardless, in those days they often said: "It's not like there's blood between us."

What was blood? Your father, Michael Beaudry Sr., widower, had married my grandmother, Virginia Mayhew née Beauvier, a widow with three girls, husband dead of cancer, and everyone had simply become, on legal documents and in restaurants, "the Beaudrys, party of six." After that awkward first year— silence in the car, silence at the dinner table—things changed and it was difficult to remember what life had been like before. You became family. Your room simply became "Michael's room," not "the room Michael stole from Lily when his father married our mother, and now we have to sleep three in a room while he, a prince, has a room to himself." Soon enough you were a typical brother, someone who ate more than his fair share of the mashed potatoes, someone who was allowed to wander around downtown afternoons unsupervised, someone who did not have to come home and put supper on, someone whose occasional chores (raking, putting out the trash) were a far cry from the day-in, day-out bitch of keeping up the household. Like any brother you were not regarded by your sisters as an official member of the opposite sex. They did not care if you saw them with their hair in curlers, with toothpaste dabbed on their pimples. They did not care if you listened to their conversations about Dave Duncan and Jess Landry and Mike Murphy, the boys they loved. You were subjected to the kinds of abuse and bribery carried out exclusively on brothers. In the afternoons your sisters stole your record player and installed it in their bedroom, took your favorite singers (how you loved to sing! James Brown, Otis Redding, the Rolling Stones) off the turntable and replaced them with Elvis, Bobby Darin, Doris Day. In the evenings when you opened your bedroom window to smoke a cigarette they ratted you out—Mom! Michael's smoking again!—or came barging into your room demanding to be given a cigarette, too.

This had been my mother's tact. She was your age. You were the babies of the family, born two months apart, in the same grade at school and in many of the same classes. You copied her homework, slightly altered the wording of her book reports and turned them in as your own. She borrowed money from you (Saturday mornings you worked at a butcher shop, packing) but failed to return it. In your bedroom, the two of you stood shoulder to shoulder, blowing smoke out the window into the frigid New England air. Your window looked out on a high hill, atop which sat the state's mental hospital, a neo-Gothic castle, teeming with turrets and crockets, with a spooky clock tower at its center whose tolling woke you hourly from sleep, and you waited, you and my mother, to be freed, just like the madmen you imagined were staring back at you, you waited and waited and spoke of nothing but escape. My mother thought of California, you of New York. The minute you graduated high school you would be gone. A duffel bag, a bus, a highway. *Gone.* The two of you standing there surveying that dark neighborhood of narrow, close-built houses, the two of you standing there talking of escape, your breath fogging and mingling, the two of you standing there hatching plans that would fail and fail and fail—wasn't this blood?

You were an uncle to us—each of your sisters with two kids apiece, all girls. You were well-schooled in the standard avuncular maneuvers: the tickling of ribs, the artful belch, the plucking of noses from faces, the revolting turning inside-out of eyelids. Every Labor Day you drove us up to Hampton Beach and swung us around in the surf (*washing machine,* you called it), bought us ice cream and T-shirts (oh, the smell of that shop, those iron-on transfers, plastic melting onto cotton). You had the most T-shirts of anyone I ever knew, shirts featuring the faces of John Lennon and Jimi Hendrix, one featuring Mick

Jagger's lascivious tongue. Over the years all of those shirts grew leprous, peeled away until it was no longer possible to tell what they had once been, unless you had known from the start, unless you had been there to see things fall apart little by little, day by day, unless you were family.

Once, because someone must have thought such things made for happy childhoods, you dressed as Santa on Christmas Eve. Which house was it that year? All those houses and apartments, all those divorces and foreclosures and second marriages, all those exes and steps, I can't remember. In any case you made an entrance, kicked open the front door: *Ho, ho!* you said, and you stood for a moment shaking your belly like a goddamned bowlful of jelly. *Sorry to use the door but the chimney was on the fritz!* You spoke in the booming sneer of W. C. Fields. This was how you imagined Santa would talk, a man beleaguered by his duties, a man sick-up-to-here with kids and with no refuge but sarcasm.

Someone, one of my aunt's husbands or boyfriends, asked you, "How's it going, Santa?" and what Santa said, what you said, was: *I'm fucking busy and vice versa.*

After a few beers you settled on the couch, pulled each one of us onto your knee. *Tell Santa what you want,* you said. You were a poor choice for the role, young and trim, drunk and stoned, and we were not fooled. Your black hair curled out from underneath your cap, your suit was too short in the sleeve and leg, the muddied cuffs of your jeans stuck out. Your gray eyes, your sweeping black eyebrows, the famous bump on your nose from the time you drunkenly walked into a sliding glass door, all of these features were unmistakably yours. Not to mention your voice. When you were only five a virus had scarred your vocal cords and ever after you'd spoken in the voice of a person gone hoarse from coughing, a voice wheezy and forced, ever after you'd sounded like a football coach making desperate pleas from the sideline, and there was no mistaking it. No, we were not fooled, not for a moment did we fail to recognize you. Nonetheless my sister and our cousins sat on your knee naming their hearts' desires. When it was my turn I only pulled at your beard, which was made of cotton balls and secured to your head with elastic, which could be pulled forward and snapped back in place, again and again.

And what would you like, Little Mary Murphy? you said. I said nothing, just looked at you. *Nothing?* you said. *Howsabout one of those diamonds your sister wants?* I pulled at your beard, pulled it right off your face. You grabbed my jaw, brought my face right up to yours. *Be a doll,* you said in your regular voice, *and get Santa a beer.*

By the time you left you were lit, as it were, like the Christmas tree. *Ho, ho!* you said. *Ho fucking ho!* Like Nixon you gave us a sweeping two-armed wave, then out you went stumbling into the snow. No one thought to stop you. We were a family of bad citizens. Drunk drivers and tax evaders, people who parked in handicapped spaces and failed to return shopping carts to their collection stands. In traffic jams we sped up the breakdown lane, then weaseled our way out of tickets by crying. For special occasions we bought new clothes and wore them with the tags tucked in, then returned them to Filene's Basement. We wrote bad checks and faked our ages for discount admission to movies, we ate from other people's plates. And so it was, silent night, holy night, out you went stumbling through the snow.

Wasn't this blood? You were more blood to us than our own fathers. All six of us cousins had fathers who had run off, these two words said so often together they became one: runoff, runoff, runoff. All six of us—Ginny and Little Ellen belonging to Lily; Carrie and Little Lily belonging to Ellen; Malinda and me belonging to Margaret—had fathers and stepfathers and second stepfathers, the beautiful Beaudry girls having, it was widely known, a penchant for marriage and an even greater penchant for divorce, the beautiful Beaudry girls being, it was said, difficult to live without but impossible, in the end, to live with. My mother was the favorite and worst of them, with five husbands. Malinda and I were born of her two-year marriage to Michael Murphy, high school sweetheart and union plumber, Sagittarius, blackout alcoholic. Next she married another Michael, the Devoted and Long-suffering Michael Collins, high school history teacher and model-ship enthusiast, Libra. Her third marriage, to a large-appliance salesman named Bud Francis, Cancer, lasted eight months and was sometimes forgotten about altogether. Her fourth marriage, to the mechanic Walter Adams, Libra, twenty years her senior and black (how fiercely this word was whispered amongst our family: BLACK! BLACK! BLACK!), produced one child, Felice Shirley Adams, who lived, blue and squirming, for less than a day. Finally she married the Reverend Les Witherspoon, a preacher she'd seen on cable television raging about the end of the world, a Scorpio if she'd ever seen one. Later in life I would try to explain these things to boyfriends, the Who's Who of the Beaudry/Murphys, all of those exes and steps and halves, those firsts and seconds and thirds, those relations once and twice removed, but no one could keep up. "How many Mikes are we talking about here?" said one. "Four? Five? It's like Faulkner threw up."

October 1980, a chill in the air, and we'd just moved—my mother, Malinda and me—out of Michael Collins's middle-class house and into the first-floor apartment of a brick fourplex. I was eight, Malinda ten. We were still young enough to go along with what our mother told us: that our new apartment was a palace, a coveted slice of real estate in a fashionable neighborhood, that things were looking up, that we couldn't help but be happy here, that soon Michael Collins would hardly miss us and that we would hardly miss him, that we had been family for a time, true, but not the kind of family that lasted forever, not blood.

Narrow but long, with glossy hardwood floors, the new apartment had the feel of a bowling alley. There we were, Malinda and me, running through the living room and kitchen and then launching ourselves down the long hallway toward the bedrooms, sliding in our socks, this was what we were doing when you came knocking. We raced each other to the door— who could it be?—and found you standing there, returned to us like a biblical character. "What a surprise!" we said. But of course it wasn't, of course we were always waiting for you.

Guess who died? you said, and stepped inside. This was your favorite game. When you showed up after a long absence this was how we caught up, saying *guess who, guess who, guess who,* like it was some kind of game show: *Guess who moved away? Guess who got married or divorced, fired or promoted, arrested, hospitalized, deported? Guess who disappeared without a trace? Guess who got can-*

cer? Guess who got knocked up? Guess who's dating a Puerto Rican? Guess who's gay?

"Who?" said my mother. She called from the kitchen where she'd been sitting at the table (in that apartment we were making do with a card table and folding chairs, with mattresses on the floor, with a thirteen-inch black-and-white television, also on the floor, with a plaid sleeper sofa we'd seen on somebody's lawn with a sign pinned to it: TAKE ME SOMEBODY PLEASE), all morning making circles in the classifieds with a green pen. "Who died?"

Sal Didonna, you said. *Cancer.*

"Jesus," said my mother. "What kind?"

I dunno, you said. *Just cancer.* You collapsed on the couch, sighed. We sat on either side of you, Malinda and me, and you put your arms around us. You stank of tequila.

"Guess who's Jewish now?" said my mother. "Julie Smith. Married a Jew."

Guess who's driving a cab at night? you said. *That midget used to live down the street, whatsisname.*

"Midgy?" said my mother.

That's right, Midgy, you said. *Midgy Laruso.*

"Guess who walked out on her husband?" my mother said, appearing from the kitchen. It was three in the afternoon but she was still in her bathrobe and slippers, matching purple velour, a gift from the Devoted and Long-suffering Michael Collins. She loved nothing better than a bathrobe and slipper set.

I heard, you said. *I kinda feel bad for the guy.*

"I kinda feel bad," said my mother, "I couldn't fit the bigger TV in my car."

That's a shit TV, you said. It was running as always, dim and flickering. It was a Saturday, which meant TV 38 was playing the kinds of movies which produced in my mother unreasonable expectations about men, romance, and the tendency for wealth and good fortune to bestow themselves by happenstance on the world's most beautiful people. My mother was a beautiful person. Hardly a day went by without someone telling her she ought to be in pictures ("You're the spitting image," people said, "of Liz Taylor. Anyone ever tell you that? Spitting image. I bet you get that all the time, don't you? Well, I'm sorry but it's true"), and she had come to believe this. She watched those movies and their stars—Doris Day, Audrey Hepburn, Marilyn Monroe—with desperate, angry longing. Other people were living the life she deserved—they were parading around in front of her in the minks and pearls and convertibles that were rightly hers, and she fumed. She studied those movies as others studied the Bible, and spent every Sunday afternoon scouring sales at Filene's Basement, standing in its open dressing room, working her way into and out of various approximations of the outfits she saw on screen. Her wardrobe was legendary, spectacular, wildly impractical, her closet was brimming with bright silks and subtle tweeds, peep-toe heels and fishnet stockings, faux furs, satin scarves. "One day," she always said, regarding herself in the dressing room mirror, "this will all pay off."

On screen Judy Garland sang "Get Happy," and a dozen men in tuxedos collapsed at her feet. She was wearing a black jacket and nylon stockings, black heels. A black fedora was tilted on her head. What she had to say was this: that our troubles were meaningless and should be cast aside, that the suffering we endured would all be forgotten in the end, would be set ablaze in rapture. A line of static scrolled up the screen, again and again and again, over and again.

Judy finished her song and you said: *Guess who's in love?* My mother sat tossing out names, offering the most brutal and heartless people she could think of—Fran Palmintere, Sheila Scalia—but you kept shaking your head. You kept smiling.

Finally my mother said, "I give up."

Me, you said, stabbing your chest with your thumb. *Fucking me.*

"Yeah, right," my mother said. She snorted, she scoffed, she said, "Bullshit." But from the way you sat there, bent at the waist and holding your head in your hands, anyone could see it was true, anyone could see you had fallen at last, anyone could see you were, as you might have called it, *fucked.*

"Girls," my mother said to us, "go to your room."

This was pointless—from our room we could hear everything. At night we lay together on our mattress and listened to every word our mother spoke into the phone to her sisters, to Michael Collins, sometimes even to our father, but we went anyway.

You talked about this girl for the longest time. Her name was Sam Keller and she was a nineteen-year-old cashier at Stop & Shop. You'd met her, you said, just like every other girl: in a bar. You'd been out with friends watching the Red Sox blow another lead and there she was, sitting across from you with a group of her friends, drinking a Shirley Temple, twirling a finger through her ponytail. *Red hair,* you said, *I'm a sucker for red hair.* You kept staring at each other. Finally you got up the nerve to ask her out on a date, and she'd agreed. On the first date you'd taken her

to a Mexican place. You'd ordered the beef enchilada, she the
bean burrito, and you'd sat at a small table covered with a red-
and-white-checked vinyl tablecloth, a table by the window looking out at the street. You'd gotten to know each other in the way
that people do on first dates: she lived with her parents, devout
members of a religion you'd never heard of; she was the oldest
of three sisters; she was working as a cashier but what she really
wanted to do was hair, beauty school, or maybe open a bed-and-
breakfast. All through dinner she'd eaten with her mouth full
and chattered on and on in a high, tinny voice about this bed-
and-breakfast—somewhere up the Cape, or maybe New Hamp-
shire, she said, a fireplace in every room and four-poster beds.
She'd stayed at a place like that once with her grandmother and
she'd wanted to stay forever.

It was like any other date, you said. You'd been bored, struggling to pay attention, stifling yawns. You'd sat scrutinizing her
features: brown eyes, pale skin with a veil of tiny brown freckles,
her lips chapped, her earlobes fat, her body short and thick.
Altogether she was pretty but not beautiful, what you'd call *fuck-
able*. After dinner you drove her home and without much longing you'd tried to kiss her—you'd rested your arm on the seat
in such a way that it was more or less around her—but she'd
slipped out of the car without your making further progress.
You watched her walk into her house, her ponytail swaying
behind her, and then you drove off feeling sure of yourself—
it seemed to you a game had begun, a game which would end
with the two of you in bed together. You'd gone out a few more
times—*ten, to tell you the truth,* you said—and each date had
ended the same way, with her stepping out of your car as indif-

ferently as she would have stepped from a taxicab. On your last date you'd gone after her, followed her to her door, grabbed her arm, but she'd broken away from you and closed the door in your face. After that you'd called and called, left messages with her mother and sisters, even with her father, but she never called you back.

Your voice was like a machine, something droning in its labor, all your words were heavy and flat and ran together. You kept saying: *I don't get it. I don't get it at all.* This girl, she was average-looking, petty in her interests, dull, young, prudish, and none of this made sense to you. *But I guess,* you said, *that's love.* You'd said you'd gone back to the Mexican place a few times, alone, and relived the date. You'd ordered the enchilada for yourself and even a burrito for her and sat there eating them both. You'd tried to remember everything you'd said, everything she said. You'd written all you could remember on cocktail napkins.

"Don't tell me," my mother said. "You're carrying around a NAPKIN in your wallet! Oh JESUS!"

She talked a lot about her dog, you said. *A corgie named Snuffles.*

"Snuffles?" My mother said. "SNUFFLES?"

I think that's its name, you said.

"Jesus!"

I know. It's so fucking stupid.

"Jesus H. Christ," my mother said. When she was baffled this was all she could think of, Christ and his various pseudonyms, derivatives, and embellishments. She laughed—a short, loud bark whose sound filled the air for a second and then died, like a popped balloon.

I know, you said, *I know. It's pathetic.* You said you'd lost your

latest job, tending bar, because you kept calling in sick, preferring instead to sit in your car in the parking lot of Stop & Shop,
watching Sam Keller ring groceries.

"Christ," our mother said, "on a cracker!"

For a while you fell quiet and Malinda and I listened to the
television. Every business in our city, it seemed, was failing,
promoting its own ruin with crazed commercials. The spokes-
man for a furniture store cried: EVERYTHING MUST GO!!! TOTAL
LIQUIDATION CLOSEOUT!!! Upstairs the neighbors called to one
another from one end of their apartment to the other, curt
phrases of inquiry and accusation. "What you do with the damn
scissors?" said the man. "I don't know," said the woman. "Get
off your lazy ass and look yourself!" The woman was hugely
pregnant and we were dreading the delivery of the baby, its
pending squalling. Long gone were Michael Collins and his
pleasant three-bedroom ranch; this was the life we were living
now, apartment life, and what one did in this life was go around
pretending one could hear nothing, and see nothing, and smell
and taste and feel nothing, and remember nothing, nothing,
nothing at all.

When you spoke again it was to ask the question Malinda and
I had been waiting to hear. *Hey*, you said, as though the idea
had just occurred to you, *can I stay here a while?*

A month later we couldn't remember life before you. Our
mother, having taken one of the jobs she'd circled in the want
ads that day (keypuncher at an electric company, nine to five
at a metal desk, entering data), turned us over to you entirely.

That fall we spent more time with you than we ever had before or would again. You were our parent. You made our breakfast in the morning, drove us to school, picked us up in the afternoons. All of our problems became your problems. When our teachers sent us home with notes (three times Malinda had burst into tears for no reason at all; I spent most of the day staring out the window and often failed to respond when called on; when Malinda and I were together, at lunch and recess, we held hands and wouldn't speak to anyone else; we tended to show up to school wearing the same clothes for several days in a row. And all of these things were considered, in the language of the school, to be "red flags"), you were the one who received and addressed them (*Quit crying,* you said to Malinda. *Quit staring out the window,* you told me. To us both you said, *Change your clothes, and quit holding hands, for chrissakes*).

In the evenings, while our mother went out for drinks with a man she'd met at the electric company (an executive ten years her senior, twice divorced, she always spoke of him with deference. "Mr. Greenburg," she'd say, "is a very important man. Mr. Greenburg is a very busy man. Mr. Greenburg is Jewish, a fascinating religion. They're very close, they're very loyal, very mysterious, lots of tradition, the Jews"), you took us all around the city in Michelle. You had friends tending bar at a number of dark places, and one after another we stopped to visit them. Your friends served you beers and Malinda and I sat at the bar beside you, spinning ourselves around on those vinyl-upholstered stools. We made meals out of tiny bowls of pretzels and cheese puffs, little plastic spears stacked with orange slices and waxy red cherries. We sat doing our homework as you talked to your friends (all of them blue-eyed and red-faced, Irish, looking somewhat like lesser Kennedys) about Sam, Sam, Sam, Sam. You reminisced, strategized, you considered and rejected advice. "What you oughta do," your friends said, "is go out and get another girl, go out and get yourself another girl and fuck her." Here they stopped, looked at us, and said, "Wope. 'Scuse my French. Bang her. What you gotta do is go find yourself another girl and bang her. Clears the head."

After the bars we always stopped for a while in the dark parking lot of Stop & Shop and sat staring at its glowing insides as though at a movie screen. On the nights Sam Keller worked we watched her standing at her register, punching its keys, we watched her chat with the other cashiers and baggers. She had a habit of making minute adjustments to her ponytail, pulling it tighter and tighter. I sat in the backseat looking at Sam but also at you, studying the changes in your expression, from rapt to wistful, from keen to plotting to hopeless. Malinda sat in front and spent the whole time fiddling with the radio. She liked the music our mother liked—Helen Reddy, Carly Simon, Diana Ross, Barbra Streisand—songs regarding the thrills and disappointments of love. She knew all the words and sang them in a voice much older than her own.

Christ, you often said, *how long do we have to listen to this crap?*

"How long do we have to sit here?" Malinda would say. "How long are you gonna stare at your girlfriend?" This was a technique she'd picked up from our mother. They fought whenever they saw each other, and Malinda had developed a talent for Socratic argument. "Do you think you're living up to your full potential?" our mother would say, frowning at one of Malinda's

failed math tests. "Do YOU think I'm living up to my full potential?" she'd say. "Why wouldn't I be?"

Back at the apartment we'd take our positions. Malinda went
to lie in our mother's bed and listened to the radio, indulging
private fantasies of fame and fortune until she fell asleep, and I
sat next to you on the couch watching whatever happened to be
running on Channel 38—*The Three Stooges, Tom and Jerry, Creature Double Features.* You'd go through can after can of Schlitz,
until you were so drunk that the distance between your dreams
and the actual terms of your existence no longer embarrassed
you. *Me and Sam,* you'd say, *are gonna get married and move up the
Cape. She wants to live up the Cape and open a bed-and-breakfast.
What I'm gonna do is, I'm gonna buy a place up there and fix it up
real nice. Then I'm gonna pick her up from work someday, a surprise,
like on a Friday, and tell her to hop in the car and then drive her down
there and show her.* For a while you'd sit around hatching absurd
plans, working the problem of Sam Keller like a rosary. There
was a solution and you would find it. You were hopeful. The
obstacles standing in your way (you had no money, she didn't
love you) were minor details if they occurred to you at all.

But as the night wore on your mood would turn. After a while
the television had the effect of a hypnotist, and you'd come to
face the truth, you'd start to talk in a droning voice. *She doesn't
want me,* you said, *and I don't want any other girl.* It was a problem, it was a pickle, it was a bitch. If there was some solution to
the whole mess, you didn't know what it was. *Fuck,* you sometimes said, and clutched your head. You pressed shut your eyes,
rubbed them with the heels of your palms, hot tears ran down
your wrists. *Fuck,* you said. *Fuck, fuck, fuck.* I listened without

answering, nodded but nothing more. *If it wasn't for you,* you told me once, *I don't know what I'd fucking do. It's like if I talk about it I feel better, it's like talking about it is the only time I can stand it, if I don't talk about it, I swear to fucking God I'll explode.*

As you talked you'd stroke my hair and in your mind, I could tell, you were stroking hers.

The thing is, you said, *the weirdest thing is that sometimes I think all this has nothing to do with her. It's like I was going along fine and then I got stuck, like I'm a car that broke down or something, and I just happened to have gotten stuck at a time and place where Sam was. It's not like she's that great, it's not like she's anything at all. To tell you the truth she bored the crap out of me. Something's wrong with me,* you said. *What I wanna do sometimes, if you really wanna know the truth, what I wanna do sometimes is die.* Often I fell asleep as you talked and woke the next morning in my own bed, with no memory of being carried there.

This went on for weeks, and all that time there was the feeling that things were strange, out of order, that the life we were living was temporary, that things couldn't possibly go on this way for much longer. And as with us, so too the world. It was a strange season, violent and foreboding. The upstairs neighbors fought so often it was like a feature of the house, like the heat coming on. They had long, screaming battles that started with obscenity—"Fuck you, you fucking motherfucker!"—and escalated beyond, into a place where words failed and there was only screaming and crashing and the stomping of feet. You, or my mother, or both of you, would call up to them—*Shut the fuck up or we're calling the fucking cops! There's kids down here!*—and they'd quiet for a bit, but never for long. From the looks of the pregnant woman it seemed she couldn't carry the baby another day, it seemed she would burst at any moment. Meanwhile American hostages languished in Iran, and Reagan was elected president. There was something about all of this—even an eight-year-old could tell—that was out of order, something about all of this that begged to be explained. The world had gone crazy.

In December the first snow fell and for a brief day everything was beautiful, for a brief day it seemed the world had released to us one of its bright secrets. Everyone was walking around pink-faced and happy, waving to one another, filled with something—hope or nostalgia or joy. When you dropped us off at school that morning you seemed happy. You honked Michelle's horn twice as you drove away and when we turned you gave us an enthusiastic wave. That afternoon you picked us up from school and drove us to Friendly's, where we sat at the counter watching the fry cooks flip burgers. We drank cup after cup of hot chocolate. One of the cooks, a skinny guy with a patch over his left eye, said to you, "Cute kids," and you said, *They're my pride and joy, I'll tell you,* as though we were, as though we were yours.

That night, while we watched from the car, you walked through Sam Keller's checkout lane with a bouquet of flowers. After she rang you up you gave them to her and tried to explain yourself, your suffering, but she only stared at you with a bewildered expression. As you spoke her eyes darted, she stood with her body turned away from yours, she chewed her gum. She said something, and then you left, walked out of the store with your head down and your hands in your pockets. At home you got drunk and talked about her, on and on, going over and over what was said to whom, and how, then launching the numerous rebuttals which you'd been unable to conjure in the heat of the moment. *She thinks I'm too old, but I'm not, if she got to know me she'd realize we're made for each other.* You went on and on. When my mother came home, and we all sat down to leftovers, you repeated the whole story, then started it again when you'd finished, on and on until my mother reached across the table and slapped your face. "How goddamned pathetic," she said, "are you going to get?" She was tired, she said, tired of this. Tired of you lying around scratching your crotch, bitching about Sam, Sam, Sam, Sam, Sam. "Jesus fucking Christ!" she said. She walked to the living room, to the couch, and yanked off its white sheet. She brought the sheet into the kitchen and held it up to your face. "This sheet is like fucking sandpaper!" she said. "Look at this! This is pathetic! This is disgusting!" She balled up the sheet and shoved it in your face.

You pushed it away. *Gimme a break, okay?* you said, and hung your head in your hands. *Christ,* you said. *In front of the kids.*

"The kids are fine," she said. "The kids aren't the ones with problems here."

They're not? you said. *They're not? You think the kids don't got any problems? You think the kids are fine? Have you even met them? Do you even remember their fucking names?*

And then you were both standing, screaming at each other, your faces red and an inch apart and Malinda and I were looking at each other, staring right into each other, it was one of those moments, searing hot and trembling around the edges,

as in the moments just before a migraine. Everything was difficult to hear, nothing was difficult to hear, all at once something was said about your debts and your drinking, your lost
charm, something was said about a girl you'd gotten pregnant
last year, something was said about your heart being bullshit, an
invented ailment, something you claimed for profit, something
you used to get out of anything and everything you didn't wish
to endure, something was said about your changing unrecog-
nizably from the fun-loving rebel you'd once been, about how
the only reason anyone was willing to tolerate you was long
gone. Concerning Malinda and me something was said about
our poor diet, our lack of discipline, our staying up till midnight, the circles underneath our eyes, the deadening amount
of violence we took in from the television, something was said
about our clothes and knotted hair, the trouble we'd gotten
into at school, something was said about Michael Collins, about
our drunk father.

You think I'm sick? you said. *I'm the one who's sick here? You never
even see your own kids. Your own flesh and blood and you never see them.*

"You don't know what you're talking about," she said. "Here I
am busting my ass to keep a roof over their heads."

Bullshit, you said. *You're out all the time with Rabbi whatsisname
who's so important.*

"The kids are fine," she said.

No they're not, you said. *They look like shit. They got no friends at
school. Alls they eat is spaghetti from a fucking can and they look like
shit.*

"Malinda could give a shit less," my mother said, "where I am
or what I do. And Mary," she said, "is tough. Mary never cries."

You have no fucking clue! You don't know what the fuck you're talking about! Your own kids!

Until the neighbors started banging on their floor and calling down to us, "Shut the fuck up! Shut the fuck up or we're calling the cops! There's a baby trying to sleep!"

And the irony got to both of you, you started laughing and couldn't stop, you were bent over with it, and while you were laughing Malinda and I slipped off to the living room and sat on the couch holding hands watching *Tom and Jerry*. In that world, which we loved, characters suffered one fatal blow after another and yet sprang up, every time, unharmed.

When you recovered my mother said, "I think pretty soon you better find somewhere else to live."

Fine with me, you said. *My fucking pleasure.*

A few nights later we were up together as usual watching TV, a football game, when Howard Cosell cut in with a voice that said something was happening. *This had better be big,* you said. *Middle of the goddamned game.* And it was. It was big. John Lennon had been shot.

Holy shit! you said. Then, eyeing me, *Sorry. 'Scuse me. Holy smokes. Holy fucking smokes.* You got up and changed the channel, as if this would change the news. On another channel a blond woman stood on a street corner and behind her was gathered a throng of people, some moving about and talking excitedly, some crying, some standing facing the camera with blank expressions, behind her sirens wailed and cars slipped past in the night, behind her was New York. We lay in bed as if in prison, stunned to think that somewhere else people were awake and walking around, driving, reporting, somewhere else someone had been shot and here we were on a foldout couch, missing everything.

I gotta go there, you said, as though something important had been taken away from you, that an injustice had been done to you personally. This man, this John Lennon, suddenly he was a friend of yours: someone who understood you, who stood for the same things you did, someone who had gone crazy for a girl and lost his mind just like you had, someone who had been one thing and then turned into another to the horror of previous fans. Already news had spread and people were standing in front of the hospital in which he'd died. *I gotta go there,* you said. *I gotta get there.*

I said the thing I always said, the only phrase I knew. In those days I was a joiner, a follower, a disciple. I said, "Me too."

You looked at me and raised an eyebrow. The next day was a school day. "We'll pretend you're sick," you said. "We'll say you were up puking all night. First thing tomorrow, we'll drop Malinda off and then we'll go."

What I remember best from that trip isn't the long drive, how John Lennon was playing on every radio station and how this made us feel like a part of something; it isn't the thrill of the city approaching, approaching, and finally appearing, tall and glimmering; it isn't the sight, from Michelle's window, of so many things I'd never seen before—a car entirely covered with bumper stickers, a man with a Mohawk so spiked it looked like weaponry, cars without tires abandoned in the street, dogs in sweaters, two men holding hands, taxicabs by the dozens, and the people, people, people, so many people everywhere it didn't seem possible to me that they could all have been born. It isn't even the Dakota, grand and towering and spooky, or the adjacent crowd in Central Park, the hundreds of people standing together in a massive huddle, most of them motionless in reverence but some wandering about, one red-haired woman sobbing and sobbing, talking to everyone and no one in particular, saying: "He's not dead, he's not dead, it isn't true, they're just saying that." It isn't the way people were singing his songs, wobbly and slow, in a rueful key. It isn't even the stupefying notion that a person, one single person, had mattered so much to so many.

What I remember best isn't any of these things, but a small moment that took place in Harlem, a world away from John Lennon and those who mourned him. We'd started for home and the driving was hard for you at first, so many cars, so many pedestrians, so many one-way streets, so many flashing lights, so many signs with symbols and names unfamiliar to us, so much peripheral noise and motion (the air was alive with horns and sirens and shouts), but then you seemed to give in to it, you seemed to stop looking for whatever it was you meant to find, and you were just driving, looking, wandering, going from street to street and neighborhood to neighborhood, each different from the last, each suggesting a million different lives. This was what we were doing when we wandered into Harlem, and suddenly it seemed we'd wandered into the shadowy remnants of a lost city. In this place there had once been businesses but many of them—most of them, it seemed—had failed. In this place people had bought and sold all manner of goods, the signs were still hanging above the doorways but the doors themselves, the windows through which one might have looked, intent on some treasure, the glass to which one might have pressed one's nose, which one might have fogged with one's lusty breathing, now these windows were boarded up, gone, so many purveyors of secondhand clothing, big-and-tall formal wear, hardware, used books and records, toys, typewriters, electronics, all of them gone. In these falling-down brownstones people had been born and had died, had been married, had made love, had slept and worked and eaten, had lived and breathed, but now these build-ings were boarded up, abandoned, many of them were doorless and looked like dead men with their mouths hanging open.

We took the first nervous breaths of people who find them-selves outnumbered for the first time in their lives. We saw that everyone, everyone, everyone was black. We saw two girls with their hair in pigtails and between them, holding their hands, a woman with a red mouth, a full-length fur coat, a fur hat slanted on her head. We saw clusters of people imprisoned in puffy coats, hooded, their faces completely obscured. We saw a man dressed up in a colorful suit and shiny shoes, a long camel-colored coat, a wide-brimmed hat, high-heeled boots. *Look!* you said, as he walked past. *Look how he walks!* It was like no walk I'd ever seen. The way we walked at home was all business but this, this was expansive, exuberant, this was like a barely contained dance.

Mostly people were going about their business, coming home from work, carrying paper and plastic bags, carrying purses, intent on dinner, their families, wondering what the kids had done at school, or turning over some problem between them and a lover. On the face of each passerby was a look of isolation, of distraction, of such familiarity with their surroundings that they might just as well have been blind. We were stopped at a red light when we saw a man walking down the sidewalk, toward us—he was wearing a woolly plaid jacket and brown slacks, a gray fedora—and as we watched him someone called out to him from across the street. We watched his face light up like a child whose birthday cake, flickering with lit candles, had been set before him, we watched him wave to his friend. "Shut up, fool!" he called, by way of greeting. Watching him you had a hungry look, your eye narrowed like an eagle's, and it was clear in that moment that what you wanted from life was for someone to say the same to you, you wanted to be a part of something like that, to have friends you might meet on the street, friends calling out to you and you answering in mock rage. New York, Harlem, what you saw there you wanted to become, what you saw there was some long-forgotten dream brought back to life. What I remember most from our trip is this, this the moment we lost you.

You hung around through spring, working long hours laying carpet in the new houses being built at the north end of town. You were saving your money. When we saw you all you talked about was New York, your dream of moving there. *You never seen*, you'd say, *so many people in your life. And the buildings, a million of 'em, and people in all of 'em, you've never seen anything like it,* you'd say. *Right, Mare?* and you'd look to me for confirmation, you'd wink. It was something between us, something unknown to others. *New York*, you'd say, to bartenders, to your sisters, to people in line at the grocery store, is where everything is happening. *You're not in New York, you might as well be dead.*

All that season you were hooked on *Sgt. Pepper's Lonely Hearts Club Band.* You filled the house with it, played it start to finish over and over and over again, sang it in the shower. I sat for long stretches looking at that album cover, all those faces, that collage of the brokenhearted—Marilyn Monroe, W. C. Fields, Marlene Dietrich, Albert Einstein, Shirley Temple, Oscar Wilde, Lewis Carroll, Marlon Brando, Stephen Crane, William Burroughs, Karl Marx, Bob Dylan, Fred Astaire. I knew their names, or didn't, it didn't seem to matter, what seemed to matter was their faces, their expressions, those far-off looks, those joyless smiles. Your favorite line from the album was something eerie and cold, and you sang it all day long, in the shower, over breakfast, in the car, during commercials, in the booths of restaurants and on the swiveling stools of diners, in the library, in waiting rooms, in bars, over and over and over again you burst out with it: *He blew his mind out in a car.*

"Would you," my mother and Malinda would say, everyone would say, "shut the fuck up?"

All that February and March our mother was home. She had broken up with her boyfriend and suddenly she was around all the time, talking on and on about the limitations of the Jewish race. "They're a closed society, the Jews," she said. "Very selfish, very judgmental. Real superior. If you're not one of them, forget it." All of the interest she'd taken in him she turned on us. Nightly she had us lie on the kitchen counter with our heads in the sink and she washed and conditioned and brushed our hair, she washed and ironed our clothes, in the morning she inspected our teeth and fingernails, wrapped scarves around us and pulled hats down over our heads. Before we left for school she took our faces in her hands and stared into our eyes. "I love you," she told us. "You're my true loves, my only true loves." She hugged us and we clung to her like fools.

When the weather broke you put an ad in the paper and sold Michelle to a guy with a handlebar mustache. He showed up at the door, head down, hands in pockets. He was wearing jeans and a flannel shirt, no coat, a green Celtics cap with a well-grooved brim. He was wearing, also, cowboy boots, and it was hard to imagine Michelle going off with a man in cowboy boots. But you gave him the keys and he went for a spin around the neighborhood. People did this back then—they'd give away their keys to a complete stranger and simply trust the stranger to return. Which he did. Runs good, he said, nodding. And you said, *She's been good to me. She could break down tomorrow, though. Who knows. I hope she doesn't but she might.*

"I trust you," said the mustached man. And you shook hands. There was a trading of money and documents. The man climbed into Michelle and drove off. We could hear her engine roaring long after we had lost sight of her, and then we couldn't even hear that. She was gone. And the next day, before anyone woke, off on a Greyhound bus, so were you.

We went for a walk after you sold Michelle, and this was the last I ever saw you. I seemed to sense it would be. I was kicking a rock up and down the street and in a trance—this was the kind of thing I did, age eight and already a mope, a loner, a drag, a slouch. You walked beside me for a while and I went through the same struggle I always did around people, tight in the throat, the struggle of wanting to talk but not knowing what to say, not knowing the first word. But it was you who spoke. *I want to tell you something,* you said. You were kicking a stone of your own now, and sometimes our rocks crossed paths, bounced and leapt over each other.

I know you don't see much of your father, you said, and I wondered who you were talking about. Mike Murphy, who came around drunk from time to time and pulled me and Malinda to his chest, who sobbed in our hair, who talked in a strange voice—ILOVEYOUMYBABIES. Or were you talking about Michael Collins, who had been our father for three years but whom we never saw anymore? (In fact I would only see him again once in my entire life, in the cereal aisle of a grocery store, where my mother had sent me to fetch a box of Special K. There he was, poor Michael Collins, bald now and thinner than ever, a small, sad collection of food in his cart, there he stood in a blue windbreaker with the name of his old high school scrawled across the back, its mascot beneath, a ferocious hornet, and the loneliness was coming off him in a wave that nearly knocked me over. Then we saw each other, and when he asked about her, my beautiful mother, it was clear that he still loved her, that she had ruined his life.)

I didn't know who you were talking about, but it didn't matter. *I bet it's tough without a dad and I'm glad I was around some. You can always write me, you know,* you said. *I'll write you and you can write me back. I wanna know how you're doing in school.*

I nodded, said nothing, kicked and pursued that fat gray stone. *You're a pretty tough kid,* you said. *You're gonna be just fine.*

When you said this it was all over. I bawled like a baby, held my face in my hands and sobbed, gasped. I stood on the street shaking and you held me, held my head in your hands. I'd never cried like this and was lost in it, hot, salty, the sorrow itself and the shame of having collapsed into it. *Don't cry, buddy,* you said, your voice cracking. *Don't cry.*

Then you were gone. This was life. This was the lesson we kept learning over and over and over, the lesson our mother was best capable of teaching us. Love—whatever else it might or might not be—was fleeting. Love stormed into your life and occupied it, it took over every corner of your soul, made itself comfortable, made itself wanted, then treasured, then necessary, love did all of this and then it did next the only thing it had left to do, it retreated, it vanished, it left no trace of itself. Love was horrifying.

We didn't hear from you for almost four years, during which time we often wondered aloud, Where were you? Where the fuck were you? And when were you coming home? Would you come knocking on the door, like you'd always done, and if so, when? Now? Was that you knocking right now?

It wasn't that anyone cared. No one would admit to that. It wasn't that we missed you. The phrase with which you were summed up went something like: "Hey, if he wants us, he knows where to find us!" It was just that Pop Beaudry could die at any moment and this was—not that it *really* mattered but in a way it did, you certainly could say it did, in a way when you thought about it, it mattered more than anything else—your father; you were, in fact, Pop's only true family, his only true blood, and what if he died, just up and died? This was possible. Pop was diabetic, he was hypertense, from time to time he suffered from shingles and gout. What your sisters couldn't get past was that Pop could die, your own father would be dead, and you wouldn't even know it. That was the thing. It was disgusting. It was unforgivable. It was, they said, something only you would do.

Finally Christmas 1984 you sent a card, and inside a picture of yourself, grown hairy as Björn Borg, your arm around your girlfriend, a pretty black girl with a red mouth, your newborn daughter held between you, swaddled. The card was full of exclamation points. *Look what I went and did! This is my kid! Meet my girls, Mary and her mother Kim!* Though we could hardly see her face amidst all those blankets we said the baby took after you. Around the mouth, we said.

Malinda said, "Which one's the baby's name? Kim?"

"Mary," I said. "Jesus."

"I'm just asking."

"Look," said my mother, "she has his eyes."

"No she doesn't," Malinda said. "His eyes are gray."

"Yeah, but the baby's are sad like his. Look how sad. Look at that face."

Your return address was a Brooklyn hotel. The aunts said:

"He lives in a hotel?"

"Fancy!"

"He must've got a good job or something."

"Too bad he doesn't invite us down, let us stay for a while."

"And to think all those nights we put him up!"

"He could at least invite us for a weekend!"

"It's the least he could do!"

They sat for quite some time imagining the luxuries of the Ritz-Carlton. They imagined a maid in a black dress coming through each morning with a feather duster, they pictured mints on the pillow, a doorman in a dark blue suit with brass buttons, a blue cap, your mail and messages waiting for you in a gleaming wooden cubby behind the front desk. They had never been to New York and didn't know what it meant to live in a hotel, a dark room at the end of a dark hallway, a mirrorless bathroom shared with a dozen other people.

That Christmas we were fool enough to expect you. On Christmas Eve Aunt Lily called my mother to read your horoscope: A TRIP TO VISIT OLD FRIENDS WILL BRING YOU MUCH JOY AND CONTENTMENT! But you never showed, and soon enough we forgot about you again. My mother kept moving us every year or so, kept falling in and out of what she considered to be love, and with all of this going on we stopped speaking your name, stopped thinking about you even in the privacy of our minds, indeed for some time it was as though you had never existed. And yet when the phone rang that day (it was a Sunday in November, just after we'd turned back the clocks, and we felt ourselves to be standing at the mouth of a cave, the upcoming months of dark and cold, the long season awaiting us, we were going to have to pass through it again), somehow there was the sound of you in it, later we would each confess that we had known from the first ring. My mother had been making meatballs—she was married again and trying to be a good wife—and she'd told me to answer. "It's for you," I said, and she held up her fingers, slick with meat and egg, wriggled them.

"Hold the phone to my ear," she said. "Be a help for once."

I rolled my eyes—those years, this was more or less my only form of communication—and she said, "Hello? Yes? Yes. Yes?" And then, "Oh. Oh no. Oh God, no." Tears down her face, and if there was any doubt it was over now, I knew, I knew, I knew it was you. My mother clutched the phone, said, "Get a pen." A grave calm had come over her—the calm that settles on us when we're burdened with a gruesome task—and she said a few more things, wrote with slippery fingers an address, a number, another number, another. Then she set about the business of calling Pop, calling her sisters. It seemed she was on the phone for days after your death. She was, at that time, married to Walter Adams and therefore not really speaking to her sisters ("Black!" they whispered. "Black, Black, Black!" And from their mouths the word seemed to lose its meaning, was less a word than a sound, an expletive). She was six months pregnant with Shirley, the daughter she would lose. Shirley was a kicker. The day after you died, while my mother was talking on the phone to someone about your death, about the procurement of your body and possessions, I felt Shirley kick. Typically my mother wasn't the kind of pregnant woman who endured the inquisitive touch, but that day she did, and I walked around for the rest of the day remembering it, quick and soft, I walked around thinking, something was alive in there. Alive.

For some time we didn't know what had happened, we only knew you were dead. Later we learned the details, how a cleaning lady found you dead in that Brooklyn hotel room, facedown

and overdosed, the bed pissed and puked on. You were entirely
alone. There was no trace of Mary and Kim. Whether they left
you or you left them no one could say. All at once we felt the
shame which should have been with us for years, the shame of
having fallen out of touch with a loved one, the shame of having
turned away from someone who needed us, someone who was
alone, a brother.

For a time my mother and Nana and Pop and the aunts made
efforts to find your girlfriend and daughter—*Mary and her
mother Kim!* They walked around your Brooklyn neighborhood
with pictures, taped up flyers, but nothing came of it. Malinda
heard from our cousins that Pop had hired a private detective,
and I imagined a man in a trench coat wandering the streets of
New York, trailing the smallest leads, until he found your girls.
But all efforts failed, and eventually we fell back on the prevail-
ing wisdom of all searching people, eventually we decided that
if we stood still, if we stayed where we were, your girls would
come to us.

For my part I was preoccupied with the room in which you
died. Often in dreams I found myself in the lobby of that hotel,
and it was a grand place, the kind of place in which Henry James
might have lived, with oak-paneled walls and birch logs crack-
ling in a marble fireplace, with satin-upholstered armchairs.
In my dreams the hotel lobby had a black-and-white-tiled floor
whose patterns shifted beneath my feet, forming whales and
clocks and chess pieces, coming together and breaking apart,
kaleidoscopic. A fine place indeed. But when I spoke to the
lobby attendant—an old man encased behind glass, glowing
yellow in his booth, much like a toll collector—he couldn't hear

me. "I want to see a room," I said. "I want to see the room where Mike Beaudry died." But the attendant only shrugged, shook his head.

I wanted to see you again. The thought of you alone in that room was something I couldn't bear to think about, and yet something I couldn't help but think about. I think of it still. I see a Cutlass or a red-haired girl, the doorbell or phone rings at a strange hour, I hear a song on the radio (*He blew his mind out in a car . . .*) and it all comes back, all of this in a rush, and how I wish I had been there in Brooklyn with you, calling your name from across the street, how I wish you hadn't been alone. Even now, across this distance between us, I want to call out to you, how desperately I want to call your name and have you answer. Just once I want to hear you say: *Shut up, fool.*

Elegy for

Elwood LePoer

(1971–1990)

Elwood LePoer, your head was a brick, a block, a lollipop. You were dumb as a stick, a sock, a bag of rocks. Your lot in life, it seemed, was to go through it unawares, your folly a perpetual amusement to others. In our dead-end school you were the village idiot, and we stood around talking about you, your latest foibles, like the weather. "LePoer, you wouldn't believe what he just did. Walked right into a glass door, fell over backwards, that dumb shit." We called you everything we could think to call you. Dipshit, Shithead, Shitheel, Shit-for-Brains. We piled on every last cliché. You were a few sandwiches short of a picnic, a pancake shy of a stack, a board short of a porch. You weren't the sharpest knife in the drawer or the brightest bulb on the tree. Your screws were loose, one of your boots was stuck in the mud, your elevator didn't go all the way to the top, you were all foam and no beer, you had lost your marbles, your lights were on but you weren't home. In ironic moods we called you Professor, Einstein, Sherlock, Your Excellency. What a knuckledragger you were, what a mouthbreather, you didn't know shit from Shinola, your head from your ass, what you didn't know could fill a book.

A number of unfortunate events marked you early, made your reputation, and for better or worse you enjoyed throughout your life a certain amount of local fame. As a toddler you once ran naked through the neighborhood, all the way down to the shops on Plantation Street, and stood smiling on the street corner while a stray dog licked your balls. Cars honked as they passed. People came pouring out of the shops and stood around you laughing, someone even taking your picture, before some kind soul, rare among us, picked you up and carried you home. In grade school you fell into the habit of trapping and torturing small animals, singeing their fur with lighters, something you bragged about at school (*You shoulda seen this rabbit, man, it went fucking crazy!*) until one day a cat got the better of you and scratched your face, a wound so deep it never completely healed, and for the rest of your life you went around with three vertical lines running down your left cheek. Some years later, on a dare, you went through the ice over Lake Quinsigamond (someone's bright idea: Hey, you think that ice can hold anyone?) and the group of kids who had put you up to it stood on the shore for a long, awful moment, some of them screaming and clutching one another, others frozen in panic, until you fought your way back to the surface and scrambled and sloshed back to shore and everyone started laughing. There was something funny about it, cruelly funny, your whole life summed up in the way you stood, shivering and bedraggled, chattering, shoeless (you had kicked off your boots and they were waterlogged somewhere at the bottom of the lake, where they remain today . . .), saying over and over again, *Oh man, Oh man, I swear to God there was something under there, some big black fucking monster like an octopus or something. I swear to God it come up to me and it touched me on the shoulder with one of its legs, and that's when I was like, Holy shit, man, I gotta get outta here, Oh man!* In the joke version of this event, as people liked to tell it, you were rushed to the hospital for a battery of tests to determine if there had been any damage to your brain, but the results were inconclusive. As a punch line the doctor threw up his hands and said: "It's impossible to tell!"

Elwood LePoer. All your life your name was synonymous with a kind of humiliating, pathetic stupidity. You were a walking joke, a sitting duck, a fish in a barrel. That you eventually died in an accident came as no surprise to anyone. When word of your death went through the neighborhood people received it as if a letter they'd been expecting in the mail. The only wonder was, they said, it hadn't come sooner.

The first time I ever saw you was the first day of third grade. My mother had just left her second husband and moved my sister and me across town to a new apartment, a new school. On the playground, before the day started, Malinda and I sat together cross-legged on the ground, communicating to one another without even needing to speak that this place, this school, was worse than our old school, the grass on the playground burned out and spotty, its swing set without swings, the school itself—a block of brick with grated windows and a flat roof—suggesting a prison more than anything else. Younger kids were running around playing games we were no longer interested in playing, though what we were interested in doing we couldn't say. We were eight and nine and we were defined, that year, mostly by what we had once done but didn't do anymore. We spent much of our time sitting around taking in the bleak landscape of our new lives as though watching a commercial, waiting for it to end and for the real show, what we hoped would be our real lives, to begin. At our new school yours was the first name we learned. Everyone kept saying it all around the playground— Elwood LePoer, Elwood LePoer—and we wondered who you were. "Elwood LePoer," we heard someone say, "is wearing a Playboy T-shirt!" And you were pointed out, a stocky kid with blond hair that hung in your face. You stood throwing a rubber ball against the windowless wall of the gymnasium, hurling it as though a grenade, your square jaw thrust out. The ball shot up and sprang back to you over and over, a pattern that seemed to enrage you—every time you threw it, it was with increased force, as though you expected to drive the ball through brick. I kept trying to get a look at your T-shirt. I had some vague notion of what "Playboy" meant—I had heard the word before and knew it had something to do with women—but when I finally got a clear view of your shirt there was something disappointing about it, just a white shirt with the black silhouette of a tuxedoed bunny printed on it. Nevertheless by lunchtime you had been summoned to the school nurse, who kept extra clothes in her office, and made to change into a striped shirt such as little boys were supposed to wear.

In the following years I saw you here and there, around school and the neighborhood. You were always alone. One of the more memorable aspects of your personality was that despite your solitude you couldn't stop talking, some feature in your brain demanding you dictate whatever you were doing as you did it, whatever you were thinking about as you thought it. Often what you were thinking about was what you had recently watched on television, or heard on the radio. Your head was full of jingles, slogans, mottoes, theme songs, indeed you were a marketing man's fantasy, you couldn't get those songs out of your head: *Oh, I wish I was an Oscar Mayer wiener,* you sang, *that is what I'd really like to be.*

Once you caught the attention of our principal, a WWII purple heart who ran the school much like a basic training camp and who was, that year, embattled in a lawsuit involving a student and allegations of physical violence. His name was Mr. K., and indeed he carried about him all the mystery and absurdity of a Kafka character. Silver-haired, acne-scarred, with the angry profile of a bald eagle, he walked the halls in shining suits and polished, clacking shoes, commanding silence in every room he entered. Often he would walk into the cafeteria and call a handful of kids away from their lunches, line them up on the stage at the front of the room, where he drilled them on the basics of American education—the states and their capitals, the dates of wars and treaties and ratifications, the terms of presidents. Most of us performed badly, stuttering and stammering, at which point Mr. K. liked to give a speech, the same one every time, about the statistical likelihood of our pending worthlessness. "In this city," he'd say, "the high school graduation rate is well below the national average. One out of four of you won't make it through. And out of the pathetic rest of you who graduate, only half of those will go to college, and only half of those will finish. Look around your tables," he'd say, "and ask yourself if you're going to make it that far." He'd stop for a moment to let us make our calculations. And when we looked around it was already clear who was who, the handful of kids taking all of this seriously, sitting at attention wondering, Is it me? Could it be me, could it? while the rest of us had already resigned, thrown in the towel, for kids like us there was no point even wondering. "The answer is," Mr. K. would say, "probably not." He'd pace up and down through the rows of tables, hands clasped behind his back. "I'm standing here today on behalf of that small handful of you," he'd say, "who are willing to work hard to become worthy of the resources spent on your upbringing. As for the rest of you," he'd say, "I hope you enjoy your lives shoveling other people's shit."

When your turn came for questioning, Mr. K. asked you to name the countries involved in the war of 1812. *I dunno,* you said, and Mr. K. told you to take your time, to think about it for a moment. *I dunno,* you said again, and Mr. K. said to at least take a guess.

Massachusetts, you said, *and Boston,* and Mr. K. stopped in his tracks. He stood for a long moment regarding you, as if seeing you for the first time. The room was silent. "Step forward," he finally said, and you stepped out of line to the front of the stage, hesitant, sensing that you were in some kind of trouble but unsure of the cause. "Look at those trousers," said Mr. K. You looked down at your corduroys, which were covered in mud. "I want you to tell me what happened to your trousers."

You shrugged.

"Did you roll around in mud this morning?" he said. "Are you some kind of pig?"

You stood looking at your feet, seeming to make some kind of calculation. *No, sir,* you said.

"Because you call to mind," he said, "with trousers like that, a pig." Here a ripple of laughter went through the room. "You think you can track mud through my hallways?"

No, sir.

"What does your mother say," he asked, "when you come home with your trousers looking like that?"

Nothing.

"Nothing?" Mr. K. said, with the thrill of a man looking for a fight.

It dries up, you said, *and falls off on the way home. She doesn't notice.*

"It dries up," said Mr. K., in his rage reduced to repeating whatever it was that you said, "and falls off." He stood staring at you, smiling, his face gone purple, a man battling to contain himself. "And your mother doesn't notice." Then without another word he turned and walked out of the room, through the swinging doors, the silence holding until we could no longer hear his footsteps, and then even beyond that. When we returned to our lunches it was with the grim silence of motorists who had just passed an accident.

What we knew, and Mr. K. didn't, was that your mother wasn't the type to concern herself with the condition of your pants, or her kitchen floor, or anything else relating to the duties and comforts of homemaking. Everyone knew your mother. Her name was Irma and she was older than most mothers, with a beehive hairdo and a face as craggy and oblong as a potato. She worked as a cashier at the am/pm and after school kids would go there for candy and soda, they'd empty their pockets on the counter, pushing their pennies and nickels toward her. Aside from her duties at the register your mother was responsible for dispensing slush drinks from a tank that, full of unnaturally bright fluid, pulsed behind her like a bodily organ, and there was a kind of thrill amongst kids our age, watching her fetch their drinks when their own mothers had long since stopped doing anything of the kind. Your mother's fingers were twisted, arthritic, the knuckles swollen to the size of gumballs, and it hurt to watch her fit the plastic caps onto the drinks and scrape change from the register drawer, in fact it was painful just to stand in her presence. She never, as far as I knew, spoke a single word to a customer or looked anyone in the eye, preferring instead to stare off at one of the convex mirrors positioned in the corners of the store's ceilings, all the traffic of the store's life, its drudgery and its petty crimes, encircled there and reflected back to her in miniature. Your mother was known to be religious, a Catholic who attended daily mass. Sometimes while she sat at the register she fingered a rosary. People said she was brain-damaged, that your father had beaten her once to the brink of death and that ever since she had been more or less disembodied, a rumor that was easy to believe. Often she forgot to remove the paper napkin which she had tucked in the collar of her shirt during her lunch break, and she sat all afternoon at the register as though a child seated in a high chair, draped with a bib, some stain or other spotted on it. Given all of this—and also given the fact that your father was an infamous drunk, known for passing out on the floors of bars—your family was thought to be cursed. It was set aside as exceptional and delinquent, which, in a neighborhood like ours, full of drunks and derelicts and deadbeats, where the margins of acceptable behavior had been drawn with a generous hand, was saying something.

The following year a plague of lice went through the school and we were all made to line up in the gymnasium for head inspections. You and I were among the small group brought to the nurse's office and kept there, largely unsupervised, for the rest of the day. You spent your time going through the nurse's supplies—pulling apart cotton balls and splitting tongue depressors in half, sticking bandages all over your arms and legs. When the nurse (a child-sized woman named Mrs. Chang who wore to school, every day, a black-belt karate uniform) finally returned to her office she was carrying a set of electric shears. She offered to shave your head and you shrugged, as you always did when someone asked you a question. She turned on the clippers and guided them over your head with the quick, indifferent strokes of a military barber. Your hair fell to the floor in clumps. When Mrs. Chang was finished you sat with your head in your hands, rubbing your palms across your skull, crying.

Then Mrs. Chang turned to me, still holding the clippers, and for a brief moment it seemed that she would shave my head, too. "You," she said, "are in bad health." She walked over to me and pressed the pads of her thumbs beneath my eyes. Then she pulled my mouth open and inspected my teeth and then my fingernails, which were overgrown and embedded with dirt. "You maybe have lice, maybe not," she said. "Your hair is too full of knots to see." My mother had been working nights that year and Malinda and I had been home alone much of the time. Left to my own devices I had been living on a diet of Coke and saltine crackers. I couldn't remember the last time I'd washed my hair. "Go home," Mrs. Chang said to me, "and tell your mother to wash your hair and brush your teeth." As far as I know you never told anyone about this, and I never told anyone that you had cried. Even at that young age we had developed between us the discretion of thieves.

In fifth grade you were held back and fell from Malinda's grade into mine, and this was when you made your only friend, Bill Yablonski, frecklefaced and bucktoothed, fat, his pants always falling down, Bill Yablonski the pyromaniac who was always lighting matches and burning them down to his fingertips, who once started a fire in his desk. Your friendship appeared to be wordless, both of you going around with your hands stuffed in your pockets, your heads down, kicking stones, or sitting quietly sharing a cigarette at the back corner of the playground, in an alcove behind a warped, dying shrub. It got so that one of you was never mentioned without the other—Bill and Elwood, Bill and Elwood, Bill and Elwood—like some comedy act, two desperate fools, Laurel and Hardy, Tom and Jerry,

Lenny and Squiggy. In science class that year we learned about electrons, the desire for even the smallest forms of life to pair up, the unstable ones hopping from ring to ring in search of a mate. We were told that this was how two atoms bonded, each completed in the other, and this was something that made sense to me, to my otherwise unscientific mind, because I had seen it in life. Yes the mind hurt, at that age, to see a person alone, indeed the sight of you talking to yourself had always troubled me. But then you found Bill and the two of you joined in my mind, you settled down, and for years I hardly thought of you.

By the time we entered high school (a sprawling, run-down building, many of its windows cracked and held together with duct tape) you were over six feet tall, broad-shouldered, hulking. Though your hair was still blond your eyebrows had grown in thick and black, the combination giving you a fierce look, which teachers took to be threatening. They sensed a defiance in you, and you wound up spending half of your time at the in-school suspension program, sent there not so much for the reasons others were (fighting, destroying school property) as for your complete lack of interest or effort in the classroom, how you almost never remembered your books or even bothered to fill out tests. Stories went around about you—how in English class you had titled your first essay "S.A. #1," how in biology you had so vexed your teacher, answering *I dunno* to such a long series of increasingly simple questions that she had burst out crying and kicked you out of the room. The suspension room was in the busiest corridor of the school. Its walls had been knocked down and replaced with glass, the idea being to put offenders on display, to shame them, but whenever I saw you there you looked perfectly comfortable, asleep on a pile of books, your mouth open in a half-smile.

Sometimes, when my sister didn't object to my following her, I stood in the same circle as you in the parking lot before classes started, where the smokers huddled together against the cold. One morning you removed your jacket to show off the tattoo you'd gotten over the weekend—your own name curved across your bicep in Gothic capitals—and when you displayed it, proud, the joke went around that you'd been compelled to tattoo your name on your arm as a means of remembering it. *Man,* you said, in your famously warped voice, which was like a regular voice projected through a tube—*Fuck you guys! Fuck you!*— enraged at first, but then surrendering to the joke, laughing, as was your only choice, your place in that circle being that of its jester. Sophomore year you bought and fixed up an old Camaro, slapped it over with red house paint, and you and Bill sat in the car before school started, the windows fogged over with smoke, the radio blasting, WAAF, nonstop rock, crank it up. As the year went on you showed up to school less and less, until one day the inevitable happened, you dropped out. I was sitting in history class when you walked in the room and handed a piece of paper to the teacher, Mr. Hickey, a mouselike character so pathetic he wasn't even made fun of. *You gotta sign this,* you said. And Mr. Hickey frowned, took the paper from you and examined it. "Are you sure," he said, in a trembling voice, "you want to do this? Have you thought about this decision, and all of its consequences?" You said, *Yup.* Mr. Hickey was slow about retrieving his pen from his pocket, slow about signing his name, which he finished off with a flourish so dramatic he might as well have been signing a death sentence. "You're choosing a very hard way to go, you know," he said, keeping the paper to himself for a moment longer, as though this might change things. *I know*, you said, and took the paper from him and walked off, your boots clomping down the hallway. If it passed through our minds what would become of you, it was only briefly. If we thought about you thereafter it was only because it was strange to see Bill— who wanted to be a firefighter and who therefore had to finish school—going around by himself. Whenever I saw him he was leaning against a wall, flicking his lighter open and closed, setting a tiny slice of the world on fire and then snuffing it out, over and over and over again.

I was surprised to see you a few months later, when I rode with my mother to take her car to a mechanic, an old friend of hers named Wade, a long-faced man who fixed cars out of his own garage, cash under the table. Wade's garage was at the end of a dirt road, and around it were several flat-roofed, leaning houses. In the yard between Wade's house and his neighbor's there were a half dozen or so old cars, parked haphazardly, and three kids were running around and through the cars, playing a game of evasion and capture, shouting threats, opening and closing doors, honking horns. I assumed these kids were Wade's and stood watching them. Until suddenly a woman I recognized as your mother emerged from the neighboring house (a simple box of a house onto which had been added, with no apparent design, several sloping additions) and called out to them—Jimmie, Davis, Ellen, get away from Wade's cars—and the kids, moaning, went back to their own yard. Your mother stood on the front porch shaking out a braided rug, a small cloud of dust rising from it, and as I watched her—hunchbacked, the flesh of her arms sagging, jiggling—I wondered how she could possibly be your mother, the mother of those younger kids. It occurred to me that she must be your grandmother. Just as I was thinking this you came rolling out from underneath one of the cars, quick as a jack from a box. You stood up and wiped your brow, nodded at me—we had never been friends and this was all we owed each other—and then looked at my mother in the frowning way that people tend to do when they first put a face with a name. For if your family was known for its troubles, mine was known for my mother's beauty and for the terrible chaos she tended to create with it. She had, for instance, broken up a marriage the previous summer. For years she had been dating a married man who was keeping her—and, it must be said, me and Malinda as well—in a lakefront condo, but things had soured between them, their fights growing more and more spectacular, resounding across the lake (When are you going to leave her, I'm not going to give this away forever you know; Baby, you already have . . .) until one night, drunk and vengeful, my mother had called the wife and given her an earful. Everyone knew my mother's story. Going through life with her—the somber, apologetic shadow that followed her around—was something like being a public defender.

You walked through Wade's garage and into his house, letting the door slam behind you. "That's my apprentice," Wade told my mother, after you disappeared inside. "Fucked in the head but the kid can fix anything." After which Wade and my mother went back to their conversation, concerning Wade's redheaded and estranged wife, her attempts to fuck him over in court, his subsequent attempts to fuck her back by hiding his assets. Wade was a man who liked to leave sentences hanging in the air unfinished. "I tell you," he kept saying, without further comment. "I tell you what . . ." He liked to stroke his chin, shake his head, gestures of bewilderment and regret. And I recognized these words and those gestures as yours, too, things you had said and done a thousand times while standing in the smokers' circle, *I tell you, I tell you what,* things you must have picked up from Wade. I recognized, I thought, your life. A kid drawn to his neighbor, to the shadowy work of fixing cars, to the refuge it gave him from his own house. I'd long been looking for something similar, and I felt in that moment a connection to you, something shared between us.

But what did I really have to do with you, and you with me? We were two people around the same age, growing up in the same failing city, walking the same streets under the same clouds, nothing much. Except to say that once, without knowing it, you did something that changed my life entirely. With the smallest gesture you altered the course of my life, split it in two, and since then I haven't been able to think of you without feeling a stab, the question of what might have become of me if you had done otherwise.

This was during the summer of 1988, the summer after you dropped out of school. My mother had recently married her third husband, Bud Francis, a man after the fashion of Burt Reynolds who gnawed on toothpicks and stopped at every mirror he passed to fluff his hair. Bud was an appliance salesman and sole heir to Francis Housewares and Electronics, a fluorescent-lit warehouse rumored to have dealings with the mob. Over the Fourth of July weekend he had put in long hours at something he kept referring to as "the No-Money-Down Independence Day Appliance Blowout," and as a reward to us he suggested a weekend at the beach.

The beach was an hour north, a place where people from our city went to sun themselves and stroll along the board-walk, a hundred-yard stretch of junk shops and restaurants, a concert hall and an arcade. There was a desperate feel to the place, not only on the part of the motels and restaurants competing against one another for a modest survival, but on the part of the tourists as well, who went around, lemming-like, after some thrill they couldn't name and couldn't seem to find. Stories were always being told about the beach—about how friends of friends had stumbled into a party at one of the motels or rental cottages, a party at which the music was loud and the beer was free, at which everyone gathered around the person in question and laughed at his jokes, held their stomachs laughing, a party at which there were hijinks, people swinging from chandeliers and lighting off fireworks, a party at which lines of blondes stood admiring the person in question, each hoping to be chosen as his prize. Hearing these stories people kept driving north hoping for the same but failing to find it, a ritual of expectation and disappoint-ment. Even at fourteen I had begun to wonder why the beach continued to thrill people. But it did, it certainly did. And so, even though it required a familial configuration the likes of which Malinda and I tended to avoid (all of us together in the car on the way up, sleeping in the same motel room as our mother and Bud), we went.

On the ride up Malinda read a magazine while I pretended to read a book, though I was really listening to my mother and Bud, who were, absurdly, still getting to know each other. They had met only months before and married in a rush, and Malinda and I had suddenly found ourselves living in a house with a man we didn't know, who didn't know us. In the first few months my mother and Bud had been charmed by the process of getting to know one another, delighted to discover mutual tastes and experiences, but lately there was an edge to these discoveries, the sense that if they had known better they might not have married. Their talk could skid without warning from the curious to the enraged, or disgusted, or spiteful, as it did that day with the passing mention of a certain Sandy D'Angelo, an acquaintance of Bud's.

"Sandy D'Angelo?" said my mother. "I know Sandy D'Angelo! We used to go to church together!"

"Man, what a bitch," Bud said.

"Really?"

"Big-time."

"How do you know her?"

"I don't know her all that good. You could say I knew her three or four times, if you know what I mean."

To which my mother didn't respond, the mere mention of another woman, or the fact that she considered herself superior to Sandy D'Angelo and therefore degraded by being placed in her company, sending her into the kind of complicated, seething mood to which excessively beautiful women often felt themselves entitled. Bud kept trying to make conversation but my mother only responded with yawns and sighs, with angry stabs at the radio's buttons. She didn't speak to him again until he turned off the highway, into the sun, and said, "Shit, where'd my sunglasses go?"

"They're on your head, dumbass."

"Why do you have to talk like that?"

"Because I do."

"Have a little class," Bud said.

And my mother burst out laughing. "You're telling me about class," she said. "I love it."

"What? What's so funny?"

"Nothing. It's just that I'm not about to take social advice from a man wearing his weight in gold jewelry."

"Jesus!" he said, and shook his head. "What the hell's wrong with my jewelry?"

"Girls," said my mother, consulting us in the rearview, "tell him."

"You wear too many rings," said Malinda, without looking up from her magazine. She was scrutinizing an advertisement whose heading read: SKIN AGING BEGINS IN THE LATE TEENS! "And your necklace," she said, referring to the slender gold leg that dangled from Bud's chain, "looks like a nose-picker."

"Jesus!" he said, and blew air out the side of his mouth. "Now you ruined my necklace! Now I can't look at it the same! Jesus!"

Bud was an ass-slapping type of man who tried to turn every argument into a joke—Hey, baby, you on your period or what?—and so when the nuclear power plant, situated just a few miles from the beach, came into view, he said, "Look out, she's gonna blow!" Not knowing our family, Bud didn't realize that my mother had always subscribed to the theory that one should, when going to the beach, get past the power plant without thinking too much about it. One should hold one's breath to the best of one's ability while passing it and then put it out of one's mind while enjoying oneself for the weekend. And yet for me there was something sickly fascinating about the plant, its fat, pale dome like a ball of risen dough, the activity going on within it—the bombardment and splitting of atoms, the release of neutrons—so unnatural it created within me both a profound nausea and an inability to look away. It was especially hard to look away now, considering what had happened only recently in Chernobyl, considering all the images I'd seen of its aftermath, the doomed city of Pripyat, its tall, slender tenements photographed from such a great height they looked like dominoes, upright but with their eventual falling so certain it made their standing seem strange, sad, like the hopes of foolish people.

"Boom!" Bud said, and turned to my mother expecting some display of amusement. But she only closed her eyes and said, "Jesus Christ."

When we arrived at the motel Malinda and I scrambled off, leaving Bud and my mother to their fate, which most likely involved, as Malinda put it, their getting drunk and fighting and then fucking each other's brains out. We spent the whole day walking the beach. Malinda was seventeen, and if she could be said to be interested in anything that year it was the study of other people, what they wore and ate and listened to, how they talked and moved. The beach was so packed there was hardly room to set down a blanket, people were lying flat, the women on their stomachs with their bikini tops untied, couples asleep next to each other, families going through their routines, the elder women sitting under umbrellas, mothers rubbing sunscreen onto the kids, distributing sandwiches and drinks from coolers, ex-army grandfathers, their arms tattooed with eagles and anchors and flags, swinging their grandsons in the surf, couples strolling with their arms around each other. One man, shirtless, kept walking up and down the beach with a boa constrictor wrapped around his torso, smiling every time someone jumped at the sight of him. Over the water a single-engine plane circled back and forth, trailing behind it a streamer on which was printed an advertisement for a local psychic, Mademoiselle Rousseau, full life reading, guaranteed accurate, $19.99. I thought of going. I had a pocketful of money I'd been saving for some unknown purpose—I imagined any number of emergencies in which I'd need to hop a bus or rent a room, bail someone out of jail, bribe an official—and it didn't seem unreasonable to part with a few dollars in exchange for a prediction of that emergency, when it would come and what its nature might be. For months I'd been stealing fives and tens from my mother's wallet—very discreetly, I thought—and I had saved almost two hundred dollars.

Malinda kept sweeping across the beach this way and that, like a retiree with a metal detector, though what she was searching for I couldn't say. She hardly spoke to me. If she said anything at all it was only to register an opinion of a bathing suit, a haircut, a laugh, a walk. She passed judgment in the swift, biting manner common to all beautiful people. For it was true that Malinda had recently become very beautiful. She was another version of my mother, dark-haired and blue-eyed, another Elizabeth Taylor. All day I had seen men looking at her, running their eyes up and down the length of her. She wore a yellow bikini with a pair of cutoff jeans over the bottoms. She had oiled her skin with tanning lotion, and she glistened. Men were so blatant in their staring it was like a scene from a nature documentary, the human animal's rituals of attraction and mating, the instinct to perpetuate life on bald, sickening display.

It wasn't until late in the day that Malinda found what she was looking for. The beach had emptied out and everyone was going up and down the boardwalk, which was so crowded that Malinda and I were often jostled apart. It was as if a great sale were going on and we were all in competition with one another to save money on a valuable item. Along the boardwalk the air smelled of popcorn and fried dough and hot dogs, and underneath all of that something else—an ancient, dark smell, such as one encounters in a tomb. "I don't like it here," I called to Malinda, for the noise was so loud that we had to shout.

Malinda said, "You don't like it anywhere."

"But this," I said, "is worse. I really don't like this."

"So go back to the beach then," she called over her shoulder. "I'm sick of you following me around anyways." She walked on without bothering to check if I was still behind her. But a moment later, when she finally saw what she'd been looking for, she reached back for my hand with every confidence that it would be there. "Look," she said, stopping short and pulling me toward her. "Look at those guys."

Walking toward us were three skinny men with long, ravaged hair. They wore black satin jackets and tight black jeans. Under their jackets they were shirtless and you could see their pale, skinny chests, their light pink nipples. The one in the middle wasn't bad-looking—he had dark hair and black eyes, a square jaw—and he wore an expression of boredom. But the others, who might have been twins, looked like greyhounds. Their eyes were brown and wet and searching. They had about them the meanness and desperation of pound dogs.

Malinda watched them coming and then turned to watch them go. Embroidered in red across the backs of their jackets was the name of an English band whose sole hit had topped the charts two years prior. "Hey!" she said, and slapped me like she always did when she was excited. "I knew it. They're in that band. I saw signs for them. They're playing here." The main attraction of the boardwalk was a small concert hall that tended to attract groups who had risen briefly to fame, then fallen into obscurity. No one actually wanted to see the bands that played there, but then again it was something, people thought, to be able to sit up close to someone who had been famous once, someone who had been on television, it was better than nothing. All along the boardwalk people stopped short as the men walked past, then burst into excited chatter. Girls pressed their fingers to their mouths. I heard the name of the band again and again, and wondered what it would be like to walk through the world and leave a wake behind you, the sound of people speaking your name.

"We have to meet them," Malinda said. We started walking toward the men, Malinda rising up on her tiptoes, keeping track of them. When they turned into a jewelry store Malinda positioned herself just outside its entrance, where there was a woman selling mood rings at a small table. Malinda examined the rings, slipped them on and off her fingers, and I stood behind her trying to remember the last time I had seen her so excited, the last time she had displayed an emotion besides contempt. Certainly it was before Bud, before my mother broke up with the married man and we moved out of the condo, which Malinda had loved more than anything else in her life. I watched the rings on Malinda's fingers, watched them swirl from blue to green to black, mesmerized.

Then, compelled by some instinct, I looked up, and that's when I saw you and Bill walking toward us. You hadn't noticed us yet, and in the few seconds before you saw us I sensed what would happen next. I sensed that Bill, who had long been in love with Malinda and who was always coming up with excuses to talk to her, offering her gum and cigarettes, who often pretended to need a light just so he could ask her for one, a tactic which eventually backfired ("Jesus Christ," Malinda had said once, "I'm not like your personal fucking match supplier, you know"), would see her, and approach her, and she would brush him off with some swift cruelty. Which is exactly what happened. When Bill saw Malinda he cried out her name as though in ecstasy. "Malinda! Hey, Malinda!" he said. "Malinda, hey! Whatcha doing?" He was so excited to see her he actually punched her in the arm.

"What's it look like I'm doing?" she said.

"You looking at jewelry?"

"No," she said, "bathing suits."

"Oh," Bill said. He was a nervous kid in the habit of shifting his weight back and forth between his legs, and he stood there fidgeting for a few seconds, trying to think of something to say. "There's a party somewhere," he said. "I think we're gonna go."

"Good," said Malinda. "Don't let me keep you."

"You wanna come?"

"With you?" she said. "No."

And then you spoke up, angry, your black eyebrows slanted together: *Why do you have to be such a bitch?*

"I don't know," said Malinda, "why do you have to be such a retard?"

Fuck you, you said, and walked off. Bill followed you. But behind your back he turned to us and gave Malinda a big smile, a sweeping wave. "Maybe we'll see ya later!" he said.

When the men emerged from the jewelry shop Malinda was poised there, a cigarette dangling from her mouth, rifling through her purse. Just at the right moment she turned to the men, as if looking for help from the first person who came along, and asked the man in the middle for a light.

The man said nothing, but he stopped and reached in his pocket and pulled out a book of matches. He looked Malinda up and down, lit the match and held it out. Malinda bent her head toward him. Then she tilted her head back so he could see the full length of her neck—men were always commenting on her long neck—and released a little cloud of smoke out the side of her mouth.

"What's your name?" he said.

"Marilyn." This was a name, Malinda believed, that stirred within men certain deeply held longings. When she turned eighteen she planned to go to court to legally adopt it.

"That's a awfully grown-up name," said the middleman.

She shrugged. "What's yours?"

"Flash." And without looking at his friends he stated the names of the other two. "These are my brothers Matt and Mike."

"Hi," Malinda said. She didn't bother to look at Matt and Mike either. She and the middleman had their eyes locked on each other, and it was all routine from there. Flash bought Malinda an ice cream cone, Malinda walked up and down the boardwalk licking it, twirling her cone against her tongue—she couldn't just eat it like a normal person, it had to be some kind of display—and then, the ice cream gone, Flash offered Malinda a drink from a flask he produced from the inner pocket of his jacket; he put his arm around her, she rested her head against his shoulder; they drank more; he said something and she laughed. It all happened very quickly. When Flash led Malinda down the boardwalk steps, then down the street, then steered her into the entrance of a hotel, it wasn't even fully dark.

In the elevator up to the room, while Flash and his brothers were laughing about something, Malinda whispered to me, "He's the drummer!"

I thought of one of the band's songs—the one that had played all through the previous summer—and could only call to mind the crooning of the lead singer and a muted trumpet. "I didn't think they had a drummer," I said.

"Well he is. He's from England."

"How *old* is he?"

Malinda shrugged.

"He looks kind of old."

"I don't care."

I shrugged back. "Have fun."

The hotel room had been done up in some grandmother's idea of sophistication, in shades of silver and mauve. The wallpaper featured a pattern of giant metallic flowers, and they glowed strangely in the dark, like flora dusted with nuclear fallout. It was a large room, a suite, and it was dark but for the light of a single dim lamp. Flash picked a pair of jeans off the floor and rifled through its pockets. "Here they are," he said, and opened his palm, full of tiny red caplets. He held them out to Malinda and she took one and put it in her mouth, and swallowed. Then took another. "Whoa," said Flash, "take it easy."

"My neck hurts," Malinda said to me. "Flash told me he had some pills."

"You want one?" Flash said, looking at me for the first time. "They make you relax," he said. "You Americans could stand to relax some."

"Especially her," said Malinda. "She's wound up wicked tight. She never says two words."

This was hard to argue with. I took a pill and swallowed it. For a long moment after I felt it in my throat.

Soon enough Malinda and Flash went into the bedroom under the pretense of Malinda needing a massage. Matt and Mike and I sat around, stolid and dutiful as Buckingham guards, in the manner of all people who sacrifice themselves to the whims of their betters. We were a class of people so common and so hardworking that we might as well have been unionized. Occasionally we grew tired of our work and we complained, carried out little tantrums, made demands—How come we never do what I want? How come we never talk about me?—but for the most part we simply resigned ourselves to our fate.

"What should we do then?" said one of the brothers. "We can, uh, I don't know," he said. He patted down his pockets and frowned as though it were only a matter of bad luck that he didn't have something in them with which to entertain a sixteen-year-old. "Christ, I don't know," he said. He turned on the TV and ran through the channels. He didn't see anything that satisfied him—a couple of black-and-white movies, the news, commercials—and sat there turning the channels. Like most of the men I had met he looked older up close. His lips were pale and badly chapped. His skin was ruddy and a pattern of purple veins stood out at the side of his sharp, bony nose. Here and there in his mess of long, frizzy hair I could see a gleam of gray. Like an old man he was in the habit of sniffing sharply, and when he breathed in there was a slight whistling sound.

"What instrument do you play?" I said.

"Don't," one said. "Neither does Rod."

"Who's Rod?"

"The guy your sister's with. That's his name."

"Oh. I thought he was the drummer."

"Naw," he said. "We're just with the band. We do the equipment and sound and all that."

"Oh," I said.

"What year are you in school?"

"Sophomore. Next year I'll be a junior."

"Sixteen, then?" He narrowed his eyes, as if concentrating on something important, as if wrestling with a momentous decision.

"That's too young," his brother said. "Sixteen. Man." He shook his head. "Too young."

"But girls are more mature," said the one.

The other shook his head. "Not that much."

"Sixteen isn't so young. Not all that young, when you think about it. When you think about it we're sending eighteen-year-olds off to war all the time."

"I never thought of it that way," said the other, sarcastic. He gave his brother a pitying look. "I'm outta here." He walked off, out of the room. When he was gone I turned to the one left and said, "Who are you again?"

"Mike," he said. He had settled on *The Three Stooges*, who were working as tailors and had found a suit full of money, and its pending loss, which was certain, set off an anxiety in me so powerful the skit's comedy was lost in it.

When a commercial broke in Mike said, "I'm gonna get myself a drink. You want a drink?" He opened the little refrigerator and bent over to inspect its contents. "We got Coke."

I was expecting a can but when he handed me a drink it was in one of the hotel's short glasses, amber-colored and dimpled. It tasted like Coke but there was something else to it, something bitter and warm. Rum, or whiskey, I didn't know the difference. I drank it down and in a minute Mike was up mixing drinks again, and then again. It wasn't long before I felt loose all over and started laughing at the least little thing. My laughter was loud and low and came out stuttering, without my adding any shape to it. It rang through the room and sounded to me the laugh of a retarded person.

I was lying on my stomach on the floor. Mike was sitting beside me with his legs crossed, but went so far as to stand up when something was funny and bend over laughing. "Fuck me, that's funny," he said. Sometimes when he laughed he grabbed his head like people did in aspirin commercials. I rolled over and watched the television upside down. "Hey," I said, "you should try this." Mike stretched out beside me on his back, then started voicing over the characters. "Hey, guys," he said in Curly's falsetto, "everything's all upside down!" And Mo answered, "You're upside down, you moron." With an almost scientific detachment I noticed I was having trouble doing more than one thing at a time, for instance watching the television and listening to Mike, for instance laughing and keeping my eyes open, for instance hearing Malinda cry out in something like pain from the next room and pretending I hadn't. And then everything was reduced to breathing. I was breathing through my mouth as though a person who had been trapped underwater up to the brink of death.

Sometime later Malinda and Flash, or Rod, came out of their room, and distantly I heard Malinda saying, "Shit! Oh shit!" Then she was pulling my hand, pulling me up and then onto my feet. I was still so far gone it was all as in a dream, wobbly and chimerical, the room looked like a place I'd never seen, Flash and Mike like people I'd never seen, and I was up on my feet being pulled along by Malinda out the door and down the hall—we were running, now, with a swiftness that seemed untenable—and when we got to the elevator Malinda pressed the down button but then couldn't wait. She kept on running to the end of the hall and banged through the door to the stairwell, which was lit by a single orange bulb. We ran down the stairs and out into the back parking lot, then around the building, and up to the boardwalk, which was empty, its lights out, its stores shut away behind grates, our footsteps like those of criminals, and Malinda saying all the while, "Shit. We're dead. It's like one in the morning. Shit." I thought of my mother and Bill pacing the motel room, calling the police. I thought of cruisers parked in the motel's lot, their spinning lights keeping everyone awake, massive resentment on the part of the other tenants.

But when we got back to the motel the lights were on and our mother was passed out in bed fully clothed, facedown and snoring. Bill was nowhere to be found. The room was so thick with the smell of sour tequila my mouth watered.

"Jesus," Malinda said. She turned out the lights and went to bed, fell on top of it, and I fell too. We curled toward each other like parentheses. When my eyes adjusted I saw the glow of Malinda's, wet and mournful. She had always been like that at night, unable to sleep, a sense of regret and sadness about her, a softness. This was the thing about her I knew that no one else did. We had a long history of lying quietly side by side, the troubles of our days—the fights we'd had, the wild swings we'd witnessed our mother go through, the drunken exaltations and rages—drifting around us, unspoken but felt, deeply felt. In the morning she would be back to her usual self. By that time we would just be two girls who'd gone back to a hotel room with a couple of older men, it happened all the time, every day, it wouldn't even be worth mentioning.

My mother woke early the next morning and went out for the paper. One of her quirks was that she liked to read the obituaries first thing every day; often she read them aloud to us either for entertainment value ("He was a man fond of playing the flugelhorn!") or for instructional purposes ("She entered the convent at fourteen, where she lived the remaining years of her life." Jesus! She must have died of boredom!). When she returned she told Malinda and me to get up and get our things together. "Move it," she said, "or lose it."

"Where are we going?" Malinda said, groggy, her words running together.

"Get up," said our mother, who was stuffing all of our things into a red duffel bag. It said Schlitz on the side and had belonged, at one time, to one or another of her boyfriends, though I couldn't remember which one.

"Where's Bud?" Malinda said.

"I don't know," said my mother. "Just get your shit and let's go."

"Where are we going?"

"Just come on." My mother was dressed for the beach, in a red bikini and sunglasses. I assumed we were going there but when we got to the beach we just kept walking. Once we'd cleared the strip my mother turned and started walking backwards, facing the line of cars headed out of town, and Malinda, her voice high with disbelief, said, "What are you doing?"

"Watch," our mother said, "and learn." She took her hair out of its ponytail and shook it, arranging it around her shoulders. Then she stuck her thumb out. She was thirty-five and looked, still, like a teenager—it didn't seem unreasonable to me that someone would stop to pick her up. She had always gotten what she wanted rather easily.

"What the hell?" said Malinda. "Where's Bud? What are we doing?"

"Bud's gone," said my mother. "Probably for good."

"What'd you do?" said Malinda, and my mother said she didn't know for sure, that she couldn't exactly remember, but that she was pretty sure it had something to do with another man.

"Oh my God," Malinda said, "this is so embarrassing." Her voice high, squealing, all the composure of the day before gone, gone. In that moment she was a child.

I turned backwards then and regarded the beach, as if some explanation might be found there for what had happened. From that angle the stretch of oceanfront property looked thin and flimsy as a Hollywood set, as if it might fall on its face. Also from that angle I could see my mother's cheek, the slice of flesh hidden behind her sunglasses. I could see that it was bruised to hell. A sharp pain went through me, followed by the pulsing sort of panic that I was prone to in those days. Instinctively I reached for my money, the stash I'd been saving in my pocket. Only then did I realize it was gone.

We walked for a few minutes, the cars passing us by so slowly that we could not only see all the people inside but determine the mood in the cars, most filled with the exhaustion and annoy-ance common to the end of family weekends, each curled in his seat and angled away from the rest, though in some of the cars people were still going at it, joking, fighting. Malinda hung her head, angled her body away from the road, the shame of being seen by someone we knew so hot within her it was coming off in waves. A few times there were cars full of men that slowed down and whistled, honked, asked my mother where she was going. But when she named our city, an hour south, the men didn't want to go that far out of their way and said, "Good luck, baby." And she said, "I wouldn't take a ride with you anyways."

We kept walking. The road opened up into two lanes, the traffic moved faster. Malinda started to complain. "Just call someone," she said, and listed all of our relatives. "Just go back and call Auntie Lily or Auntie Ellen. Or call Pop or something. God, this is so fucking humiliating!" But my mother wouldn't give in, she just kept walking backwards, saying every now and then, "What's this, what's this? This looks like it could be good," though the cars kept going by. Then, in one of those rare moments when the world's fools are vindicated, you and Bill drove past in your red Camaro, radio blasting as always. Bill leaned out his window and shouted at us, "Hey, Malinda, you need a ride?" and Malinda looked up. Her eyes went wide with relief. She raised her arm up and waved, started jogging toward you. But there was some disagreement between you and Bill—you kept driving forward and I could see you reaching for him, trying to pull him back inside the car by his shirt. He turned toward you and said something, you said something in return. The car slowed, and swerved toward the side of the road for a moment, and Bill leaned out the window again, waved us toward the car, but then, in some impulsive defense of yourself and your kind, some protest against the way people like Malinda had always treated you, you steered the car back onto the road and sped away. You left us there in the dust.

We stood there stunned. The air of adventure—the cinematic flair that had so far been coloring the trip—was gone and we were truly defeated. We had behaved poorly—not just this weekend but always—and we were being taken to task, humiliated. I don't know how long we walked, each of us in our private misery. In my case I was so lost in it—wondering how we would get home and then afterward, where we would go—that when I saw a car pass us, then pull to the side of the road, it took me a moment to realize that the driver was stopping for us. It was a beautiful old car, an Oldsmobile '88, with a long body and gently rising fins. There were two men in the car and they were black, I could tell even from a distance.

The driver went so far as to get out of the car—usually people didn't do this, just waited for you to approach—and even put a hat on his head before walking toward us. He cut something of a figure. He was tall and slender and very well dressed, in a pair of gray slacks with a seam pressed down the center and a white dress shirt. A red feather sprang from the band of his fedora. The brim of the hat, and its shadow, concealed much of his face.

"Good afternoon," he said.

"Good afternoon," said my mother.

"You ladies," said the black man, "look to be in need of a ride." His voice was deep and his speech exact. He could have made a living as the voice of God in movies. "Where are you heading?"

My mother spoke the name of our city. She said it in the formal way, instead of the way everyone else said it, letting the word go soft and lazy in their mouths, and the way she said it now sounded like a place I'd never been, a place in which something like this would never happen.

"That happens to be," said the black man, "where we live. My son and I." He tilted his head toward the car and for a second I could see the man's face, long and thin. Two deep lines were carved around the sides of his mouth as though with a knife. His eyes were extraordinary. They were resinous in color, almond-shaped, and there was an intensity to them, a sharpness I had rarely seen before.

"We don't want to be any trouble," my mother said in the modest voice she used whenever she was meeting someone for the first time.

"No trouble," the man said. He looked at his watch, a heavy gold one of the sort that men are given after twenty-five years of service to their employers. My mother was fond of saying that you could tell a lot about a man by his watch. And what you could tell about this man was that he was steady, reliable.

"We've found ourselves," my mother said, "in an unexpected predicament. I'm sorry to be so improperly clothed."

"Not at all," said the man, and motioned us toward the car.

"It's a relief to meet a real gentleman," said my mother. "You've no idea how rare you've become." And I turned my mother's phrasing over in my mind—so improperly clothed, how rare you've become—wondering who this person was, my mother, what disease she suffered from, to be able to change herself like this, again and again, to spend her life this way.

When we approached the car the man's son—also tall and thin, with the same eyes as his father—got out and regarded us. He wore an expression of barely contained hatred, and when

his eyes met Malinda's I saw pass between them a look of understanding, a half-lidded disdain for the situation, their parents.
In a flash I recognized it as a look I would see go between them
again and again.

All my life I'd suffered from strange flashes in which I saw
the future. Little scenes appeared in my mind, lightning-fast,
that sooner or later played out in real time. Often these scenes
were so ordinary and predictable that their eventual playing-out
came as no surprise—my mother standing in the living room
folding up a purple housecoat, packing her suitcase, calmly
preparing to leave her second husband, Poor Michael Collins;
Malinda, sick in bed with a high fever, pulling a yellow blanket tight around her, her teeth chattering. But sometimes the
scenes were so unpredictable, so extraordinary, there seemed
no way I could have seen them coming except that I had some
kind of strange ability. Once I saw a dog with a missing ear sitting on a fire escape. And years later, when my mother moved
us to a building with a fire escape, I knew he would appear, and
he did. I'd told my mother about these visions and she'd advised
me to do what I could about lottery numbers. But the things I
saw never had to do with good fortune. They were always small,
private moments of resignation and regret. Several times that
year I had seen a grassy field filled with small puddles, a set of
bare feet walking through them, and I'd been preoccupied with
what this might mean. Someone was wandering somewhere, in
sorry circumstances, but I couldn't say more than that.

How it would happen that my mother and this stranger would
come together I didn't know. The odds were against it. This man
was much older than my mother, and serious, not at all the type

she usually went for. On top of which he was black, which seemed to complicate things, at least for my mother. Once, when I was young and we were driving into a black neighborhood for take-out, I had asked my mother why black people all lived together in one part of town, and whites in another, and she had tried to explain the difficulty between the races. According to my mother it wasn't that she, and the rest of our family and friends, had a problem with "the blacks," as she called them, it was just that we didn't know them, we had no experience with them. Part of the problem, she said, was that they had their own way of talking, and dressing, and they watched different shows on television and listened to different music and danced and even walked differently. And so sometimes it was hard. For example, one of the recurring conundrums of her existence was that she happened to love the fried chicken at this particular walk-up takeout window more than any other food in the world. It killed her sometimes how much she loved it. They must have done something magical to that chicken, it was spicy and crispy and the meat fell right off the bone and the bones themselves, you could suck them. She wanted to eat this chicken every day, she said, but there was always a crowd of blacks standing around in front—Nothing against them! she said—it was just that when she walked up to order she had to stand around waiting and it was hard sometimes, to talk with black people, partly because she didn't understand what they were saying and partly because when she did understand them, she didn't know what they were talking about. Bid whist, for instance, she had no idea what bid whist was. One of the men in particular who was always there had a slow smile that made you feel like you were being made fun of but didn't realize it, like a joke had been made against you which you failed to comprehend. "And it's not just me!" she said. "A lot of my girlfriends say the same thing. So you see," she said, "it can be hard."

Yes, it was hard to imagine. I particularly couldn't imagine how this serious man would tolerate such a frivolous woman as my mother, except to say that underneath his fine clothes and good manners must beat the heart of a fool. My mother kept leaning forward into the front seat and asking inane questions—what year the car was made, who was singing on the radio, what the boy liked to study at his college, whether or not the Red Sox were going to do it this year, finally—and the more she talked the less likely it seemed she and this quiet, polite man would ever take an interest in one another. Nevertheless I had seen it, it was there. I knew it would happen.

At first I blamed you, Elwood Fucking LePoer, for leaving us there on the side of the road and delivering my mother straight into her fourth marriage before she had even finished her third. But in the following weeks and months—after we got our things and moved yet again, as my mother and Walter Adams began at first a friendship and soon enough a romance—I came to value Walter's presence: reasonable, sobering, like that of a police car parked on the side of a road on which people tended to drive too fast. To make his living he worked as a mechanic, but in his spare time he read and listened to music, played chess, whittled sparrows out of fallen branches, wrote letters to friends in Germany, where he'd been stationed during his ten years in the army. Often he gave me books to read (*The Plague, The Idiot, The Trial*) and then, after

I'd read them, asked me about the characters over a game of chess. I never knew what to say—the world of those novels was so distant and intricate, so thoughtful, so far from anything I knew—but in the process of that slow, quiet game, he'd manage to draw out of me the thoughts he suspected were buried in my mind. Overall I was a poor chess player—I never thought of advancing against my opponent—but I had a talent for evasion which Walter said would take me far. We became a club, of sorts, two people who went out to the front porch when my mother's moods were intolerable.

I suppose it must be confessed here that for a number of months prior to Walter's arrival I had stopped speaking to anyone but Malinda and the occasional complete stranger. It had started as a game, something to drive my mother crazy. But the longer I played it the harder it was to stop, until eventually the part of me that spoke to other people was gone, and I was knocked out cold, a chloroformed cotton ball dropped into the jar in which I lived. Once I'd been forced to meet with my high school's counselor, who informed me that if I didn't snap out of it I'd end up working in one of the city's factories, folding shirts or assembling boxes alongside the dregs of society, murderers and mental defectives, ex-priests, and I had more or less resigned myself to this. Many a life had passed this way and I didn't see what difference it would make if I did the same. But with Walter around I started to imagine a different kind of life for myself, a possible future, away from that place and those people, maybe even college. With Walter I found that I had things to say. Whenever I stopped to think about how chance our meeting was, how I would have turned out if I'd never met Walter, I thought of you, Elwood LePoer, I saw your battered red Camaro speeding off, and I felt for you a begrudging fondness.

It happened that in the months before you died I saw quite a lot of you. I had graduated high school and taken a summer job checking groceries at the Super G, where you worked part-time in the meat department as an assistant butcher, arranging cuts of meat on cotton pads, in Styrofoam trays, then running them through a machine that sealed them in cellophane. After my shift ended at the grocery store, but before I had to show up for my second job, I often sat in the grocery store's break room drinking coffee from its vending machine, which was awful but which I couldn't stop drinking, something about the Styrofoam cup dropping down and the two streams of liquid—one oily and black, the other steaming hot water—striking me as clever. This was the time of day when I sat thinking over the question of what I would do with my life. My mother had already left Walter Adams and moved in with someone else, her life fully absurd now, her last chance blown. She was irredeemable. I was saving money and trying to decide whether to use it for college or to go off in search of Malinda, who had left home the day after she graduated high school and hadn't called or written in a year—we had no idea where she was. Most of the time I told myself it didn't matter. Malinda had turned wholly cruel by then. If she spoke to me it was only to tell me to fuck off. She had barely graduated high school. In the months before she left she had been going around with an older guy who took her to bars every night, and her movements and speech had taken on a languid, melting quality. She had stopped eating, stopped showering. One day she woke up with a tattooed snake wrapped around the entire length of her left arm and told me she had no recollection of getting it. By then she didn't care about anything, anything, anything at all, and to find some-one like that—to defer one's own life, to uproot oneself and go off in search of a person like that—wasn't something lightly undertaken.

Sometimes you came into the break room for a soda, and a few words would pass between us. Rumor had it that, even though a war was brewing, you had gone and signed up for the military, that you were just wasting time until you left for basic training. All that year the army had been running advertisements—"Be All You Can Be"—and I imagined they must have appealed to you in the same way that other commercial slogans had. People talked about your enlistment behind your back, but I never heard anyone ask you about it personally. "Jesus," people said whenever you left the room, "that dumb bastard."

The last time I saw you you were especially animated. You had a secret, something you couldn't wait to tell someone, and you burst through the door of the break room hoping for an audience. When you saw only me sitting there you looked disap-pointed, but you went ahead and took what you could get.

You wanna see something gross? you said. And I said, Okay. You waved me toward you—*It's back here*—and you walked out of the break room and through frozen foods, behind the meat case and through the swinging doors into the cold of the meat room, which smelled of flesh and fat, the bitter stench of old blood. It was a wide-open room with white walls and a concrete floor, a steel table at its center, a hulking steel machine off to the side, the grinder, I guessed, and a wide steel sink at the back, at which stood a skinny man in a white coat and a white hat in the shape of an ocean liner. He was cleaning off a stack of metal trays. *That's José,* you said. And José, rat-faced, looked up and nodded. The radio was going, the ecstatic wailing of Robert Plant. You walked past José and disappeared through a doorway covered with vertical plastic slats and when I followed you through them it was into a dark freezer, biting cold, with three sides of beef hanging from the ceiling, red muscle wrapped in yellowish fat, still alive somehow, it seemed, something glowing about them, and I thought about a book I had read as a child in which the world was controlled by three amorphous beings who sat alone in a dark room, receiving and enduring millions upon millions of tiny communiqués, measuring them, keeping track by the second of the amount of life and death in the world, its beauty weighed against its suffering. In the world of that book the fate of the universe depended upon good outweighing evil—the world would end, it was said, the very instant that evil tipped the scales—and it was a vicious battle, the world being saved sometimes by a single act of kindness, a smile bestowed upon a stranger.

You walked through the room and out its back door, which opened in a burst of light onto a concrete platform, up to which a truck had been pulled, a small ladder running up its back side. *Delivery,* you said, and jerked your thumb at the truck. *Go ahead and take a look.* I climbed the steps and looked over the top of the truck, which was open, and down to its insides, in which lay a skinned horse, its muscles painfully red, intricately woven, its eye still intact, lidless, staring. "Jesus," I said, and climbed down, my face screwed up in disgust.

Hamburger, you said. *Cheap meat.*

"No way."

Way. You fished a cigarette from the pack in your coat pocket, lit it, dragged with the scowling intensity of all smokers.

I said, "I heard you joined the army."

Yeah, you said. *I leave in a couple weeks.*

"Oh," I said. As usual I wanted to talk, to say something expansive, but couldn't find the words. What I said was, "Have fun."

Where you living now? you asked, a discreet way of acknowledging that we had moved yet again, the fifth time since I met you. My mother had moved in with a golf pro ten years her junior, and we were all living in a carriage house at the back corner of the grounds of a country club.

I said, "I don't know. Somewhere around." Because the truth was I sometimes forgot where I was going and started walking toward Walter Adams's house, sometimes I still went there to sit on the porch with him and play chess, his chess set so oversized—the kings and queens standing six inches high—that my mistakes could be seen from a block away.

What's up this weekend? you said.

"Working. Here and Friendly's."

Yeah, you said. *I seen you there.*

I had seen you, too. On weekends you and Bill and Bill's new girlfriend—a squat, short-haired girl named Jeanine—came in for burgers and ice cream. The sight of the three of you together had struck me as wrong somehow, and clearly it struck you the same way. As Bill and Jeanine sat with their arms around one another, feeding each other spoonfuls of ice cream, you sat looking away, a pained expression on your face. In fact your expression was so wounded it had caused me to wonder if you'd joined the military out of spite, like a rejected lover.

You blew smoke out your nose, as if some sign of disapproval. *I gotta fix Bill's car tomorrow,* you said. *Then me and him are going up the beach.*

"Oh," I said, the memory of what we had done to you, and you had done to us, flashing through me. "I heard there's a party up there somewhere." The kind of lie I was prone to telling in those days, anything to keep up a conversation.

Yeah, you said. *Well, see ya.* You took a last drag of your cigarette, tossed it down into the parking lot. Then you belched long and loud, and without another word walked back inside, through the freezer and cutting room, out the swinging doors with their circular plastic windows, whistling all the while a tune that was familiar but hard to place, the notes sent off slow and halfhearted, just shivering in the air, and it took me a moment to recall the lyrics—*I wish I was an Oscar Mayer wiener, that is what I'd really like to be*—this song trailing you all the way out of the store, Jesus, Elwood, what a farewell, what an exit. It was the last time I ever saw you. Because the next morning, when you went to fix Bill's gas tank, which had a leak and which was, he assured you, bone dry ("Bone fucking dry," he kept saying afterward, crying at the funeral, in bars and stores and the bank and post office and wherever else he ran into people, "I swear to God it was bone fucking dry"), when you got on your back and squirmed underneath the car and touched your soldering iron to the tank it exploded, it killed you.

"Jesus," people said when they heard the news, "that dumb bastard."

At the wake, on a table draped in white cloth, stood a gold-framed picture of you, from your last year of school. In the picture you were staring off, openmouthed, your dark eyebrows pushed together in an expression of strained effort, as if you were trying to recall someone's name, or multiply in your head. Those pictures had, I remembered, been taken in the gymnasium, and we had stood in long lines waiting for our turns in front of the camera. When we finally got to the front of the line, and were seated on a wooden stool in front of a marbled blue backdrop, our friends had stood next to us saying things to make us laugh, and I imagine as your picture was taken someone had told a joke you didn't get, and the photographer, hating his job, having grown weary of waiting, had snapped the photo in the second before the joke's intentions announced themselves to you, the second before you smiled.

At the funeral the priest spoke of you, and your death, in somewhat surprising terms. "Glory be to God!" he said. "One of the Lord's gentlest lambs has returned to his shepherd!" Your mother sat with her head turned toward the window, staring off as always. She fingered a rosary.

After the burial people stood around saying how pointless your death was, how stupid. We did a poor job of mourning you. Mostly we spoke of the last time we saw you. (The last time I saw Elwood was at the Laundromat, he was sitting there eating sardines and the smell was so bad I almost puked . . . I saw him just a couple days ago, I was walking to work and he was driving around and he honked at me and he yelled out the window, *What's up, motherfucker!* . . . I saw him in the library just sitting in one of those big-ass chairs, and I said what's up and he said he was just there for the air-conditioning . . .) The nature of our talk had more to do with fear—with the feeling that death had swept down and taken you and we'd been standing right there, more or less right next to you, it might just as well have been us—than with grief. "That dumb bastard," people kept saying, looking down, their hands stuffed in their pockets. "That dumb fuck."

At no time did anyone mention that there was something more to be considered, that factoring into your death was not only a large measure of stupidity but also of trust, of faith. To take a friend at his word, to position oneself on one's back, in the dark, in service to that friend, to do this knowing that if your friend was wrong, if the tank wasn't completely dry, it meant your life—there was something sadly noble about this, something beautiful. But we were too small to mention it.

A week later I went off to college and for a long time I didn't think about you. Then in my junior year I came across your name in a French literature class, given to a hapless, doomed character much like yourself. Le Poer, a variation of *le pauvre*: the pathetic, the pitiable, the poor. By then I had seen wealth and had realized at last that we were poor. You, me, that whole miserable city, that godawful place, bleak and ugly as hell, we were all poor. We could hardly be otherwise. Our city was a landlocked settlement that had failed long ago, that had built its factories—dozens of them, red brick, leaning smokestacks rising up from their rooftops—without taking into account its lack of waterways and the added cost of transportation this made necessary, all of its exports—wire, textiles—having to be carted out by horse, and so it was only a matter of time before these factories folded to their competitors, the city folding soon after. And of our ancestors, the people who chose to stay behind after the factories shut down, what could be said of them except that they were foolish, stubborn, hopelessly stupid, what could be said of them except that they were poor? By the time we came along, generations of decay later, the place was falling down, a third of its population jobless and walking the streets, drunks and drug addicts, crippled veterans, raving lunatics. We were poor, our lives filled with the stupid things that poor people did, the brutalities we committed against each other, the violence, the petty victories we claimed over one another, crabs topping each other in a basket instead of trying to climb out of that basket; the desperate, impulsive lurches we made at love, no matter what the cost to those around us or how fleeting we knew that love would be; the indifference; all that we drank and smoked, the serums we shot into our veins; the hours we spent at grueling, mind-numbing jobs, one day after another, how, in order to survive these jobs, we scraped our minds clean like plates, cleared them of all thought; our prayers, if we prayed at all, sent off in rages, Jesus Christ, Jesus Christ, Jesus god-damned Christ. We were poor.

There wasn't much chance for you (or Bill, who killed himself a few years after your death) to turn out much differently than you did, the pathetic, the pitiable, the poor. In order to turn out any differently one had to leave that place. One was, for a time, glad to do it, one was free—free!—one felt oneself weightless. And yet something about being poor stayed with a person and managed to trouble that person's new life no matter how far away she traveled. If a once-poor person, say, was taken to a dinner party, and the party's host picked up a small bell and rang it, and if, theoretically, at the sound of this bell a servant came into the room dressed in a humiliating outfit, then retreated, then reappeared producing whatever it was that the host required, perhaps a sugar spoon, the once-poor person would most likely have to excuse herself from the table on the pretense of needing air, would most likely walk back through the kitchen and sit for a long time, an unreasonably long time, on the plastic bucket being used to prop open the kitchen door, because the once-poor person—myself, yes—would have just then realized how absurd it was, the party she was at, the life she was trying to live, how miserably out of place she was there. To be poor, it marked a person, it cast its shadow across the whole of her life.

No, there was no getting away from that place, one always returned and returned always. How strange it was to realize that everyone I had known, everything I had seen and done, was still with me. How closely, after all, we were bound together. Years later, when visiting the graves of my family, I remembered that you had been buried in the same cemetery, and went looking for you. I tried to remember which plot was yours. In poor cemeteries there are no large markers by which to orient oneself—no statues rising up to testify to the greatness of a sin-

gle lost life—and it took me a long time to find it. I walked up
and down the rows, reading the names, Santangelo, Cosentino,
Stephanopoulos, and the biblical scraps beneath them (Come
unto me, I will give you rest . . . I will fear no evil . . . The Lord
is my shepherd, I shall not want), all of the headstones more or
less the same, many of them leaning and seemingly forgotten.
Only the occasional grave showed any evidence of pilgrimage, a
tiny flag, a plastic bouquet speared in the soil. The ground was
soaked from the morning's rain, little puddles everywhere. My
shoes were so waterlogged that I had to take them off. I walked
barefoot through the green grass.

When I finally found your grave, along with a few of your
relations, clustered together near the cemetery's back fence, I
saw that I had circled back almost exactly to the place where I
had started, that your family had been laid to rest very close to
mine. Soon enough, I thought, there would be almost no difference between us. I stood for a long time before your head-
stone, inscribed with your full name, Elwood Eugene LePoer,
and beneath it something your mother must have chosen, the
last, false hope of the long-suffering: *Blessed are the poor in spirit,
for theirs is the kingdom of heaven.*

Elegy for

Carson Washington

(1972–1993)

Fat and black, fat and black, did I have any goddamn idea, you asked, what it meant to be fat, to be black, any goddamn idea what a drag it was sometimes, what a lack, everyone else going around getting pats on the back and what you got, right in the face, was a slap, all your life alone dancing with a hat rack, what a kick in the ass it was, what a rip in the slacks, to be fat and black indeed.

This was 1990, your first and only year of college. You were eighteen. You had come to the state university (that fine, fine place conceived and built and haunted by a president, with its green lawns, its flower beds and cherry trees, its magnificent brick buildings, the money so thick there you could smell it in the air like a blossoming crop) on scholarship from your dusty hometown, population nine hundred, where you lived with your mother and father and sister and her infant son in a four-room cinderblock house. Your father worked in the fields—tobacco, hay—your mother and sister part-time at the county nursing home, and the same sort of life was expected for you. Until you'd gone and shown a talent for school, until the teachers had made a fuss over you and sent you off to that place where we met, roommates, and lived together for a time.

The first thing you ever said to me was: *That all you got?* A phrase of assessment and disapproval. I was standing sweat-soaked in the doorway of our room, holding a blue duffel bag. You had already arrived and made up the bed by the window with bright pink sheets, you had already tuned your wood-paneled thirteen-inch television set to one of the few channels that came in. *Casablanca* was playing. Humphrey Bogart slouched over a drink.

All you got's a duffel bag, for real?

"I took the train," I said. " I didn't want to carry too much." I stood there staring. You were the fattest person I had ever seen, so fat I wondered how you moved. Two suitcases lay open on your bed and you were busy fussing with their contents, shaking out clothes and putting them on hangers. You wore a purple smock-like dress that snapped up the front, and your head was wrapped in a purple scarf.

Boy, you said, *you took the train? Your parents didn't even drop you off or nothing?* You shook your head and laughed, like I was some kind of joke. You looked me over, up and down and up again, and when our eyes met I saw that yours were strange, different from any I'd seen before, amber-colored and gleaming, shot through with flecks of yellow.

Then—having reached a decision about me, having seen in my eyes no kind of threat or even resistance—you started in talking like we'd known each other all our lives. *You just missed Daddy and Sharon and Regis,* you said. *Momma stayed home 'cause she on shift at the nursing home. She and Sharon work all day wiping asses down at the county home and they figured me too but I said I got better things to do than wipe an ass, thank you very much, so here I am.* Your talk was quick, high-pitched. You rifled through one suitcase, then the other, until you found what you were looking for—a plastic bag full of snapshots and a roll of tape. You started taping the pictures to the wall over your bed. *This is the only picture anyone have of my father, Merriweather Washington,* you said. You held up a three-by-five snapshot of a short, stout man standing with his arms crossed, seething and shirtless, in front of an old rust-colored Mercury. *The only picture of him in the world except his driver's license. Otherwise he hate to take a picture. Why I'm hanging it up I don't really know. It's not like we get along so good. You should see his temper. Break a dish and look out, spill something and look out. One time he even threw a cat out the window. The only person he got any patience with is Regis.* Here you produced a series of wallet-sized photos of your sister's baby, fat and smiling, fat and smiling, fat and smiling. *This is my sister's kid. We had all kinds of pictures done. Regis in sailor suits, Regis in a ball uniform.* You held them up. *Regis in his christening gown. Regis butt naked.*

"He's cute," I said. I moved to get a closer look, dropped my bag. That smile!

He's a pain in the ass is what he is, you said. *Going around the house turning everything upside down, screaming, like it wasn't a small enough house to begin with before he came along, let me tell you.* You taped up the pictures of Regis in a star pattern. The walls were cinderblock, painted white, the kind of walls you wanted to cover over with something, but when you did the effort looked sad.

You held up another picture, a beautiful girl with a sly smile, with long, wild hair like the tentacles of a squid. *Here's his mother,* you said, *my sister Sharon. She the dumbest thing on two legs if you want the truth. Dropped out of high school. All she does all day is sit watching TV in some kind of trance, twirling her hair around her finger, you should see her sitting there with her mouth open, ten hornets could fly in there she wouldn't even notice.* You turned Sharon's picture and looked at it for a moment, then put it back in your bag. *I don't need her looking at me all the time,* you said. *Staring over my shoulder, no thank you.*

You kept talking. On and on about your family, immediate and extended, taping up their pictures. Your father had thirteen siblings and you named them all, named their spouses and children, a biblical litany of names. In fact one of them was named Jesus. *Jerome, Penny, Louisa, Sherman,* you said. I stretched out on the bed and used my bag for a pillow, half listening to you and half wondering what I had gotten myself into, what I could have possibly been thinking when I'd left the house that morning and walked in the dark to the train station, past the bars on Shrewsbury Street with their signs still lit, with muffled music still coming from their insides; past the diners glowing yellow, their patrons slumped on their stools and staring down into their coffee mugs, and finally the train station itself, at five-thirty in the morning no less, a depository of lost souls, some-one in blue coveralls mopping in a corner, some old man in a dirty trench coat bent over with his arm deep up the bowels of a vending machine, making desperate straining noises. All summer I'd wondered whether I'd leave home or not, and had more or less decided against it. But then again I'd taken note of the train schedule, so that was something. Up to the last min-ute, when I boarded, I was going back and forth. Then I got on and settled in, the train lurched, and it was done. I watched that wretched falling-down city—its brick factories with their crumbling smokestacks, their busted-out windows—pass by and felt, surprisingly, nothing. When we passed my neighbor-hood I thought how my mother and her boyfriend were still sleeping and wouldn't wake up, wouldn't know I was gone, until past noon.

When I'd finally stepped off the train it was into some south-ern translation of the life I knew—leaning houses with peel-ing paint and burned-out lawns, sagging porches, rusted cars parked helter-skelter in the front yard, kids going around shirt-less and barefoot. But as I walked toward the campus the build-ings straightened up, grew larger and more polished, their lawns filled out, there were flowers spilling out of window boxes, there were mailboxes painted to resemble the houses whose mail they stood to collect, there were waxed cars gleaming in driveways. And then, finally, there was the campus itself, every leaf, every blade of grass bright and smacking, impeccable, people going around in blue blazers and white pants and tasseled loafers, blond people walking in large groups talking riotously, laughing, one of them exclaiming to another, "We used to summer there!" and all up the brick walkways, in my T-shirt and jeans and flip-flops I dragged my bag behind me, having long since given up carrying it on my back, then in front of me like a corpse, sweating and exhausted I dragged myself to the dorm, stopping now and then to consult a small campus map I kept unfolding and then folding and then unfolding again, as if looking at it would explain what I'd done, what I'd been thinking that morning when I left home. The last light was in the sky, pink and violet, and it was too late to go back.

Now here I was, arrived at last, having done something significant for the first time in my life, but it didn't matter. However far I had traveled and what I had left behind was of no significance in that room, which was yours from the start, entirely. You were still talking. *My second cousin,* you said, *hardly any blood between us, she went up to Washington with a boyfriend and got herself killed in a parking lot 'cause she got mugged and wouldn't give up her purse, which was ugly, you ask me, you wouldn't see me getting killed for no patchwork piece of shit purse like that, I'd be standing on a corner trying to give it away.* You held up a picture of the dead girl, pigtailed and smiling, and shook your head. *No kind of sense,* you said. *And here's Emily who died in her crib, poor thing. And here's a picture of Uncle Clarence who died of natural causes at ninety-four, a pervert if you ever met one. And here's Aunt Fanny and Aunt Florence, dead and also dead, twins, one of them or the other, I can't remember, was working in the fields and got struck by lightning, it came out of the ground and up through her leg and out her shoulder, and from then on she could speak French, nobody knows how come.* You were taping all of the dead people some distance above the others, as though the dead were floating in heaven. *Here's a kid from my high school, Wallace Hudgins, dead of a heart defect right in the middle of a basketball game,* you said, and taped him up—skinny and bucktoothed, red-haired, freckled—off to the right of your family, in a separate heaven for white people. *Pathetic,* you said.

Those days I was having a problem seeing my way out of whatever moment I happened to be in, and for a long time I lay on the bed, staring at your dead relations as if held in thrall. It seemed to me that the whole year would pass this way, you talking and me listening, you going on and on about people I didn't know and would never meet. I saw myself in some warped translation of *A Thousand and One Nights,* held captive to your stories in and out of a year, yes, I was in for it, there was no escape, I saw you talking and talking and talking, and a dread settled on me, I saw myself swallowed up, my own life erased and yours written all over it, I saw these things as truths and as self-evident, which they were: indeed, that year, this was pretty much what happened.

Those first weeks of school, during which we both failed to make other friends, we fell into the habit of sitting together for hours in the cafeteria at a table by the window. How we loved that cafeteria! Other students stopped there to eat as little and as quickly as possible, complaining all the while about the food in loud voices. "I'm supposed to eat this?" they said, stabbing their fork into blocks of lasagna, peeling layers of cheese off the tops of casseroles to inspect their insides. "This is bullshit!" But for you and me that cafeteria was some kind of dream. One could sit and eat to one's heart's content; one could eat, for instance, bowl after bowl of every kind of sugared cereal known to man, bowls topped to the brim with the coldest, whitest, wholest of milk. And we did. We sat there eating cereal until closing. I was up and down a dozen times refilling our bowls. *Gimme some of that Cap'n Crunch,* you'd say. *Go get me some of that marshmallow cereal, you know, the kind with that faggoty leprechaun mascot. Go get me some Sugar Smacks, some Corn Pops, some Froot Loops, some Honeycombs, some Trix.*

You talked the whole time we ate. Your favorite subject was the folly of passersby. *Don't she think she something,* you'd say of a girl walking past wearing some ridiculous outfit, an argyle sweater and a pair of crisply ironed khaki shorts, a set of pearls, a pair of tasseled loafers, a giant ribbon in her hair. *Walking around like she Miss America or something. Please.* There were groups of people walking everywhere at all hours, out enjoying themselves, off to concerts or movies or bars or volleyball games, to chess club and choir practice and keg parties, a never-ending parade of people walking past the cafeteria window, and you mocked them all. When groups of boys walked by you liked to ventriloquize them in a voice so surprisingly not your own, so deep and precise, so white, that I could hardly believe it was you. *What kind of asshole are you?* you'd have one say to another.

I'm the kind that likes to torture small animals. As a kid I used to sit in the driveway frying ants with a magnifying glass.

I'm the kind, said the first, *with a limp little dick. But I'm so rich someone will marry me anyway.*

I'm the kind, said a third, *who's gay but won't admit it. I'm going to run for office so I've got to find somebody here to pretend to be my wife.*

Let's go drive our convertibles, said the first.

Yes, said the second, *and then let's go polish our money.*

After that, said the third, *let's go buy some more khaki pants. I don't have anywhere near enough khaki pants.*

Mostly I left things to you but now and then I'd mutter something cutting. "That girl," I'd say of a trotting bucktoothed blonde, "is what happens when a horse fucks a rabbit." And you'd say, *I knew it. You one of those quiet types who got all kinds of nasty things to say, I knew it the minute I saw you.* Once you even raised your glass to me.

Each night we stayed and ate until everyone was gone but the janitors, those skinny black men in their blue coveralls, who brought out the mops and buckets, who turned the chairs up onto the tables, who slopped that cold gray mop water all over the floor, as if it did anything. Everyone, everyone working those service jobs at the university was black, and you liked talking to them. They were, you said, *your people.* You spoke to them in a country accent so thick I struggled to understand it. *Hi you doing,* you said to them, and I sat turning that phrase in my mind, wondering if it was a clever shortening of "Hi, how are you doing?" or if someone somewhere had misheard the word "how" and started going around saying "hi" in its place. While I was thinking about this I was also thinking about how hard you would laugh at me if you could read my mind.

Your conversations with these men were all more or less the same, and acknowledged in one form or another that life was an undertaking to be trudged through, and trudged through, against great opposition.

"I keep on keeping on," the janitors said.

And you said, *You gotta keep rolling on, that's right.*

"You know how we do," they said.

You just keep putting one foot in front of the other.

"No one stopped me yet."

Ain't nobody can.

"I tell you what, I dare somebody."

That's right.

Whenever it came time to introduce me you always claimed we were sisters. *This here's Mary,* you said. *My twin.* Which always got a laugh.

"If you twins," they said, "so's me and the president."

You know it!

Something started to happen in my mind whenever I heard you talk to those janitors. When you talked to them it was like music, and like music it played in my head for hours after. The quick back-and-forth of it, the understanding and agreement— I'd never been a part of anything like it. In my family everything was terse, accusatory. And I wondered what I would sound like, who I would be, if I talked like you. Early one morning I stared at myself in the bathroom mirror and said, ever so quietly: "Hi you doing?" And answered myself: "I just keep on keeping on." But it was ridiculous, from my mouth it sounded ridiculous.

It got so that your voice was in my head all the time. I had a job that year working at a sad, failing place called Donut Land, weekday mornings from five to ten, and all through my shift, even though you were home sleeping, I could hear you making comments, putting down the place and its patrons with your two favorite words: *Pitiful! Pathetic!* Indeed everything about Donut Land was pitiful and pathetic. The Donut Land uniform—a short-sleeved white shirt and brown pants, a brown visor that said "Donut Land" in pink and red—had been copied more or less exactly after the style of our national donut competitors across the street, thriving, whose name we didn't speak, absolutely did not speak, as if speaking its name would stop our hearts. The owner of Donut Land, a fat woman with oil-slicked hair and beady black eyes and rotten teeth named Deborah McGhee, left every day during the morning rush and walked over to Dunkin' Donuts to study their wares. "They got black-frosted donuts over there with little orange jimmies on 'em," she said one October morning. "Halloween Donuts. We got to get us some Halloween Donuts to keep ourselves competitive." This was her soul's sole preoccupation, the keeping up with and eventual surpassing of Dunkin' Donuts. Never once did she strike preemptively against them; at Donut Land it was always a matter of catching up with whatever move was made by our betters. "They got themselves special napkins with their names printed on 'em," Deborah always said, staring out the window, grief-stricken. These napkins, they were Deborah's greatest sorrow. "We should get ourselves some Donut Land napkins is what we should do, but the printers want an arm and a leg, I'll tell you." She said this ten times a day. The fact that she had said it only moments before did nothing to stop her.

My job was to run the cash register and keep the coffee brewed, and I grew to hate it like nothing else I had ever hated before. The kind of person who preferred Donut Land to Dunkin' Donuts was the kind of person who liked to wallow in his own sad sack, the kind of person who stood at the register talking of his ex-wives chasing him down for child support, about the refrigerator college he was planning on enrolling in which would change his life immeasurably for the better. These people were, in short, my people, and I hated them. All the while I was there and half the time I wasn't I felt this hatred throbbing in my veins. *Donut Land!* I thought, a thousand times a day. *Fuck you!*

I had a problem with washing my Donut Land uniform, which is to say I never washed it. The shirt was crawling, thick as skin, smeared over with icing and coffee stains, a map on whose surface was marked the grim terrain of my days. Deborah kept telling me to wash it, threatening to fire me if I didn't, but then backing off on the grounds that she wasn't likely to find another person so steady as me in my dedication to Donut Land, my ability to come in at five in the morning: no one else in her seven years of running Donut Land had shown up so dependably for so long. "Most people," she said, sighing, "can't be counted on for more than a week." A person who would show up every day to a job like that (in that kind of person dwelled levels of foolishness and desperation and self-hatred in just the right measures, shifting, hydraulic) wasn't easy to find, she said, sighing again, no it wasn't, to find someone like that, someone like me, it surely wasn't easy.

You had a problem with my working at Donut Land, with my alarm going off at four-thirty, then four-thirty-five, then four-forty and four forty-five, with my slapping around at it like some deranged drunk. But then again there was a fringe benefit to my employment—there was the dozen chocolate-frosted donuts I brought home each day, which we ate in the evenings after the cafeteria closed. The thing about Donut Land, you said, licking your fingers, was that its donuts were actually better than Dunkin' Donuts', but no one would ever know because no one would ever go there on account of what you called *the cheapness of its imitation*. You could turn a phrase, when you wanted.

Carson, I wonder what might have happened if you had put the least bit of effort into your studies. You hardly ever picked up a textbook and when you did it was during a commercial break from one or another of the soap operas you followed with the passion of a saint. You'd read for a minute, sigh, read another minute, sigh again and toss the book on the floor. You had intended to major in business, then open up a restaurant, but you couldn't for the life of you figure out what one had to do with the other. What a business needed most, you said, was a sense of style, a personality, and there was nothing in those books worth looking at or getting to know.

Instead you devoted yourself to the careful study of checkout aisle magazines, which your mother sent you every week in a fat envelope. Magazines devoted to things bizarre and surreal, things defying physics, things which the government attempted to cover up in vain. Your favorites were the magazines devoted to the glory and scandal of Hollywood celebrity. Best of all was *People*. You sat reading it front to back to front again, keen and hungry, as if some secret to your future wealth and happiness might be found there. You didn't know how or why, but you saw it happening, saw yourself smiling on the red carpet, saw your name in lights.

By November you were failing all of your classes and word had spread up through the ranks. I took messages for you from various academic officials offering their help. One of the people put on your case was our resident assistant, a pale and skinny senior named Belinda Wimpy who was, at the age of twenty-one, still a Girl Scout. She had her own troop of Brownies and was always going around campus with them. They walked in a line, holding hands, their brown sashes crossing their chests, their little caps tilted on their heads, and even these Brownies, six years old, appeared to sense already the lameness of scouting, indeed to be seen in this kind of procession caused them to look down at their feet in shame. But not Belinda. How proudly she wore her green sash, how thoroughly covered it was in badges and pins. She wore the Girl Scout's green beret, as though she were some kind of secret operative. On Wednesday evenings the Brownies crowded into her room or sat outside the dorm in a circle. One Saturday they even slept outside in little orange tents.

In a different era Belinda Wimpy would have been the kind of woman to volunteer in a military hospital. She would have nursed men through the last agonizing moments of their lives, would have convinced them they were bound for heaven. But since this was peacetime she was merely a troop leader and a resident assistant, and the person she was charged to save—to assimilate into the habits and glories of university life—was you. Several times a day she knocked on our door—two enthusiastic taps—and then opened it without waiting for us to respond. "Hello, ladies!" she'd say. "I was just on my way out for a nature walk and wondered if you'd like to join me!" Or, "I'm off to study group! Free pizza! Any takers?"

Every time she asked us out you had some clever answer. *I'd love to,* you said, nodding toward the TV, *but I'm staying tuned for an important message from our sponsor.* Belinda's face always flickered with disappointment, but then broke out in a hopeful smile. "Maybe next time!" she'd say.

Next time for sure, you'd say. After she'd closed the door you'd add, *Next time for sure I'm gonna turn you down again.* Behind her back you called her *Thin Mint.* As in, *Go lock the door so Thin Mint don't come barging in here again.* There was a comfort in mocking her. Maybe we weren't thriving, maybe other girls on the hall only talked to us when they needed to borrow a stapler, or use our phone because theirs was being hogged by an inconsiderate roommate, maybe there weren't red carpets unraveling at our feet, leading us toward bright futures, but we could count on one thing: We were better than Belinda Wimpy.

One Sunday morning you announced it was your birthday, and to celebrate we took the bus down to Shoney's all-you-can-eat, six-ninety-nine breakfast buffet. For the sake of frugality we agreed to eat off the same plate. *When the waitress come,* you told me, *just say you ain't gonna eat. Look at you, ninety-eight pounds soaking wet, a drowned rat if I ever saw one, anyone gonna believe that. Then you eat off my plate and we only pay once.*

So when the waitress came that's what I said. Nothing, thank you. And though the waitress could not possibly have cared less whether we paid for one plate or two, whether I ate or not (anyone could tell she had her own problems; apart from working at Shoney's she was what you liked to call *poor white trash,* with bruises all up her arm, even thinner than mine, about the size of a mop handle, and her two front teeth missing), you weren't quite satisfied. You wanted that waitress to know we were absolutely *not* planning on both eating from a single plate. You said to her, *Don't you think she should eat something? Look at her. She pitiful. Tell her to eat something.*

The waitress rolled her eyes. "Juice," she said, "or coffee?"

You took your time going through the buffet line, picking up a link of sausage with the tines, examining it, turning it this way and that under the orange glow of the heat lamps, then placing it back and choosing another. You heaped your plate with meat and eggs, with fried potatoes, with fat triangles of Texas toast, all of it slick with grease.

The trick was to take bites off your plate when no one was looking, and we made a game of it. I ate like Charlie Chaplin ate, a thief stuffing food in his mouth as soon as the grocer turned his back, stuffing in those morsels with the quickest, nimblest gestures. *Hold up,* you'd say. *Here come the waitress.* You liked to believe she was monitoring our every move, you liked the thrill of it. When the waitress slapped our check on the table you told her, *I couldn't get her to eat nothing. I tried, I tell you, I tried and tried but she stubborn all right.*

For a while we sat in our booth, painfully stuffed, watching people standing in the buffet line like nuns queued up for communion: solemn, reverent, intent. They stood in their Sunday best, polyester slacks with elastic waistlines, button-down polyester shirts with winged collars and swirling paisley patterns, brown leather shoes scuffed at the toes. It seemed to me that everyone there was wearing the same clothes, and working the same jobs, and aching the same aches that they had worn and worked and ached twenty years before, and with horror I saw myself, having dropped out of college and committed myself full-time to Donut Land, standing in the same line twenty years hence. I had the feeling that the same thought was passing through your mind. "I better get back," I said, "and study."

Me too, you said. *I'm in some kind of mess.* Your voice was low, deflated. This was the first time you had spoken of your struggles with any measure of regret. *I guess if I don't hustle they're gonna kick me out.*

But the last weeks of the semester went by and still you didn't crack a book. You were quiet for long stretches and lay in bed watching television, falling in and out of sleep. You started to talk about leaving school, about not returning after break. *I don't know,* you kept saying, *what's the point of all this.* You said when you opened your restaurant, Carson's Cafe, you'd be back in the kitchen, cooking and plating food, and who needed a degree for that? *Here's your college-educated pot pie,* you said. *Here's your business-major chicken salad with a history-minor side of fries.* You said, *Please.*

It wasn't until the very end of the semester that you started to ask about me, as if it had only just occurred to you that I was a person. The last night before you left for break, after we'd turned out the lights and gone to bed, you asked: *Don't your folks ever call you? Don't they ever send you nothing?"* I tried to explain about my sister, how she'd left home the day after she graduated high school and we hadn't seen or heard from her since, not once, not a single word. I tried to explain about my mother, how she wasn't the type to call or write, being too busy with her own pursuits. I explained about the four husbands and all the boyfriends in between. Each husband I tried to sum up in the briefest, coldest demographics: first husband Michael Murphy, white male, eighteen years old, high school prom date, blue tuxedo with ruffled shirt, shotgun wedding, degenerate drunk, missing in action; second husband Michael Collins, thirty-something, high school history teacher, Knight of Columbus, Old Spice cologne, left brokenhearted; third husband Bud Francis, white male, late thirties, appliance salesman, Tom Collins with a swizzle stick, capped teeth, gold rings, left my mother during a family vacation when he discovered her in bed with a younger man; fourth husband Walter Adams, black male, fifty-three years old . . .

Here you sat straight up in bed. *Your momma married to a black man? For real?*

"Used to be," I said. "But he wasn't really black."

How come he wasn't really black?

"He was one of those white kind of blacks. He's got black skin and everything but if you talked to him on the phone you'd think he was white."

No I wouldn't.

"Yes you would."

Would not, you said. *No way, no how.*

"Trust me," I said. "He listened to Bach."

His last name's Adams?

"Was," I said. "Is, I guess."

That's a dead giveaway, you said. *Don't you know the first god-damn thing about black people?*

I shrugged.

Don't you know when the slaves were set free they named themselves after presidents?

"I know," I said. "I know that."

You always saying you know things, you said. *When you don't. Which is exactly your problem. You don't know shit about shit, is your problem.*

"My problem," I said, "is that my mother left him and went off with some new guy everybody hates. Which is why I came to school all the way down here."

What's it like, you asked, *your mom goes off and gets married and you got to move in with some guy you don't know?*

"I don't know," I said. "Weird, I guess."

Weird is right, you said, and whistled in the universal manner of impressed people.

Then you wanted to know about my father. *You mean to tell me your own father alive and well and walking around the same city as you, and you never see him?*

"Never," I said.

But you know who he is?

"Yup."

And you met him a few times?

"He came over a few times but he was always drunk. Except the couple times he was in AA and trying to make amends and he came by sober and promised to take responsibility for us. That's about it." I said these things in a yawning, dispassionate voice, like I could hardly remember what I was talking about.

So you seen him, like, ten times your whole life?

"Pretty much. A couple times we ran into each other."

You run into him? You run into your own father by accident? You laughed, snorted. *Like maybe you standing in line at the grocery store and you look up and there he is in the next lane, reading the* TV Guide *and shit?*

"I think it was the library," I said.

What's he doing in the library?

"How the fuck should I know?" I said. Though I knew. In an instant, in one of those moments in which you rise out of yourself and see everything with perfect clarity, I'd seen him and all of his trappings, spread around him at one of those giant wooden reading tables, scratched and scuffed and softened as driftwood, I'd seen the names of those books: *How to Win Friends and Influence People, Ten Steps to the Life You Deserve, What Color Is Your Parachute?*

About your own father you had little to say. You said your father could be summed up rather easily: that he looked, walked, talked, dressed, and conducted himself exactly like James Brown. *He knows it, too,* you said. *He rides around in his Mercury all the time with James Brown blasting out the windows, he listens to James Brown all the time at home and at work.* You said he worked in the fields, here and there, now and then, all around the county: cotton, tobacco, soy beans, grapes. *One of those little men,* you said, *hellbent on making himself bigger than he is, is what he is. He's like one of them tiny dogs jumping around barking all the time all nasty-like.*

You said he called you names: Lardass, Crisco, Hubba Bubba. I said, "Don't let him talk to you like that!" and you clucked your tongue. Like a man could be stopped from calling you something. Like this was the worst of your problems. You said you had scars on your back from where he'd whipped you. For talking back, for breaking a dish, he whipped you until your skin was crossed over with bleeding gashes. Sometimes, you said, he even beat you for no reason. You'd be asleep and he'd come in the room and turn on the lights and get you out of bed, screaming. *Says I'm too lazy,* you said. *Says he gonna teach me to lay around all day eating and watching TV, says he gonna teach me what's what, goddamn little man is what he is.* If it wasn't the switch, you said, it was the belt. I had seen those scars once as you turned away to change, as you struggled to close your bra, those long raised-up scars all across your back which gave the impression that you were a person assembled from scraps, a human quilt. I can see them now. I didn't know what to say about them then, I still don't.

It's not like I expect you to understand, you said. *You got no idea what it's like, no goddamn idea.* Fat and black, you said, you grew up in a shack; fat and black groceries on credit; fat and black winter coats on layaway; fat and black and the bank calling for the mortgage; fat and black and your father gone missing with his paycheck for days, weeks at a time; fat and black with one pair of shoes, canvas, collapsed outward at the sides; fat and black you escaped in daydreams, saw yourself thin and famous, having sold your life story to the big screen, you saw yourself walking the red carpet in a twinkling gown, thanking the academy; fat and black you dreamt of the lottery, of driving around in a Cadillac; fat and black behind your back the boys called you names—Aunt Jemima, Mammy Two-Shoes, Mrs. Butterworth; fat and black when you sat on the bus the boys all went running to the other side, saying they needed to balance the freight; fat and black those same boys came around knowing you wouldn't turn them away, what they wanted from you was practice for other girls, or relief from the way the other girls strung them along. They took you out back, into the woods and fields, and you came home with wisps of cotton clung to your clothes; fat and black all around that town of yours, you said, was cotton, and at harvest it took to the air, long white wisps of it floating everywhere, twisting and lifting in the breeze, catching in the limbs of trees, in the condensers of air conditioners and the grilles of cars, in the spokes of tires, in people's hair, in screen doors and in shrubbery, it was everywhere, fat and black the first time you went out in the fields with a boy you came home with these white wisps clinging to your clothes, your hair, and your sister had known right away, she knew what it meant, she picked them off you before your mother could see and beat you blind; fat and black this was what it meant, only the beginning of what it meant, and I had no goddamned idea, you said, no goddamn idea at all, not even for a second, and never would.

Then you did what you always did when you'd talked too long about yourself and your problems. You picked up the phone and pretended to dial it, pretended you'd been patched through to the direct line of the President of the United States. *Hello, Georgie?* you said. *Georgie Porgie, Pudding and Pie? It's me, Carson. Why yes, you're right, it* has *been too long, we* should *have lunch. But listen a minute, George, I'm calling for a favor. What I want is a national holiday. That's right, in my name. Uh-huh. Uh-huh. January out of the question with Dr. King and all, I understand. February already tied up with Black History. March? No I can't do March, March don't work for*

me. April? April's good. Let's say April. Carson Washington Pity Day.
Sounds good, sounds good, you keep it real now, Georgie.

You had a doll, Betsy, which you had slept with since childhood. She was blond-haired with a pink plastic face and a set of icy blue eyes that closed when you lay her down, then sprang open when you sat her up, and you lay there tilting her up, down, up, down, her eyes opening and closing, opening and closing, making the sound of a marble hitting another marble. After a time you said, *Boy. Four husbands. Huh.* And I fell asleep to the sound of those doll eyes opening and closing and opening again, opening and closing, and opening, and closing.

The next morning when I left for Donut Land I wondered if I'd ever see you again.

When you returned in January it wasn't, as I first thought, to make good—it was to ride out whatever time you had left on your scholarship, spending your days however you pleased, a free roof over your head and no one telling you what to do. You only went to the first week of classes, then started to skip, then quit altogether. You did this with the full knowledge that doing so meant you would fail out of school and be sent back to that town, that four-room house, that life you hated. The time you had remaining at school was like a joyride in a stolen car. You could do anything you wanted, and what you wanted to do was nothing. It got so that you hardly left the room, hardly got out of bed. It got so that the TV was running twenty-four hours a day.

For the most part you occupied your days with game shows

and soap operas. Whenever you were bored—every few hours or so—you called home and talked to your mother. How two people could talk so much I didn't know. Often you and your mother talked on the phone while watching the same television program, commenting back and forth on the folly of your favorite characters—the desperate, plotting mavens of daytime television. On screen an aging woman with giant sculpted hair and shimmering red lipstick would look off in the distance and drum her fingers together, would speak under her breath some bitter warning—I'll get you, my pretty—and you and your mother would howl. *You better watch it, lady,* you'd say, *You got another thing coming!* And in moments like that it always seemed to me that you had never really left for college, had never really intended to go off and make a new life for yourself. Rather, you were merely living your old life at a distance.

After you talked to your mother you always asked to talk to your nephew Regis. You kept him on the phone as long as a person could keep a toddler enthralled, saying the kinds of things that adults say to children, things implying that what you wanted to do most in the world was to eat him. *Who's my little pumpkin muffin?* you said. *Who's my crumb cake, my cream puff, my chocolate pudding pie? Is it you? Is it?*

The evenings went by in a blur of reruns, Archie Bunker griping in his chair, Redd Foxx faking heart attacks, Flo the Waitress yelling "Kiss My Grits," J. J. Walker going "Dy-no-mite!," Jack Tripper writhing in all kinds of misunderstood humiliation, the same laugh track running through everything, periodic bursts of merriment, of hilarity. I fell asleep in the flickering blue and part of that rerun world seeped into my dreams. Toward morning I'd wake to the whine of the off-air signal. When I turned off the set it was hot to the touch.

It wasn't long before the authorities, as you called them, were on your case. The phone started ringing throughout the day, various advisors and counselors wanting a word. You'd pick it up and say, "Carson? No, Carson ain't here right now." You'd examine your fingernails, turn your hand this way and that. "I'll tell her," you'd say, "if she ever gets back from the strip club."

Then came a series of letters making various threats and promises. Your favorite letter was from an assistant dean, James Findley Ramsey III, whose name amused you. You said it over and over, in various different voices, most often with a British accent. *James Findley Ramsey the Third.* James Findley Ramsey was a good cop, and his letter was full of hope. All kinds of options were available to you: incompletes, tutoring, counseling. Whatever difficulties you might be experiencing could be overcome in a variety of pleasant ways. If only you would reach out, Mr. Ramsey wrote, and experience everything that the university had to offer. "There's something for everyone!" he said. "I hope you're enjoying our campus during this beautiful season, enjoying the fine spring air. It won't be long before the cherry trees are in bloom!" The fine spring air! You read this and laughed. *Oh James,* you said, *you do tickle me.*

Sometimes I sided with James Ramsey and said, "Shouldn't you study? Don't you have a test, a report, a paper? Aren't you, you know, failing?" And you said, *Why don't you mind your own business? Don't you have anything better to do than sit around wondering what I'm supposed to be doing? Don't you got any friends? Don't you got to go to hide away in the library again down in the basement*

where no one would ever find you if you died, no one would find you
until you start decomposing and stinking up the whole place? Don't you
have a test, you said, *a report, a paper? Aren't you one to talk? Aren't*
you failing, too?

It was true that I was failing. Having no idea what I wanted
to do in life, I had signed up for an absurd variety of classes:
Astronomy, History of Jazz, Physics, Human Anatomy, Postco-
lonial Literature. Each of these classes seemed to have been
designed specifically to undo every fervent belief and vague
assumption I'd ever held. All my life I'd looked at the stars and
listened to music, fallen down sets of stairs, lived and breathed
and eaten and slept and read, all without understanding what
I was looking at or listening to or doing—the physics involved,
the math, the angle at which I approached things and they
approached me, the distance between myself and everything
else. And instead of being thrilled at understanding these
things now, or at least beginning to, I was filled with an almost
crippling embarrassment, I was humiliated, I suffered like a
person does after performing badly at a party, replaying afterward every mishap and foible one has committed. I was stunned
to the point of paralysis in all of my classes. In particular I was
stuck in the middle of a paper on *Heart of Darkness* but couldn't
finish it. The assignment was simple—a five-page analysis of the
book's symbols—but I fell into it like Alice into Wonderland,
plop down deep into a well, and couldn't get out. In the world
of that paper nothing was right-sized and everything shifted.
Every time I wrote something it occurred to me that its opposite
was also true, and it got so nothing could be said at all. And yet
everything. The paper grew to twenty, twenty-five, thirty pages.

Then I'd throw it away and start over. I sat at my desk for long hours bent over that book clutching my head; several times I even came to tears.

What's that you reading? you asked at first. Then, after it became clear that the book was all I could read and all I thought about, that the book had become everything to me, you said: *You still reading that* Heart of Darkness? *What the hell's wrong with you?* At some point while I was out you must have picked up the book and read it, because you started offering advice. *If I was you,* you said, *which I thank God I'm not, I'd have a thing or two to say about that Kurtz character and his obvious homosexuality.* I stayed up late into the night, every night. Every so often you'd rouse from sleep and tell me, *Mister Kurtz, put him down. He dead.*

Finally I turned in a forty-three-page paper and got a D. On the bottom of the final page my professor—a bitter German obsessed with Kafka—had written, in block letters that stood in stark contrast to the paper's looping, fuzzy logic: GET A GRIP.

By then spring was in full bloom. In the quadrangle beneath our window people threw Frisbees, rode bicycles, played football, and their lively cries rose up to our room. There was a general sense of happiness and excitement in the air, but for us everything seemed to be taking a grim turn, lapsing into a minor key. One of the janitors we always talked with in the cafeteria—an ancient and painfully thin man named Leroy, who had trembling yellow eyeballs—developed a wet, pesky cough, and for a few days he could hardly get through a conversation. He was always taking a handkerchief from his chest pocket and spitting into it, great globs of bloody phlegm, and you kept telling him to see a doctor. "Ain't got time for no doctor," he'd say. Then he went missing for a week and when we asked after him we were told he had checked into the hospital and died the next day.

The news of Leroy's death plagued you. *I told him,* you kept saying, angry. *Didn't I tell him see a doctor? Goddamn,* you said. It was as if Leroy's death and your failure were bound up together, you saw these things in the same light, his struggles— I keep on keeping on!—and your failures, they were mutual. After the news of Leroy's death you fell into a foul mood you never recovered from. You started to complain in a general way about white people. Under your breath, in an almost constant stream, you listed their flaws. *Look at them eating their yogurt,* you said, *drinking their little bottles of water, wearing their shorts, their loafers, their hand-knit Irish sweaters, riding their little bicycles to the library, sitting all quiet in class taking notes, balancing they checkbooks, it bores me to tears just watching them, I'd rather die,* you said, *than be a white person.*

Sometimes you took care to excuse me from these faults on the grounds that I was pathetic. But other times you turned even on me. I'd be reading and you'd mutter, *Pretty little white girl think she got problems. I'll tell you about some problems.* And I'd say, "I can hear you, you know." And you'd say, *Good for you.* We started to quibble like siblings elbowing each other in the backseat of the car. You complained that the sound of my pencil scratching on paper was interrupting your enjoyment of your favorite shows, I complained about how loud you kept the television. You started turning up the television even louder, I started bringing home plain glazed donuts instead of chocolate. I let my alarm go off for longer stretches each morning before hitting the snooze button, you picked my clothes off the floor and set them in a pile on my bed, told me to stop being such a disgusting slob; on the same pretense you washed my Donut Land uniform in the bathroom sink and hung it to dry in a shower stall. *You should've seen the water,* you said, *all thick and gray, three times I washed it and the water was so murky it could hardly get itself down the drain, you pig.*

Which was the last straw.

I started staying out later and later at the library. When I came home we fought like jealous lovers. *Where you been? You must've been at the library again 'cause I* know *you ain't been out with friends. You don't have a friend in the whole goddamn world 'sides me. Your own* family *don't even like you. When's the last time anyone call you, or mail you something?*

"At least," I said, "I'm not getting letters from James Findley Ramsey the Third."

At least, you said, *people care what happening with me. Nobody even notice you. Nobody care what you do or fail to do, you ever notice?*

"What's your fucking problem?"

I'm not the one with the problem. You the one with problems. Nobody like you at all. Thin Mint don't even like you and Thin Mint like everybody.

"At least," I said, "I get out of bed in the morning."

Good for you, you said. *Just a minute while I call up the president and tell him about it. Hello, Georgie?* you said, thumb in your ear, pinkie extended toward your mouth. *Hey, George, it's me again, what's happening? I'm just calling to tell you my roommate, Mary Mur-*

phy? Look like a walking corpse? Uh-huh, that's the one. I'm just call-ing to tell you she get out of bed this morning. Uh-huh. What's that? You gonna give her the Medal of Honor? Oh, George, you too much.

"Fuck you," I said.

To which you of course responded: *You wish.*

"Why don't you go hang out with the other girls, then," I said, meaning the heiresses all up and down our hall, blond and blue-eyed and rich, one indistinguishable from the next, their closets so overflowing with clothes, with silks and velvets, with tweeds and cashmere, that many of them had been obliged during the first week of school to go out and purchase addi-tional bureaus. By which I meant the girls you had spent the entire year making fun of, referring to as *Blondie* and *Barbie* and *Baby* and *Bitchface.*

And so you did. You dropped me in the coldest way you could think of—by making yourself popular. When I came home from the library one night you were sitting in the lounge with a circle of girls gathered around you. You were telling their fortunes—reading their palms—and had dressed the part, your head wrapped in a red turban, gold hoops dangling from your ears. You sat running the sharp edge of your fingernail along the girls' lifelines, money lines, love lines. On successive evenings crowds of lovesick girls lined up to see you, standing in line in their satin Doris Day pajamas, their faces covered in mud masks, their hair in curlers, wanting to know—they held out their palms to you, desperate and helpless—whether they were loved by certain boys, boys with names like Preston Car-rington and Wesley Knoxville. One of the girls, the loudest and blondest of all, was named Lacy Winterson, and she was in love

with a boy named—in all official, Confederate seriousness—
Rhett Butler. "Does Rhett Butler," said Lacy, "love me? Is he the
one?"

Let's see, you said. *Sit down.* You took her hand in yours, peered
at it, lifted an eyebrow.

"What!" said Lacy. "What's it say?"

Quiet, you told her. *This one special. I need to concentrate on
this one.* You tortured her, studied her palm for five whole minutes without saying anything, pulling at her skin, bunching it
together and then stretching it out, bending her fingers back.
Well, you said, finally, *that's what I was afraid of. I don't see any way
out of it.*

"What?" said Lacy.

You gonna get married all right, you said. *And you gonna be happy
for a while.* You stopped, got up and crossed the room, picked up
and flipped through a magazine while Lacy sat on the edge of
the couch, her mouth hanging open.

"Then what?" she said in the softest voice.

Well, you said, *I can't say for sure. But after a certain point you
ain't gonna be happy no more.* Though this was the vaguest possible fortune, and bound to come true for more or less everyone
on earth, Lacy felt doomed in a very particular way, as though
she alone had been singled out to suffer a rare disease. Her eyes
brimmed with tears and she shut herself away in her room.

You were wildly popular. "Carson," the girls told you, "we had
no idea you were so awesome!" They invited you to the private
pizza parties they held in their rooms. Each night these girls
had pizza delivered to the dorm by other students who didn't
have money, and so worked as delivery drivers, students who suf-

fered the indignity of wearing uniforms equally as bad as Donut Land's, and you sat on the other side of this divide quite regally. You sat in those rooms telling all kinds of stories. I could hear you talking and the girls erupting in laughter. They liked to call you "girlfriend." "Hey, girlfriend," they said. You made a habit of exclaiming, in a voice so loud it was sure to carry into our room: *It sure is nice to have some fun for a change!*

One night you sat in the lobby in your gypsy wear but didn't have any takers—the thrill was gone and everyone was studying for finals, which you didn't have to worry about because you had already failed. You returned to the room and took your suitcases out from your closet, started taking clothes off their hangers, went fussing about the room. You took the pictures down from the wall, picked the little circles of tape off their backs. When you were finished packing you sat on your bed and sighed. This was my cue to say something like, "You're leaving already? You're not staying through finals?" But I didn't. I had one talent in life and it was staying silent through a grudge. In all my years fighting with my sister and mother I had never once broken first.

There was a *Creature Double Feature* running on the local channel, some black-and-white horror film involving the destruction of a city by a giant reptile. The music soared in what was supposed to be suspense, but the effects were laughable. *Pitiful,* you said. It was a long time before you spoke again, and when you did it was with annoyance. *Gimme your hand,* you said.

"Why?"

To read your fortune, dummy.

It had never crossed my mind that you could actually read

a palm—I'd assumed that you only claimed to read palms as a means of telling people what you really thought of them, as a means of dooming them toward unpleasant futures, out of spite. But I let you anyway.

Average, you said. *Nothing too exciting.* Then you examined my other hand, turned it this way and that in the light of the television.

This here's not too common, you said, tracing a line that slanted across my palm, left to right. *Not too common at all. Fact I never seen this here in real life, just in books, never up close in person.* An extra line, you claimed. Strange. Like a sixth finger.

"What's it mean?" I said.

It could mean one of two things. People think different ways about it.

"What do they think?" I wanted to know but you were coy. *I don't think anybody really know what that line mean. It's too uncommon for anybody to say for sure what it mean.*

"What's it mean?" I said. "I'm gonna die any minute, right? It's okay. You can tell me. I don't believe in this stuff."

No, you said. *Not that.*

"Then what?"

I tell you what I think it means, you said. *My personal opinion. And I already thought this anyways from the minute I saw you. What I think it means is you gonna be famous.*

"For what?" I said.

Can't say, you told me. *You don't have any special talents far as I can see.*

We watched as a giant lizard reared up on its hind legs and bit the spire from the Empire State Building. *Maybe,* you said, *you'll be one of those people who breaks a record. For the longest finger-nails or something. Maybe you'll live to a hundred and fifty.*

"What's the other thing?" I said. "You said it could mean two things."

I forget, you said. Then you got up and snapped off the television. That was the thing about you. You talked and talked and talked, but as soon as someone wanted you to talk, you clammed up and turned your back.

We lay in the dark, quiet, for a long time. I was turning a question over in my mind but didn't know how to put it into words. I kept trying to think of what to say, and failing, until finally I had the feeling that if I didn't hurry you'd fall asleep and I wouldn't get to ask you, and so I burst out with it: Why? Why, why, why? Why were you going back to that place? Why had you thrown it all away? For what possible reason? I wanted you to give me one good reason why.

It was a long moment before you answered me, and when you did it was more than I'd bargained for. *I'm gonna tell you something,* you said, *and if you ever tell anyone else I'll kill you. Even after I'm done telling you I don't wanna hear a word out of you, I don't wanna hear a single peep. You just keep lying there quiet like always. Not a word. You say a single word and I'll kill you.* And then you told me why. You told me how Sharon, your sister, had given birth years ago to a baby but had lost it in labor, and after that couldn't have any more children, though a child was what she had always wanted most in life. So when you'd gotten pregnant in your junior year there was at first talk in the house of adoption, of sending you off to some home and telling everyone you'd gone away on scholarship to some fancy summer school, but the more you talked about this with your mother and Sharon the worse it seemed, with Sharon not being able to bear children and all, and here you were with one you didn't want, here you were with college and a bright future ahead of you ruined, it started to seem like a good idea to give your baby to Sharon. It seemed reasonable to keep you both in the house claiming illness, mononucleosis, reasonable to tell everyone, after you had the baby at home, that it was Sharon's. *The point is,* you said, as if I hadn't already figured out the truth, as if I weren't already aching with it, *the reason why I'm going home, the reason I can't stand it here, Regis belong to me.*

"Oh, Carson," I said.

And you said: *Shut up, fool. Didn't I tell you? Didn't I tell you not to say a word to me? You ever say one more word to me again I'll kill you. I'm leaving in the morning, my daddy's driving up to get me, and if you say one goddamn word to me I swear to God I'll scratch your eyes out. We're done here.*

The next morning you were up early, stuffing your sheets and blankets and pillows into a white trash bag you'd pilfered from the bathroom wastebasket (*White trash,* you said to yourself, and chuckled), going around the room pulling out drawers again and again until you were satisfied that no trace of yourself remained. You made trips outside, carrying down your suitcases, then the television. Then you came back up and stood in the window watching for your father. I sat up in bed and said hello, but you didn't say anything. A long time passed until finally you saw what you were looking for, the stout figure of Merriweather Washington making his way toward the dorm, and you up and left.

Bye! you said, and slammed the door behind you.

After you left I stood at the window watching—you knew I would. Your father was walking on ahead of you carrying the television and your bag of bedding, slouchy and weary as Willy Loman. You were following lazily behind him, a suitcase in each hand. Just when I thought you weren't going to look back you set your suitcases down, you turned and called up to me, hands cupping your mouth. *Hey,* you said, *I forgot to tell you something!*

By now you had attracted the attention of clusters of students walking past, the normal kids who were out enjoying the fine spring air. They stopped and stared, some looking at you, some looking at me.

"What?" I said.

"You better work on being famous," you called. "Otherwise you gonna drown."

A few days later it came time for me to see James Findley Ramsey III, who was my academic advisor and therefore responsible for helping me with the selection of fall courses. I had failed to register for anything and this had come to his attention; he had sent a letter. It was funny to see him in person, more or less exactly as we imagined him, pink and plump as a Christmas ham, blue suit, white shirt, blue-and-orange-striped tie, silver hair, false teeth, hot handshake. He was the jovial "Come in, come in! Sit down, sit down!" type who you couldn't help but oblige. "Mary Murphy," he said, and opened a manila folder stuffed with papers. I wondered what was in there. "You've taken quite a variety of courses," he said. "Which is what liberal arts is all about, isn't it?" He chuckled. Then sighed. Then frowned. He said that he regretted the necessity of settling down and focusing one's efforts on a single field, but that it was time to do so. It was time to start thinking about what I wanted to do with myself. Had I thought of this?

I said I had.

"And what," he asked, "did you conclude?"

I said I had concluded that I had no particular talents and couldn't imagine myself in any type of job whatsoever.

"Well," he said. He leaned forward, clasped his hands together in little fists. He was getting excited. His skin flushed and he appeared for a moment to be on the verge of cardiac arrest. A challenge! An academic soul in need of direction! "People with no particular talents," he said, "don't win full scholarships, do they?"

I regretted to inform him that, in some unfortunate cases, it appeared that they did.

"Nonsense! You must have some special abilities." Desperately he scanned my file. "French!" he said. "You placed out of French! A nice, high score, too. That's special. What about French? Have you thought about French?"

"Sure," I said. Though I'd never really seen French as a skill. I'd taken it in high school and only done well because my grandparents were both first-generation French immigrants, and I'd spent a lot of time with them as a kid. My grandparents had always spoken to each other in French when they didn't want me to understand what they were saying, but over the years I'd picked up a working vocabulary. "Get out of here," I learned to say. "Give me a break; Stop screwing around the house and get out of my hair; I've had enough; You're driving me crazy; Leave me alone; Where are my keys; You've had too much to drink again; When is their mother picking them up, when is she going to stop fucking around and take responsibility for things; It's not my fault; It's never anybody's fault, but it has to be somebody's." My grandfather was a bus driver, and in my teenage years I'd spent my afternoons riding around the city with him, on the seat behind him, and he'd taught me more. "Look at this guy about to get on," I learned to say, "what a pathetic bastard, his spine so crooked he looks like a question mark. If I ever get crippled like that I want you to kill me immediately." I had always enjoyed the language—how it had a way of softening even the most grotesque phrases, of lending an air of sophistication to the mundane life around me—and I told James Ramsey that I supposed its virtues were worth further study.

"Excellent!" he said. "How do you say 'excellent' in French?"

"Excellent," I said.

"Right-o!" he said.

Suddenly he was plotting my entire future, flipping through the course catalog and choosing courses on Hugo, Voltaire, Flaubert. "These aren't in translation, see?" he said. "The whole text is in French. Quite a challenge! Wow, right?"

"Wow," I said.

"There's a good buck in French!" James Ramsey said. "Kidding, kidding. There's not a good buck in French, of course. But you could teach. Maybe even on the college level. That's a nice life. I taught history here for a number of years and found it very satisfying." He rubbed his hands together. I stood up, and he actually gave me a little hug. I had made his day, he said.

He had saved my life in under five minutes and he was going to go home and tell his wife about it.

And so, because I was nothing if not suggestible, I spent the next three years as a French major and with characteristic French selfishness more or less forgot about you. Sophomore year I became an R.A. myself, became the French-major version of Belinda Wimpy. I lived alone in a dorm room smoking French cigarettes one after another through a foot-long ebony holder. I wore black turtlenecks and listened to French music and read French newspapers and watched French films. Whenever two or more people gathered in a room and started to enjoy themselves, I knocked on their door and reminded them of the dormitory policies forbidding their behavior. I quit Donut Land and took a job checking books out of the library, which was more like Donut Land than I cared to admit. In both cases people had to go through me to get something they wanted, and I didn't want to let them have it. I sat in judgment of them. I was silent and huffy with the date stamp, I slid the books across the counter with a glare that said: You're lucky I'm letting you have this. I made a habit of hating everyone and the time passed quickly.

In my junior year, in a class on Tocqueville, I met and went crazy for one Roger Preston Fairbanks, political science major, son of an ambassador, former prep-school classmate of Dan Quayle's son. Roger had been to Dan Quayle's house, had even been to George Bush's house in Kennebunkport, Maine, and believed that this was all one needed in life to be successful. And indeed this seemed to be true. After my first date with Roger I went back to my dorm and stood in front of the bathroom mirror and said, over and over, *I am Dan Quayle's son's friend's girlfriend!* mostly realizing how pathetic I sounded but also secretly thrilled.

Roger said that he liked my look, as if it was something I'd cultivated, some kind of anemic chic. We dated all through junior year and spent the summer together at his Maryland house, at which there were yachts. Yachts! And though these people—these friends of Roger's with whom I had nothing in common, and who furthermore seemed to be in some way responsible for the misery of everyone in my family—were not my people, I was, in truth, desperate to know them, to become one of them, to speak and dress and carry myself just like they did, I had never been so desperate in my life. But then Roger dumped me the next year, as soon as he got into law school, saying that he wanted to arrive in New Haven focused and unattached.

Dumped!

I had been dumped!

I spent the rest of the semester in my dorm room and only left when I absolutely had to. These instances I dashed from place to place, wearing sunglasses and headphones, so that if I ran into Roger or any of his friends I would not have to speak. I went so long without talking to anyone that I started having trouble with things as basic as purchasing groceries. The exchange of money at the register, the back-and-forth with the cashier, was becoming difficult.

In the afternoons I crossed the street to a Chinese restaurant, the Dragon Lady, which sold giant bowls of wanton soup for a dollar, and I sat there for hours eating that soup, long since turned cold, thinking that it was strange to be alone in a restaurant so much, although slightly less strange, on the whole, than sitting alone at home.

One night in April there I was at the Dragon Lady, reading as always, but occasionally staring out the window, and in the way that we sometimes notice things we have overlooked a thousand times before I noticed a phone booth in the parking lot. I could see its fat directory dangling from a metal cord, twisting slightly in the wind. I sat and tried to think of someone to call. I thought of my family—a person could always call family, I thought. But I didn't know where Malinda was, and my mother wasn't really my mother anymore. Earlier that year she had suffered a religious crisis and gotten married for the fifth time, to a preacher from Atlanta whom she'd seen on cable television. She'd started calling me every day to encourage me to accept Jesus Christ as my personal lord and savior. Now she spent her days running her husband's church's child care center, a service the church provided, my mother said, to make sure that its dearest, most innocent lambs got the love and compassion that all of God's creatures deserved. The last time we'd spoken I could hardly hear her over the chatter of so many children in the background.

"Any word from Malinda?" I'd said.

"God's looking after her," she said. "I have that as a comfort."

"What?" I said. "I couldn't hear you over all that screaming."

"God is a comfort," she said.

"I can't hear you," I said. "I guess you'd better get back to your new family. Don't let me keep you."

People walked in and out of the Dragon Lady in pairs, talking and laughing, and I sat trying to think of a single person I knew well enough to call, and what I might say. No one to call! It seemed to me that if a person couldn't think of a single person to call, then that person was in trouble.

Finally I thought of you. And when I did it seemed you were the answer I'd been searching for, it seemed that if I could talk with you, make some kind of connection with someone, then something might change, I would be okay again.

I didn't have your number, but how many Merriweather Washingtons, I thought, could there be in that one-stoplight town, in fact in the world? I went to the register and bought a roll of quarters, then out to the pay phone. Everything was automated by then and I had to give that name, Merriweather Washington, to a robot. But the robot had trouble and kicked me out of its system to a human being—WHAT LISTING, PLEASE?—and I had to say it again, Merriweather Washington, and then the number came up, the robot speaking again, and I had to listen twice because I was having trouble holding things in my mind. In fact I had trouble believing that one could punch numbers into a machine and, as a result, actually speak to someone. The fact that the phone rang and someone answered fairly bewildered me.

"Is Carson there?" I said, my voice tight from disuse. There was a moment of silence.

"You kidding?" said the voice on the other end, a woman's. "Who is this?"

"A friend from school. Does Carson still live there?"

And then she, your sister I suppose, told me the news. "Carson don't live here no more," she said. "She dead."

I slammed the phone down in its receiver, as if by doing so I could change things. A hot shame came over me, a pounding sort of panic. I sank down and sat on the floor of the phone booth, my knees pulled into my chest. In brief flashes I convinced myself that there had been some kind of mistake, that I had misheard, but the voice on the phone came back, and back, and back again: she dead, she dead, she dead.

Some days later I gathered the nerve to call again and this time your mother answered. I told her my name, told her I was a friend of yours. "Of course," your mother said. "I remember you, Mary. Carson talked about you all the time." When your mother spoke of your death, the year before, she used the word "expired." When she spoke of the car crash, the boy you'd been with who ran off the road and into a ditch, she used the word "misfortune." I heard Regis scream in the background and my throat went tight, I couldn't speak, I managed to thank her and hung up the phone.

I kept thinking of all the things you'd planned to do—raise Regis, open your café, see your name in lights—and I couldn't believe you were gone. Not long ago you had lived and breathed. You were a living body, you heart beat, blood pushed through your veins, cells split and multiplied, you ate and drank, you thought and spoke, you were alive—and now you weren't anymore, now you were dead, now your image was taped to the wall hovering amongst the departed, and I couldn't get my mind around it, I couldn't believe it. I could hear your voice in my head with such clarity. I kept hearing you talk about the Oscar you were going to win one day, the moment they would call your name. *I'm sitting way up in the back probably,* you said, *and then they call my name and the music playing and everyone looking around, saying, "Who the hell Carson Washington?" and it take a month and a half for me to get myself down the aisle and up on stage, and then they try and tell me I ain't got time left to thank nobody but I say, Listen, baby, I'm three hundred pounds and you just try and move me, that's something I'd like to see.* And I couldn't believe you were dead, I couldn't believe it.

In some strange way the news of your death saved me. I started to wonder what I wanted to do. I had only the vaguest idea of my future. I was scheduled to start graduate school in the fall, in French language and literature, after which I imagined teaching high school, living a quiet life in a tiny apartment, probably with several cats. But now I saw very clearly what was missing—the things I would regret if I never did them.

First on the list was reconciling with my sister, and so I set about the business of finding her. I looked in the classifieds for a car and found a Buick Centurion for two hundred dollars. The car's owner was a man in a cowboy hat, and he seemed reluctant to sell. As we took the car on a test drive he listed all of its flaws: the heat and radio didn't work; the wipers dragged; the tires were bald and the brakes iffy; there was a bit of trouble with the transmission, the engine overheated and so it was best to drive at night if I was planning on going farther than ten miles. "She might break down on you tomorrow," he said. "I'd hate to see you stuck on the side of the road. You better look around some more."

But I bought the car and packed it up with everything I

owned in the world, with clothes and books, a sleeping bag and pillow, my old clarinet (long dead in its coffin), a fifty-year-old manual typewriter I'd bought at a pawnshop along with a spare ribbon. I imagined that this was the last ribbon on earth suited to the machine, and sometimes grew preoccupied with the problem of the ribbon, and the notion that within so many feet of black fabric I would have to say all that I had to say because when it ran out there would be no replacing it. Though this was ridiculous—one could write by hand, for instance, one could always find another typewriter—it filled me with anxiety.

As I was leaving campus it occurred to me that I might first drive down to that town of yours, that awful place that had held you captive. At the exit to your town I pulled off the highway and drove for miles and miles through yellow fields. The town itself was small and it wasn't hard to find city hall, where I stopped for your address, and from there it was just a short walk to your house, a small white block of a house with a red door and red shutters. To the mailbox by the road, your father had affixed the Washington name with reflective foil stickers. A small bicycle lay on its side on the front lawn. Regis had been a baby when I'd known you but now of course he was old enough to ride a bike. This troubled me. The windows were open and I could see your mother's curtains, white lace, lifting and falling with the breeze. In back of the house was an aluminum swing set, blue, with two white plastic swings dangling from it. A sprinkler was running, though it couldn't have been for the grass—the grass was long dead—it must have been running for a child, for Regis, but there was no one out.

I walked around some more. There wasn't a building in

town taller than a single story—all of the houses and shops and municipal buildings were squat and flat-roofed. Even the church—the First Assembly of the Fire Baptized—was this way. It had been converted from a house and still had a screened-in porch at the front. There weren't many people out, but now and then I passed someone and they'd nod to me, seeming to wonder what I was doing there, who I was, what I wanted.

At the center of town there was a small grocery store and I walked through it. Everything had been priced with a gun, little flags of white paper with numbers printed in purple, the way things used to be years ago. I picked up a loaf of bread, squeezed it. I picked up a variety of cans—half pears in lite syrup, fruit cocktail, sliced pineapple—and examined them, placed them back on the shelf. I thought of you shopping there, going through the aisles. I found the pastries, the donuts. I found the cereal. Though I knew it was ridiculous I was compelled to touch everything. On my way out of the store I waved to the cashier—a fat woman in a flowered dress—who remained expressionless, as if she couldn't see me.

I walked to your house again, knocked on the door, even looked through the living room window, but all was quiet. Which I told myself was for the best. I didn't know what I'd say if someone had answered.

By the time I left town the sun had gone down. On the southbound road away from that place I drove past the county nursing home where your mother and sister worked, a single-story building made of red brick that had obviously once been a motel. It had a large central lobby and a long wing extending out on either side, each room with a door opening right out into the parking lot. All the rooms were dark and only the lobby was lit, by light of the television. When I drove past I saw that all of the home's residents had been wheeled to the lobby in their wheelchairs and arranged around the television in a horseshoe. They sat with their backs bent, their heads bent, and they seemed like spineless creatures languishing under the sea. I pulled to the side of the road and looked for a long moment at that place. Black women in pink scrubs walked about, going in and out of the lobby, and I thought perhaps one of them was your mother. Around that nursing home wasn't a stick of life. It sat in the middle of a giant paved lot. Rising above it was a tall sign that had once said something but now no longer did, now it was only a giant white sign that said nothing. A chill went through me. To live in that town one's whole life, to die there— one of those long, suffering deaths, day after day after day in bed looking out the window into an empty parking lot—it was unimaginable. I sped off as though fleeing the scene of a crime. But the picture of this nursing home stayed with me for many years, dogged me, it raised the hairs on my neck every time I thought of it. In dreams I saw the home glowing green, saw myself in it, and woke in a sweat.

A bit farther down the road (would I never get out of this place?) there was a train coming and I had to stop for it. The clanging of the signal, the traffic arms coming down, the blinking lights, the bright light shining out in front of the train, and then it came into view. The ground shook. The train was slow-moving, car after car after car, some piled up and overflowing with coal, some piled with crushed automobiles, some of the boxcars with their doors flung open, empty. It occurred to me then as it always did when I saw an open boxcar to run after it and jump inside it and ride on to wherever it was going, to make a new life there. As I sat watching it—slow, slower—I saw something twisting in the air, it went in and out of the path of the car's headlights, one of those white wisps of cotton you'd mentioned. The cotton seemed propelled by some inner force. It turned and lifted and curled and fell, turned and lifted again, twisting. Just when it seemed about to disappear, sinking down, it lifted again; it would never come to rest, it would never settle anywhere, which was a problem I knew something about, the problem of being weightless. I watched that cotton for I don't know how long, hypnotized, and then the train was past and the cotton, the last trace of you, swept along with it, and I crossed the tracks and headed north.

Back home I stayed with Walter Adams, and went about the city tracking down Malinda's old friends. "God, Malinda," people said, shaking their heads, "we were wicked tight for a while but then one day she just dropped me." Somehow the fact that I was looking for Malinda escaped these people and they wound up asking me how she'd been, what she'd been up to all these years. "I don't know," I told them. "I haven't seen her in five years."

"You mean," they said, "you haven't talked to her in all this time, your own sister?"

One person sent me to the next, then the next, and I spent two weeks hunting people down at their jobs, I walked the long hallways of hospitals and hotels, I went up and down the aisles of grocery and discount stores, in and out of restaurants, until eventually a story came together—that Malinda and a group of her friends spent their summers in the resort town of Ogunquit, Maine, working in the restaurants, where they made enough money in three months to support themselves for the rest of the year.

When I got to Ogunquit I went to all of its restaurants, showing Malinda's picture around until late in the night, but no one had ever heard of her. After all of the restaurants had closed I took a long, despairing walk on the beach. It seemed I had reached a dead end, it seemed I would never find her. I put my feet in the water and felt the pull of the tide. I decided to swim for a while. Without thinking too much about it I swam out farther than it was reasonable to swim. I could see the shoreline, curved and winking, but it was vague and out of reach, like some dream I'd once had. Then I was suddenly tired, out of breath, and it seemed I would never fight my way to land. I lay on my back trying to gather my strength and I started to wonder what the point of swimming back might be. It occurred to me that I might as well just float away. Though moments later, propelled by some primal instinct, I would start back to shore, and make it—at the time the sky was black and the water too was black, at the time I was floating on my back with my ears sunk underwater and it was quiet, quiet, at the time I felt utterly, hopelessly, infinitely alone, at the time I was going slack and I knew then, just for a moment, what it was like, I knew what you meant, I knew what you said was true, I knew I was drowning.

Elegy for

James Butler

(1952–1996)

Northern Arkansas, 1952. Oh that you had been born somewhere, anywhere else. A swamp of a town, as you told it, its inhabitants like the creatures of a swamp, primitive and slow-moving, with the stupid smiles and heavy-lidded stares of frogs. No place for you. *A person with a bit of taste,* as you called yourself. *A person with a bit of class.* Throughout your childhood you waited like a customer in line at a complaint window. Somber, patient, holding a numbered ticket in your hand, you believed there would come a day, one day your turn would come at the head of the line and you would be given the chance to explain to someone, a surly employee in blue coveralls, your predicament. *I believe some mistake has been made. I do not belong here.* And there would be no doubt. One look at you would tell the story. You were a short, slender boy with an oversized head; you were pale, with hair so thin it was colorless; you had a soft, sibilant voice, a lilting cadence; you were nearsighted, with thick glasses in tortoiseshell frames, your eyes strangely magnified behind them; you were weak, pigeon-toed, with a funny, shuffling walk, and no, no, you did not belong here, you were not the right kind of boy for this place, anyone could see.

To be a boy in your town, a proper boy, was to be out-doors, running barefoot and shirtless through the woods, to shoot down squirrels and birds with slingshots, to wrestle and fight with other boys—those writhing, muscular, brainless organisms—to flick open and closed, open and closed, the blade of one's pocketknife, to move through the world mud-covered, dirt thick under one's nails, to spit on the ground, to piss against trees. Meanwhile there you sat on your grand-parents' front porch, in a cane rocking chair, reading from your encyclopedia set, listening to classical records on the Vic-trola. Every afternoon you sat there in your linen shirts and trousers—preened and polished, your nails clipped, your hair oiled and parted to the side—you sat sipping tea from your grandmother's rose-trimmed china cups, and when the other boys passed you by on their way to and from the woods, they called out to you the worst name they knew—Fairy!—and the word and its name became one, the word floated in the air, glimmering and alive, the word settled like dust around you. Though it would be many years before the troubles of sex introduced themselves to boys your age, they knew already the difference between you—Fairy, Fairy, Quite Contrary—they knew already, you were not a proper boy.

There was nothing for you to do but wait. Wait and perform those duties necessary to your survival and eventual escape. Through one decade and into the next, through grade school and junior high, through the long, yawning stretch of high school you waited, practicing your piano in the mornings and evenings, the metronome knocking out time as you ran your scales and arpeggios, ascending and descending and ascending again; you waited in the front row of every classroom with your hand raised; you waited with your hands folded through Baptist services every Sunday, you waited while you waded into the town's cold lake to be baptized, fell back into the arms of your preacher, even with your head submerged underwater you were waiting, waiting, waiting for the day you would leave for college and renounce that place and everyone in it, everything you had said and done and pretended to believe within its borders. And when finally the day came (like Ulysses you escaped from your cave under the aegis of an animal), when you left to study music in New York, you watched from the window of the Greyhound bus as the porter loaded your suitcases into the luggage compartment, you watched as your grandmother stood waving a kerchief, you looked back and told yourself: *I am never coming back, I will never see this place, these people, ever again.*

Of course I knew none of this at first—at first you were nothing to me but another in a long line of strange characters I met the summer I went off in search of my sister. This was in Ogunquit,

Maine, a quaint beach town whose streets were lined with historic houses, with little shops and restaurants. It was the type of place I'd only seen before on postcards, and in fact everything there looked not quite real, as if it had been staged by a photographer, an adman. Tourists strolled around in perfect ease, their hands in their pockets. They wore white pants, bright polo shirts, tasseled loafers. They were fat and pink and exuberant, smacking of health and abundance. In a place like Ogunquit it was easy to believe that life was effortless, beautiful, that there was nothing to it but riches. It was exactly the kind of place, I thought, Malinda would run off to.

I had spent two days walking around town, sneaking behind all of its restaurants, to their back entrances, where the dumpsters were kept, where employees sat smoking on overturned buckets, for it was in these shadowy, stinking corners that life's drudgery was hiding. I'd shown Malinda's picture around, and almost everyone had the same reaction, which was to look at her and whistle: "A girl like that," they said, and paused, "a girl like that I'd remember."

This is how we met, on my second evening in town, when I had started to give up hope. When I first saw you, you were leaning by the side entrance of a fancy seafood place that overlooked the water. You were so remarkably small, so short and slender, that for an instant I had the impression you had stepped out of another dimension. As a child I had always suspected that a race of small people was working behind the scenes of what I took for ordinary life—behind a scrim they pushed buttons and pulled levers, controlling the traffic, the weather, the moods of my mother—and now, it seemed, here you were, an elf out on a cigarette break. You had an elf's pinkish skin, and an elf's delicate upturned nose. Your hair was parted elf-like on the side, slicked down with pomade. Though you were formally dressed—in a dark blue suit with a yellow bow tie—your small size gave the suit the look of a costume.

I caught your eye and we stared at each other for a second. I wonder, now, what I looked like to you—some wastrel, some crumpled vagrant.

May I help you? you said. Your voice was high, snide.

"I'm looking for this girl." I held out Malinda's picture and you fairly snatched it out of my hand. When you saw Malinda a corner of your mouth turned up.

What is it you want with Malinda? you said. *If I might be so bold as to ask?*

"You know her?"

I might, you said. *I might not.* Your voice seemed to me like the recording of a voice—it was too loud, and there was something plastic about it. *She doesn't have any money, if that's what you want. If that's what you're after, you can just forget it.*

I wondered how bad off Malinda was. If there were people coming by her workplace looking for the money she owed them. I didn't doubt it. The last time I'd seen her she was so drunk her eyes were swirling in the manner of a cartoon character hypnotized by a mad scientist. She'd come home in the middle of the night and woken me up. "Can I have some money?" she'd said, and I'd gone to my bureau drawer, where I kept a roll of soft, dirty bills rolled up inside a tube sock. I'd pulled out a twenty, thinking how it represented five hours of standing in front of a register at the grocery store, five hours of my life I'd never get back. She'd grabbed it and stuffed it in her pocket and said, "See ya." Which was little enough of a parting sentiment, and she'd delivered not even that kindness. The next night I'd come home from work to find the rest of my money gone.

Hello? you said. You stepped toward me and snapped your fingers in front of my face.

"Could you just tell me where Malinda is?" I said.

I don't think so. If I were you I'd turn around and go back wherever it was you came from. You made a shooing motion with your hand. *I have half a mind to call the authorities. We don't allow loitering on the premises.*

I looked at you murderously. I had an image of gripping your throat, strangling your neck. I wondered who would win in a fight between us. Since my junior year of college I'd suffered bouts of insomnia, and I'd spent long nights on the couch in the dormitory lobby watching nature documentaries on public television. One animal was always fighting another, and I could never tell which one would survive. Sometimes the smaller animals were faster and got away, other times their size worked against them and they were devoured. You were, I thought, smaller and more delicate than I was, and I had an advantage there. But then again you were angry, and sometimes anger was enough. It was a toss-up.

Have you had a stroke or something? you said.

"Sorry," I said. "I forgot what we were talking about."

Then you burst out laughing, a high, stuttering kind of laugh I'd heard before only in cartoons. "Oh God," you said. "You're the sister, aren't you?"

I nodded.

"Oh, this is rich," you said. You laughed again, threw your head back and cackled. "You're exactly like she said."

"What'd she say?" I asked.

Oh, you said, *nothing much. She said she had a sister but that you were polar opposites, you were like a deaf mute, all you did was sit around reading books.* You swirled your cigarette around in the air, as if conducting yourself. *She said you froze up during conversations and sometimes started crying for no reason, you couldn't help it, you should be pitied.*

"That's not true!" I said. "I don't cry!"

She said you were probably on the street somewhere, sitting on the sidewalk shaking a paper cup full of change. You know, a charity case. One of those people walking around with a sandwich board. Some kind of crazy message painted on it. The apocalypse or whatnot. Don't worry, you said, *she didn't say much.*

"I have a college degree," I told you.

You looked me up and down. *I'm sure you went to a fine institution,* you said, your sarcasm so sly I almost missed it.

Then you started reminiscing about Arkansas, something I'd soon realize was a compulsive habit of yours. *Of course we had our own lunatic back home—every town has one, that's what I told Malinda, the world wouldn't be the same without crazy people walking around asking for change. The funny thing about Arkansas, though, is that everyone does everything backwards. Our lunatic was a fat man who went around carrying a sign with something or other drawn on it, every day something different, a flower, a rocket ship, a dog wearing roller skates. Things of that nature. No one knew who he was or where he came from, but he stood at the town center, holding up his sign, and whenever you passed by he'd try to give you a quarter.* You stopped to drag on your cigarette. You looked up at the sky, squinting, as if a scene from your childhood was playing out there. *I took a quarter from time to time, bought myself a soda, but it never tasted right. There was always something funny about it.*

"I'm not a lunatic!" I cried. Though the sound of my voice, high and pleading, wasn't exactly convincing.

Of course not. You gave me another cutting look. *I never said you were.*

"I just want to find Malinda."

She's not in town yet, you said. *But we're expecting her hourly, my dear. Hourly.*

With that you flicked your cigarette butt into the air, and it soared into the dumpster. I imagined a fire breaking out. *At the present moment, however,* you said, *I have a show to put on.* And you turned on your heel and disappeared through the door.

I wondered what to do—whether to stay in town and wait, and if so, how to pay for it. I would have to get a job. I imagined working at that very restaurant, side by side with Malinda. We'd reconcile, and she'd realize how unfair she'd been to turn away from me, she'd sob with regret . . . My head was swirling with plans when suddenly you appeared in the doorway again. *Well, are you coming to the show,* you said, *or what?*

I followed you through the kitchen, bright and hot and clattering, and then through the dining room, dark and cool, where tourists sat dismantling lobsters. They had little plastic bibs around their necks, and they were working at the lobster claws with nutcrackers and tiny forks. In their concentration they stuck the tips of their tongues out the sides of their mouths, like children in an art class.

Adjacent to the dining room was a bar, and in its far corner sat a baby grand. Small tables were clustered around the piano, and several couples sat waiting for you. They applauded when you settled yourself on the bench.

Thank you so much, you said, *Thank you, I love you all.* When your voice came through the microphone it was entirely different than it had been just moments before. It was low and mellifluous, and laced with such a false humility that it made me wince.

I sat at the bar, and a man who looked very much like Humphrey Bogart asked me what I was having. I looked in my pocket to see how much money I had. "Can I get anything for three dollars?" I said.

The bartender stared at me with Bogart's wearied indifference. "I suppose you could get a Shirley Temple," he said.

"Then I guess I'll have a Shirley Temple."

He made an elaborate display of serving my drink, setting down a little napkin, then resting the drink just so on top of it. He waited until I took a sip. "Everything satisfactory?" he said.

"Quite."

Printed on the napkin was a cartoon drawing of you—a tiny man with a large head. In the drawing you were smiling, and your teeth nearly overtook your face, like the Cheshire Cat. THE OASIS BAR, the napkin read. FEATURING THE PIANO STYLINGS OF JAMES BUTLER.

I sat listening to you for hours. Your strength as a performer had nothing to do with any particular quality in your own voice, but in your ability to mimic the singers you covered—the gravel and glee of Louis Armstrong, the low suavity of Dean Martin.

You chattered with the couples between songs, the kind of banter common to performers. *Where are you folks from?* you said. *Are you enjoying yourselves? How long have you been married?* You spoke in the most earnest, delighted voice, like it was the greatest privilege of your life to be in their company.

From time to time, as a little joke to himself, the bartender came over and suggested high-priced bottles of wine, glasses of single-malt scotch. "Perhaps I can get you something to eat? An appetizer? A lobster dinner?"

"No," I said, affecting an indifference that had nothing to do with money. "Not at the moment."

Eventually there was only one couple left in the dining room. The woman had white meringue-like hair that stood up in peaks, and her pink lipstick was drawn far outside the lines of her mouth. Her husband was a fat silver-haired man who sat with his legs spread, his hands in his pockets. As you sang he stared at the floor, probably wondering about his stocks. In between songs you kept assuring these people that there was no need for them to leave just because the place was empty and it was midnight. *I have all the time in the world,* you said. *I'm here just for you.*

The woman kept requesting Gershwin songs. As you played—lightly, dreamily—the woman sat staring at you with her hands pressed together, as if in prayer. Whenever you finished a song she stood up and clapped—Marvelous, Marvelous, she said—and you stood also, and gave her a little bow. Finally the man led his wife away by force, and as they left she kept turning and blowing you kisses. "I can't remember," said the woman, "the last time I so enjoyed an evening."

Well, thank you, you said. You bowed again. *You made my evening as well.*

When they were out of earshot you said, in the high voice that was your own, *That miserable cunt. Two hours she sits there clapping her claws together and do you think she leaves a tip?* You had lit a cigarette and were waving it in the air. *I'm done,* you said. *I can't take it anymore. I quit. I fucking quit.* You emptied out your tip jar. You lined up the bills and counted them angrily, pulling them from one hand to the other.

Seventeen fucking dollars, you said. You sat down on the stool next to me, and the bartender poured you a vodka. *Did I not play every goddamn Gershwin number ever written? Was I not flawless? Was I not charming?* Your voice was loud now, hysterical.

"You were charming," I said.

From the inner pocket of your suit you produced a silver pill case. You opened it and offered a pill to the bartender, who took one and popped it in his mouth. *Would you care for a pill?* you asked me.

I inspected them—there were pills of all different shapes and colors. "I don't really take pills."

Why not? you asked, as if everyone in the world took unidentified pills from complete strangers. *How on earth do you get through a single day?*

"I don't know."

These, you said, swallowing one, *are simply marvelous. I take one every night after work.* You shook another pill into your palm. It was pale blue, shaped like a flying saucer. *They have a marvelous effect,* you said. *They're very relaxing. Other people become tolerable.*

I took the pill and swallowed it. "Hell is other people," I said.

You raised your eyebrow, looked me up and down. *I'm sur-prised you're educated,* you said. *No offense. But considering who you're related to, I wasn't exactly expecting Sartre.*

I shrugged.

I guess Malinda got the looks, you said, *and you got the books!* You laughed, amused with yourself. *Being an only child, of course, you might say that I got it all—the looks, the brains, the whole package. I could have done anything I wanted in life, anything. I had the grades, the talent, the charisma. I could be President of the United States right now if I wanted.*

Humphrey Bogart scoffed, but you ignored him.

Or an actor, you said to me. *I would have had great success as an actor. People sometimes make comparisons between me and Paul Newman. Of course I never laid eyes on Paul Newman until I got to New York. We didn't even have a theater back home. The world could have ended and we wouldn't have known it. You know how it is in Arkansas.*

I'd never been to Arkansas and did not know how it was. But this didn't matter to you. You carried on about the faults of your hometown—its narrow-mindedness, its poverty, the general stupidity of its population, its problem with mosquitoes, the chemicals sprayed on its crops by low-flying planes and your ensuing skin rashes, respiratory problems. *Which is why,* you said, *naturally I had to move on. A person of my abilities trapped in a place like that. It's amazing I survived.*

One of the great curses of your life, you said, was that your brain was configured in such a way that you never forgot any-thing, and so Arkansas was as present to you as the glass in your hand. Every day of your life was preserved and filed away in your memory, a veritable card catalog. *I plan to donate my body to science,* you said, *so that my brain can be studied.* You claimed to have memories of infancy, of being held, of grasping your grandmother's pearls in your fist, of being rocked, you claimed to remember the dark shade of your pram casting a shadow on your face, the hot sun on your fat bare legs, you claimed to have spoken full sentences at the age of one. *Twelve months old and I was reciting the King James Bible,* you said, *and by the age of two I was reading it.*

I had questions I wanted to ask you—I wanted to know more about Malinda, how she'd been—but you were caught up in your reminiscences. Your stories kept pouring forth, all of which portrayed you in the light of a biblical character, someone whose fortunes had taken wild and unprecedented turns. It was a blight, you said, to have been born a genius in a place like Arkansas. But then again there were moments in which you felt the full weight of your power. The time a tornado flattened all of the houses on your street except yours. The time you sat down at your grandmother's piano, age five, and spontaneously composed a song so beautiful that it brought the entire household to tears. *The next day Grandmother hired a piano teacher,* you said, *and within a week I was playing Beethoven.*

The bartender chimed in now, too. "My kid played piano," he said, "but she's gone now, she moved to Tucson with my ex-wife and her new husband. Whenever I talk to her she just asks me for money."

He'd just begun talking, and obviously had more to tell, but you interrupted him. *That's a charming story,* you said, *but I can't sit around chatting all night. I have to get my beauty sleep.* You hopped off the stool—your feet didn't quite reach the floor— and started for the door. I followed you, out through the restaurant, and then up the street.

"How well do you know Malinda?" I said.

Oh, completely, you said. *Completely.*

"Do you know where she stays when she gets in town?"

Probably with some boyfriend, you said. *When she arrives for the season, you never know who she'll bring with her. She passes through people quite frequently.*

"I know," I said. "I haven't seen her in a long time."

That's a shame, you said, and yawned flagrantly.

"We were really close when we were younger. But then she left home, and we never really knew why. We always thought she'd come back any day, any minute, and then all of a sudden you turn around and it's been years." The pill you'd given me had kicked in, and I saw my past as if a long corridor lined with doors, each opening up into a separate memory of Malinda. "Looking back," I said, "I should have known she was leaving. She was burning her bridges. Not long before she left our father came to visit—we didn't see much of him but occasionally he'd stop by—and as he was sitting on the couch and telling us how sorry he was that he hadn't been around for us, Malinda just got up and went to the closet and got a hammer, and she very calmly walked outside, and then all of a sudden we heard this smashing and crashing, glass breaking, and we ran outside and saw that Malinda had broken his car windows, his windshield, she'd put dents in the hood. He was too scared to go near her, he just stood there holding his head and waited until she was finished and then he got in the car and drove away, with no windshield or anything, he must have been sitting on glass."

Someone else's dog, you said, *used to follow me to school every morning, and every afternoon when school was released it was waiting to walk me home. It couldn't get enough of me.*

"That's so cute!" I said. Though I never used words like "cute."

I hated it, you said. *It had this stupid smile on its face all the time, its hair was all knotted and mangy, one of its eyes was crazy.*

I started to get the feeling you were talking about me. "It's just that I don't have anywhere to go," I said.

Well what were you planning on doing? you asked. *If you didn't find Malinda. Or for that matter, if you found her?*

"I don't know," I said. "I hadn't really thought about it."

Well where were you planning to sleep? you said.

"My car?" I said. I'd spent the previous night in the parking lot of a grocery store, and had barely slept. In the morning I'd woken up with my face stuck to the vinyl seat.

Well this is absolutely pathetic, you said. You stood with your hands on your hips, the universal posture of disappointment. *You're just going to have to come home with me.*

Your grandparents' was the biggest house in that small Arkansas town, a three-story Victorian with a turret on its west side, a wraparound front porch. Your grandfather, who had made his money in paper and envelopes, was the richest man in the county, and he had built for himself a house so big, and so like a museum, that it was referred to by name—"the Butler

Place." Your grandmother was always having boxes delivered to the house, large and small, from all kinds of foreign destinations, and people wondered what treasures lined the walls, the china cabinet, the bookshelves. They came to the door under the pretense of selling raffle tickets, of seeking charitable donations, of wanting petitions signed, of looking for work, and they stood craning their necks, wanting to see inside. But your grandmother allowed no one in except the handyman and the maid, a married black couple who lived on the outskirts of town.

Mostly what your grandmother ordered were educational materials—books and music. She had been raised by what she referred to as "people of nobility"—many of her relatives had held positions of governance within the Confederacy—and though her family's stature had fallen into decline, she was determined, through her marriage and offspring, to redeem it. Your mother, unknown to you and shrouded in mystery, had proved a failure, and was never mentioned apart from the passing reference to the shame she'd inflicted on the family. Now you were your grandmother's only hope. She was obsessed with your proper upbringing, your education and advancement—it was her particular wish that you become a senator.

Before you started grade school you could read and write, add and subtract. You could identify all of the world's countries and their capitals. You could say *Hello, Please, Thank you,* and *Farewell* in ten different languages. By the time you were six your grandmother had already given you the social training of a diplomat. She kept a first edition of Emily Post's *Etiquette* laid open on a wooden stand, and whenever you violated a rule she made you stand before the book and recite the relevant passage twenty-five times. *When gentlemen are introduced to each other they always shake hands.*

Music was your grandmother's one indulgence, the closest you were allowed to leisure. In the afternoons the two of you sat in your rocking chairs on the front porch, listening to records. She had records delivered to the house from shops all over the world, and by the time you were five you could name and recognize dozens of different composers. The summer before you entered the first grade your grandmother began to import, once a week from the nearby university, the services of a professor named Mr. Svevo, who taught you piano and foreign languages. Mr. Svevo was a thin, bald, dour-looking man who arrived every Saturday morning in a blue Cadillac. He dressed in fine suits, he wore polished shoes, cuff links, fedoras with bright feathers springing from their bands. Rumors swirled around this man, concerning his identity and his place in the household—it was supposed that he was your grandmother's lover, a Nazi war criminal, one of your grandmother's downtrodden relatives looking for Mr. Butler's money.

You'd taken an immediate liking to Mr. Svevo and adopted many of his airs. On the first day of grade school and every day thereafter, you arrived in a blue suit with a red pocket square. You made a habit of speaking in foreign phrases in front of your teachers and classmates. *Zut alors!* you said disgustedly whenever they exasperated you, *J'en ai marre!* Before you sat on a chair, you wiped it off with your handkerchief in an effort to protect yourself from the germs of commoners. You were, of course, despised.

Under Mr. Svevo's instruction you learned Mozart, Beethoven, Bach, you learned not only their notes but their feeling. You developed an ear, an eye. With Mr. Svevo's help you eventually started composing your own music. *A prodigy, I suppose,* you said. When you were ten years old Mr. Svevo took you to give a concert in Fayetteville, and your performance was so celebrated that you were invited to play once a week, every Sunday morning at noon, on the local radio station. Each week you wrote a new composition. *Little nothings after the fashion of Mozart,* you said. *But oh, I was famous. The ten-year-old composer. People recognized me everywhere, just everywhere. Once when the maid and I were in the grocery store they announced over the intercom that a special guest was in the store—me, an honored guest.* The grocery store's checkout clerk was a six-fingered woman, and going through her line, seeing that extra finger, had always nauseated you. After your appearance on the radio station she'd ventured to pat your head, and a chill had gone through you from which you'd never quite recovered. Partly it was the extra finger which chilled you. But it was partly something else. The feeling that you were special, noteworthy, the feeling that someone couldn't help herself from reaching out and touching you.

When the time came to send you to college, Mr. Svevo spoke to your grandmother about a connection of his at Juilliard. Your grandmother was reluctant to send you to New York, where you might fall under any kind of influence, but Mr. Svevo convinced her that with the proper instruction you might become one of the world's great composers. This wasn't exactly what she had planned—she was still tied to the idea of your becoming a politician—but in the end Mr. Svevo persuaded her. She bought you a set of luggage, five new suits, and sent you off like a bride. As you boarded the bus that would take you to school, your grandmother stood straight-backed, her face contorted in an effort not to cry. When the bus pulled away she waved a handkerchief at you, and its frantic movements amounted to the most outward and desperate display of emotion she'd ever given you.

In Maine you lived at a boardinghouse called the Bavarian Inn, a large white cottage with dark wooden trim, about a mile's walk from the restaurant. To distinguish itself from the countless other motels that ran along the same stretch of road, the Bavarian offered what it referred to on its sign as "Old World Charm." Its first floor was a common area consisting of a dining room—where breakfast was served each morning on German pewter plates—and a living room, furnished with antiques, its walls lined with a vast selection of leather-bound classics. One of the corners of the living room was devoted to a baby grand of a rare tone and quality, which you claimed was the only reason you took your lodgings there.

There were five rooms upstairs, all of which shared a common bathroom. Years ago, when people had been willing to tolerate shared baths, the Bavarian's charms had attracted a great many people. But in recent years tourists had since drifted off to motels with other features—with private baths and swimming pools, air-conditioning, cable—and now the Bavarian was more or less abandoned.

The proprietor of the Bavarian was a German woman named Mrs. Strauss, who seemed to be operating under the delusion that she was still a girl living in a prewar village nestled at the foot of the Alps. She wore her gray hair in two braids which she looped into buns above her ears, and she dressed in the same girlish outfit every day—a white short-sleeved shirt and a pair of khaki knee-length shorts, a pair of bright red socks pulled up to her knees. Mrs. Strauss had the naïve cheer of a child, a child's sincerity. She talked of almost nothing but her girlhood village: farming, singing, hiking, goats. She told long apocryphal stories about the village and its characters, their difficulties and their inevitable triumphs.

On the night that you brought me to the Bavarian Mrs. Strauss was sitting in the living room, crocheting an afghan, like a mother waiting up for her child. When you introduced me, and informed Mrs. Strauss that I would be staying for a while, she acted as if she'd been expecting me her whole life. "But of course you'll be here with us!" she said. "Your room is already made up and waiting for you."

She showed me upstairs to a small room just large enough to accommodate a twin bed, a nightstand, and a dresser. The bed was covered with a white matelassé spread, which Mrs. Strauss informed me she had made herself. On the nightstand was a blue bowl and pitcher. "For the purposes of washing one's face," said Mrs. Strauss. There was also a leather-bound collection of fairy tales. It was in just such fairy tales, I realized, that I had seen rooms like this before, and I knew that the characters who lived in them were always happy, for a time.

The next day you made a phone call and got me a job washing dishes at the Oasis, seven nights a week, from six to midnight.

The kitchen was run by a man named Houston, a retired wrestler who was so oversized he often bumped into people and sent them reeling. His wrestling persona had been that of a madman, an escaped mental patient who liked to bite the heads off of small animals. One of the prep chefs had an old newspaper clipping that showed Houston in a unitard, crouched in a stalking posture, a chicken strangled in one of his fists. "The Inmate," it read, "Is Back and Out for Blood!" In the picture his head was shaved, and he wore a long mustache that extended well beyond the corners of his mouth. He looked menacing, bloodthirsty. Since then he had grown back his hair and shaved his mustache, but he still had a seething look about him. He was always in a furious sweat. It was hot in the kitchen—giant vats of water were kept boiling for the lobsters, the grill was fired at all times, hissing—and as Houston stood over the grill drops of his sweat would roll off his forehead and onto the fillets he was cooking, and although he never went so far as to smile, it seemed to me this satisfied him.

Houston wouldn't tolerate any form of what he called "fraternizing." The waitresses would hang around talking to the lesser chefs and he'd say, "Y'all stop your fraternizing," and point a spatula at them in a threatening way. What annoyed Houston most was the way that all of the kitchen workers would gather around and eat the leftovers sent back by customers. A plate of mussels would come in from the dining room, a few of the shells abandoned in the buttery broth, or a lobster with one of its claws still intact, and the workers would stand around prying out bits of meat, stuffing the scraps in their mouths. Houston would lose his mind. He'd come charging out from behind the

grill with a knife. "Y'all get along!" he'd say. "Ya'll stop fraternizing. Y'all making me sick in here."

I never did any fraternizing. I watched quietly from my corner of the kitchen as the waitresses went in and out, talking
about the tables they were serving, the petty requests of spoiled
customers, the amount of money people were throwing away on
kids who didn't appreciate their food. They talked about their
kids, their boyfriends and their boyfriends' kids and ex-wives,
problems with money and sex, and I just stood in my corner of
the kitchen, listening.

Washing dishes wasn't what it had once been—it merely
involved scraping off plates and stacking them in a machine,
then pulling down a hood and waiting for the cycle to run.
When the dishes were finished I restocked them in the kitchen,
brought hot glasses out to the bar. Occasionally I dropped
something and had to sweep up its remains. When it was slow
and there were no dishes there was always something else to
do, and Houston would set me about the business of filling up
the salt and pepper shakers, mixing together salad dressing,
filling a pastry bag with sour cream and coiling little flowers
of it into small plastic cups, to be served on the side of baked
potatoes. I fell into deep, thoughtless trances and was reasonably happy. Everything I'd learned in college seemed to me now
ridiculous. I had only been out for a few weeks but already I'd
forgotten, or locked away, the entire history of the world, its
religions, its people and its languages and its literature, its scientific advancements, its philosophical principles, its artwork,
the conclusions and predictions of its noblest minds—how far
away it all seemed now, how useless!

Pills went around the kitchen, passed between the cooks and waitresses and bussers. There were different kinds—some were white, aspirin-like tablets, some were pink and shaped like eggs, some were red capsules, some were clear capsules with tiny yellow balls inside—and people swallowed them without knowing what they were taking or what the effects might be. There were different features to each of the pills, but they all shared the quality of making work slip by very easily. Everyone went about the kitchen with swift, balletic movements—they lofted heavy trays in the air and chopped vegetables and sautéed scallops and plunged lobsters into their boiling, hissing deaths—they did all of this beautifully, effortlessly, the way we move in dreams.

I sometimes wondered where the pills came from. They were always there, always, and it didn't seem to me that anyone actually paid for them. It wouldn't have surprised me to learn that the owner provided them, to grease the wheels of his machine. He was a short, skeletal man who dressed like the captain of a ship—in white pants and a blue blazer with gaudy brass buttons—and he wandered around the restaurant like the Ancient Mariner. Ten times a night he'd come through the kitchen checking to make sure that all was in working order, and he moved with the same easy fluidity that we did. Rumors went around about him—that he had dealings with the mafia, that he had once stood trial for killing a man—and I had no trouble believing any of them.

Within a few days word got around to all the employees that I was related to Malinda, and people started coming around to talk about her. She had provided a great deal of amusement over the past few years, and people missed her. Because of her beauty she was always getting invited to parties on yachts, or in the expensive homes along the beach, and she'd often bring the rest of the waitstaff with her. These parties never ended well—people were kicked out, the police were called. Twice Malinda had been arrested and had to be bailed out of jail. Another time she had woken up in the backseat of a car in New York, with no memory of having been driven there, and she'd had to call one of the waiters to come pick her up. Several times each season someone came storming into the kitchen—a spurned lover, a jealous girlfriend, someone from whom Malinda had borrowed money but never repaid—and there were violent, spectacular, thrilling arguments. "God, I miss Malinda," people said.

I tried to press them for details about her—where she went in the winters, who she lived with—but it was hard for people to say. She always took off with whomever she happened to be dating at the time—she'd gone to Florida one year, Arizona the next—but no one could remember where she'd gone at the end of last season. She had a boyfriend whose name no one could remember, because he'd simply been referred to as "the Lesser Castro."

"One of those guys who went around in military gear," said one of the waitresses. "He had this full beard and everything. God only knows what Malinda saw in him. I think he was actually a Communist."

All of these conversations ended in the same way. Whoever was talking would give me a look, like I was some kind of impostor or criminal, like I was the reason she hadn't shown up. "How do we know," said one of the cooks, "you're not just some crazy person off the street, how do we know you didn't kill her and, like, eat her? And that's why she ain't here?"

During my first few shifts I expected Malinda, as you said, hourly. I imagined her showing up unannounced, kicking the door open from the dining room and abusing the chefs about a late order. She'd pile up her tray with food and settle it on her shoulder. Then she'd turn and see me, and drop everything. The kitchen would come to a halt and not even Houston would dare to speak. "Now that I see you here," Malinda would say, "I can't for the life of me believe I ever left you." She'd cry, fall at my feet. "Forgive me!" she'd say. "I never meant to leave you!" All the people who had looked at me skeptically would say to themselves, "I guess we were wrong. I guess they're sisters after all. I guess nothing can keep them apart. I wish I had something like that in my life."

At the restaurant you were something of a petty celebrity. You were an employee, like the rest of us, but of a higher caliber— you didn't have to get dirty, serve other people, and your work was confined to the cool elegance of the bar. On your breaks you walked through the kitchen so you could smoke in the back alley, and as you passed through you were greeted by the other employees with a mixture of respect and disdain.

Houston always took his breaks with you—fraternizing with you was the single exception he allowed to his general rule—and the two of you sat outside smoking. Apart from being southern and longtime employees of the Oasis, you and Houston seemed to have nothing in common—in fact you seemed to hate each other. The back door was always open, and since the washer was right next to it, I often overheard you and Houston talking. Not once did I hear you talk about anything substantive—you dealt exclusively in sarcastic comments about fucking each other, and members of one another's family.

"Don't be calling your momma too early tomorrow," Houston would say, "I'm gonna be keeping her up late tonight."

I can tell where you learned how to wrestle so poorly, you said, *your momma just lays there and takes it to the count of three.*

"Fuck you," Houston said.

Anytime.

"Suck my dick."

Right after I'm done with your daddy's.

Mornings, back at the Bavarian, you were a completely different person, and it took me a number of days to get used to it. In everything that you did there you conducted yourself with the quiet dignity of a butler. You rose very early and attended to yourself in the bathroom, leaving behind the strong scent of grapefruit—your aftershave, imported from France. Then you walked down the street to a convenience store and returned with the *New York Times,* which you read aloud to Mrs. Strauss over breakfast. Between articles you and Mrs. Strauss passed comments back and forth, always amounting to more or less the same sentiment. *What people won't do,* you said. Your speech at the Bavarian was very refined, and held no trace of the southern drawl you spoke with in the evenings. At times I even detected a slight British accent.

"Yes," Mrs. Strauss would say, "what the world is coming to these days."

Often a news article would remind Mrs. Strauss of something from her native village, and she'd carry on at great length about things which couldn't possibly be true. Once she told a story about her brother Karl and a prize watermelon. "He watered that melon, and watered it and watered it, until it grew bigger than he was and in order to water it he had to climb a ladder!"

Every day was the same. After breakfast you took a walk, which you referred to as your *morning constitutional,* and returned with a bag of groceries, which Mrs. Strauss made into the afternoon's meal. You'd read a book in the parlor, or on the front porch (that summer you were working your way through Nietzsche), then retire to your room for a brief nap. Before work you sat at the piano and played the classical pieces that you loved so much, but that weren't to the taste of the *philistines,* as you called them, at the bar. You made frequent reference to a symphony you were composing, which took the brooding and passion of Beethoven and sifted it through what you called a *reduction machine.*

"Interesting," I'd say.

I don't expect you to understand, you'd say. *But someday you will, someday the world will understand.*

After the first week, when Malinda still hadn't shown up at the Oasis, it occurred to me that she might have taken a job somewhere else in town, and I spent my days walking around the shops and restaurants, showing her picture around. I stopped at every hotel, every bed-and-breakfast, and came to know the town quite well. One of the most notable features of Ogunquit, it turned out, was its gay population. The town had been one of

the first in the country to declare itself—its hotels and its restaurants—friendly to gay couples, and it had since become so
popular with them that now it was a shock to the system to see
a man and woman holding hands in the street.

    This was 1994, before the widespread use of protease inhibi-
tors, and so that year there was a subset amongst the gay
population—the men who were dying of AIDS. These men
were wasted down to skeletons. They went about with canes,
with aluminum walkers, they went about in wheelchairs. They
wore long pants and long-sleeved shirts with cardigan sweaters,
they wore hats pulled down over their faces. Their skin, what
you could see of it, was pale, translucent, so ghostly that it made
the robust health around them—the suntans and the exposed
flesh—seem in poor taste. These dying men were always surrounded by friends, enthusiastic and gregarious people who
seemed to do nothing but point out the pleasures of their surroundings. "Smell that fresh ocean air!" they said. Or, "Taste
this! It's divine!" But I never saw any of the dying men look anything but completely indifferent to his surroundings. A dying
man could see straight through the fleeting distractions of the
life around him. Whenever I locked eyes with one of them it was
as if I could see, for an instant, what they saw, and it was chilling.
The party we were all casually strolling through—the health we
enjoyed, the sunshine, the freedoms, the fine foods—this party
was temporary, this party was over.

The Bavarian attracted the occasional guest, and whatever
variety we had in our daily life was their doing. For two weeks

in June a gay couple, Mark and Addison, stayed at the Bavarian and swept us up into their bizarre, tumultuous love affair. Mark and Addison looked like brothers. They were both short and trim and well-muscled, they both had deep tans and sparkling white teeth and blond hair, which they gelled into perfectly vertical spikes. Like brothers, they fought all the time—it seemed their relationship depended on it. Sometimes they'd sit side by side complaining to me about each other. Mark, Addison said, had a problem with going off in the middle of parties with other men. Addison's problem, Mark said, was that he tired too easily and always wanted to go home right when things were starting to get rolling. Also, he was too possessive. The problem with Mark, said Addison, was that he was shallow. And stupid. And couldn't hold up his end of even the most trivial conversation. "Never go to a movie with Mark," he said. "The movie ends and you ask him what he thought and he says, 'The popcorn was too salty.'"

"Well, his ass," said Mark, "is getting fat."

"Well, fuck you," said Addison.

"You wish," said Mark.

"No, you wish."

"You're the one who's going to be sorry."

"You think for one second I can't find somebody else?"

"I'm sure Mary here would be happy to date you. And your fat ass."

"Oh please. Don't make me vomit."

Whenever Mrs. Strauss appeared Mark and Addison would change entirely. She'd come through the door with a pan of strata and start filling our plates, and Mark and Addison would sit up straight and smile. "Thank you, Mrs. Strauss," they said. "Thank you, Mrs. Strauss." During breakfast they listened attentively as Mrs. Strauss relived one or another of her childhood memories. "When I was a girl," she'd say, "Father used to start off every morning with a raw egg. He'd crack it into a short glass and then swallow it in one gulp, right down the hatch, and Karl and I would be squirming in our seats. Oh, we thought it was horrible! But Father swore by it. You've never seen anyone in such health!"

Mark was a compulsive sycophant who always encouraged Mrs. Strauss to keep talking. "That's fascinating," he said, "I should try that. I've been trying to eat a healthier diet. I'd like to put on some more muscle."

"That's a wonderful idea!" said Mrs. Strauss. She practically leapt up from the table and disappeared into the kitchen, then reappeared with an egg in a glass, its yolk bobbing.

"Down the hatch!" Mark said, and swallowed it. Something like this would soften Addison, and by the end of the meal they'd be holding hands under the table.

Almost every breakfast ended with Mrs. Strauss saying how much she loved having boys in the house. "Such nice, strapping boys!" she said. She believed that they were brothers, and so fond of one another that they couldn't bear to sleep in separate rooms. "It is so good for brothers to love each other so much!"

Once, when Mrs. Strauss was back in the kitchen, they started kissing at the table, and you sat staring at them in disgust. *Excuse me,* you said, *but some of us are trying to eat.*

"Hey," said Mark, "why don't you come out with us tonight? We'll fix you up!"

Oh please, you said, and went back to your newspaper. *I'm retired.*

It was only by comparison with Mark and Addison that I realized I'd come to think of myself as a resident of the Bavarian. I regarded the hours they kept, and the noises they made, as interruptions to what I considered our usual routine. "They don't understand," I said to you once, "how we like to have harmony in the house. We really don't like all this bickering."

Every night, when I was finished in the kitchen, I sat in the bar and watched your act. Once the season was in full swing, and the town was full of gay men, you changed your repertoire and sang show tunes, Barbra Streisand, Barry Manilow. Between songs you made sexually suggestive jokes about the customers, the same jokes every evening. A handsome man would be sitting in the audience and you'd stop mid-song and ask if he was choking. *I think this gorgeous young man is choking on his shrimp cocktail,* you'd say. *Does anyone know the Heimlich? No? No one? Do I have to do everything around here?*

Toward the end of the evening you'd stop to remind people that a full dessert menu was available in the bar. *We have a very talented waiter who'll take care of you, his name's Foster, he'll set you up with a banana. If you like chocolate, there's the ever-popular Whitman's Sampler.* I wondered how you could keep cracking the same jokes, with the same enthusiasm, night after night. I suppose it was the crowd's laughter. At the sound of it your face lit up, in a brief flash, and the satisfaction registered there never diminished.

After the last customers left I sat at the bar and took a pill
with you and Humphrey Bogart, who always stood silently polishing glasses with a rag. You talked endlessly about your childhood, making your way chronologically through the memories
of your life. There was something overdone and unbelievable
about the cast of characters you described. The way your maid,
Lottie, doted on you as if she were your mother, how she cried
in the evenings when she had to leave you and return home to
her own children. *There now,* you'd tell her, wiping her tears
away with your silk handkerchief, *I'll be right here when you get back
in the morning. Right here.*

The villain of your childhood was the local sheriff, fat-bellied
and swaggering, who had a son your age and who believed that
you were afflicted with something communicable, that your
"nature," as he called it, might be catching. In your stories you'd
be walking down the street, minding your own business, and
the sheriff would pull you by your ear into an alley. His dialogue
was straight out of a country western. *You stay away from my boy,
now, you hear? We don't want any more of your kind around these
parts. I don't care how much money your grandaddy has, I'm still the
sheriff!*

Though you sometimes stopped to acknowledge me—*It's so
nice to have someone educated to talk to,* you'd say, *you have no idea
what a cultural wasteland this is*—for the most part I had the feeling that anyone would do, that you had practiced all of your stories on dozens of people before me and would practice them on
dozens afterward. Indeed as Humphrey Bogart stood polishing
his glasses he often rolled his eyes, as if he'd heard these stories
many times before. *I should write this all down,* you often said. *Or*

rather, have someone take it all down for me. I don't care to be bothered with the writing itself.

Days went by, one after the other, all of them the same. With all the pills I was taking I couldn't tell one from the next, and yet at a certain point I realized that something had changed, imperceptibly. I had stopped thinking about Malinda as if she were scheduled to arrive at any moment, and had begun to think of her as some kind of figment of my imagination, some character in a story I told myself. I had more or less come to think of her the way children think of Santa—a person to be dreamed of, but never confirmed. If she had walked through the door of the bar—if she had actually appeared in the flesh—I would have felt myself in violation of the natural order of things.

I had also lost any interest in going to graduate school. I was suffering, I suppose, the kind of existential crisis common to people in their twenties, the kind which often results in the rejection of entire systems of government, of moral and societal values—the kind which often results in a person's permanent employment in a kitchen. Life was simple at the Bavarian—as simple as the happily-ever-afters described in fairy tales—and I started to imagine staying there through the winter. I saw the three of us snowed in, gathered around the fireplace, reading aloud to one another from books, singing songs. I believed I had found a place where I was known, understood, and the idea of picking up and leaving for yet another strange town now struck me as preposterous.

My car had been parked outside the Bavarian all summer—I hadn't driven it once, and doubted it would start when I finally tried. It had begun to look like a car that would never go anywhere again. I imagined weeds growing up out of its hood. Everything I owned was in it—all the things I'd brought from college, and had planned to take to graduate school—and sometimes I stood looking through the car's window, as if at a museum exhibit, as if at the relics of an ancient people.

At school you had been considered a promising talent. You weren't the best piano player in your class, not the most inventive composer, but your work was more meticulous, more structurally complex than others', and you were thought to have the kind of unusual personality that often resulted in greatness. At a time when other students went around in T-shirts and jeans, in thrift-store rags, you went about in your tailored suits. Equally out of place were your mannerisms, your formality, your comportment, the rigidity of your carriage. People fussed over the way you talked—the phrases of old society turned out in a southern drawl, finished off with the sibilant lisp common to gay men. Rumors went around about you—that you were the son of a senator, a governor, that you were heir to an oil fortune, that you had been raised in Paris—and you made no attempt to correct them. It wasn't long before everyone at Juilliard knew your name. Often you heard it spoken as you walked about. That's James Butler, people said, and you imagined this was only the beginning—you imagined your name spoken the world over.

You developed a good reputation with your teachers and became one of their particular favorites. In your first year you composed a piano concerto that worked through slow and careful building, through the repetition of seemingly identical phrases that were in fact slightly different. Through a process of almost imperceptible shifts over the course of the work, everything changed, and by the end the listener arrived at a place that was, musically, in perfect opposition to the place he'd started. It was a theoretical work that appealed to the mind more so than the heart—very much the fashion of the time. Your teachers agreed that with the appropriate inspiration, perhaps a summer in Europe, you would make something of yourself.

People were always trying to befriend you, but you rebuffed them, thinking them common, foolish, spoiled, talentless, crude. Often when people approached you, you dismissed them with a comment which they at first took to be genuine, but later felt the sting of. *I hadn't realized,* you'd say, *kerchiefs were back in style. How quaint.*

You lived in a small room in a boardinghouse, nothing more than a bed, a dresser, and a small desk. Your suits hung in your closet, two blue and two black, one gray. On top of your dresser you kept a silver grooming set—a brush and comb, a razor and dish—that your grandmother had bought for you. Other than this your room was unadorned. You believed in keeping yourself free from distractions. The music you hoped to compose was spartan, meticulous, and you believed it would only come to you in an environment of perfect order.

Of course there were difficulties to city life. The noise of your neighbors, the blare of sirens and horns coming up from the street, the rush of planes overhead. For the isolation you needed you stayed late at school each night, working in the practice rooms, but this had its downside: On the walk home you were often taunted by groups of teenagers. "Hey, little man," they said. Once you were mugged at gunpoint by a mere boy, probably ten years old. You'd handed over your wallet without protest but even still the boy punched you in the stomach, and you'd folded up and fallen to the ground. After that you'd stopped carrying a wallet and never kept more than five dollars in your pocket, but you were mugged, still, for sport. Three more times.

You allowed yourself the occasional indulgence—you were human, after all. Your grandmother sent you a check each month, and you got into the habit of spending almost all of it in a single evening. You took yourself out to fine restaurants, and later to clubs, where you engaged in what you referred to as *the pleasures of youth*. You took up with different men, and sometimes went home with them to their rooms. But none of this really mattered, you said, not now, and not even at the time. You were determined to make something of yourself, to become the greatest composer in the world, and something so small as love, you thought, would never distract you.

Then, in your junior year, you fell in love with one of the school's professors, a middle-aged composer whose name you couldn't bring yourself—even twenty years later—to speak. There was nothing particularly special about this man. Many times you'd recalled the moment you'd first met him, and thought little of him. On first impression he was nothing more than another balding, nearsighted professor in a tweed jacket. You'd met him at a cocktail party thrown by another professor, and you remembered overhearing him talking about the end of the war. "Everyone knows," he'd said, "it's a positively Malthusian model of warfare." You'd thought him arrogant, dull. You'd spoken with him briefly and you'd noticed that his teeth were stained, that he gave off the odor of a stale pipe.

After the party he didn't cross your mind again until you recognized his name as you registered for spring classes. When you saw him again, in the classroom, he gave off much the same impression as before. Halfway through calling roll he'd quit the process and thrown up his hands. "It doesn't matter," he said. "I'm not going to learn any of your names until you impress me with something you've written." Several weeks later, after he'd looked at your work, he invited you back to his office so he might play a line of music for you, and after that you met every week to listen to records. He took you out for coffee. You took long walks in the park, talking of music at first, and then other things—books, politics. You said little. Every question the professor asked you turned back to him. You made note of all his habits and adopted them as your own. You tried to pretend that all your life you'd been reading and drinking and eating the same things he did. He read *The New Yorker,* you read *The New Yorker.* He drank espresso, you drank espresso. He gave you gifts, rare recordings. You used your grandmother's checks to buy him gifts. A fountain pen, a rare cloth-bound Molière. *And you can imagine what happened from there,* you said. *I'll spare you the details. Suffice to say there were moments. There were moments of great passion. I became, I suppose, obsessed.*

Naturally there were complications. This man, this professor, was twice your age, and married with two small children. His wife was a plain woman with a great fortune. The quality of this man's life—the relative luxury and leisure he was afforded—

was due to her. He would never leave her. You understood this. But sometimes in bed you spoke of the future, of traveling together. You couldn't help yourself.

One day toward the end of the semester you met for coffee and he told you he couldn't see you anymore. My wife, he explained, my children. My job. *I would never,* you said, *I would never betray you.* But he told you he was ending things, that it was the right thing to do. As you sat across from him you felt part of yourself collapse, fall away and crash like a wall of ice from an iceberg. You lost your hearing for a moment. In a daze you removed a bill from your wallet and tucked it beneath your plate. You wiped the corners of your mouth with your napkin, placed it on the table. You stood to leave and the professor said something—made a protest or an appeal of some kind—but you didn't hear it, you had lost your senses.

You spent an entire week in your room, in bed, trying to recall every moment you'd spent with him. You wrote down every scrap of conversation you remembered, everything you'd worn, every gesture you'd made. You dragged your notes for clues. Had you said something? Had you betrayed a lack of intelligence, of taste? You were sick with shame, with grief, and you couldn't return to class. You missed your finals, took incompletes in all your classes. All of the music you'd been working on flew out of your head. You thought about dying. You wanted to die.

You had one friend at school, a rich girl named Tweedy Livingston—one of those tall, horse-faced socialites for whom nothing had ever been difficult—and to save you from your misery she invited you to accompany her to Ogunquit. You spent the month of July at her family's rented home, living in opulence. You'd eaten every night at fine restaurants and had never seen, the whole time, a bill presented to Tweedy—she was one of those people who kept open tabs. You spent nearly the whole month in dining rooms, smoking and drinking, cracking open mussels and lobsters. One night you ate at the Oasis and on your way out saw its baby grand sitting empty in the corner of its bar. Tweedy had asked you to play. All evening you took requests, and as you played you felt at ease for the first time in months. At the end of the night the restaurant's manager offered you a job—their player had just quit—and you agreed to start the next day.

Initially you only planned to stay for the summer. But when August came around the idea of returning to school was still too painful. You decided to play at the restaurant until it closed in October, then return to New York and finish your compositions. You settled in at the Bavarian. You made a decent living, you had time to work on your music. You started to compose a symphony, and soon it obsessed you. You thought of it all the time, even in dreams, and there were days that it played so loudly in your head that you were obliged to take a sleeping pill just to dull its effects. You kept imagining the day you finished your symphony and put it into the hands of your advisor, who would immediately recognize its genius, stage it, record it. You imagined the prizes you would win. Upon your return to New York—after a long, self-imposed exile during which your reputation as a brilliant eccentric was solidified—you would be celebrated, redeemed. You imagined the look on your lover's face when he heard your masterpiece performed. You saw him collapsing in tears, falling at your feet. You spent long hours playing out these scenes, and they appeared so vividly in front of you that you sometimes reached into the air to touch them. If you could only finish your work. All that season, closed up in the Bavarian with Mrs. Strauss, you were just on the edge, you sensed, just on the edge of breaking through.

But fall had turned to winter, then to spring, and before you knew it you were back at the Oasis for another season. By then Mrs. Strauss had stopped charging you rent in exchange for your help around the house. You had become family. Sometimes when she called to you from the kitchen she accidentally called you Karl, and often in your mind you thought of her as your grandmother. Your real grandmother had disowned you—when you left school you had broken her heart—and Mrs. Strauss had replaced her.

During your second year in Maine you'd started taking a regimen of pills. You took pills to stay awake and pills to sleep, pills to enliven and pills to settle your nerves. At times you believed that the pills were the only things keeping you alive. Other times you convinced yourself that the pills were killing you and you stopped taking them. But then you'd be overtaken with shakes, or sweats, or bouts of intense, insufferable panic, and you'd start all over again.

You had taken on other lovers, from time to time, but had found all of them lacking. What pleasure they offered to you, eventually, amounted to far less than their inevitable disappointments. *Love,* you said, *is for fools.*

With your work you'd gone through phases of striving and phases of abandon. But it hardly mattered now—you had struggled too long and now there was no solution. Even if you finished your symphony, it would have taken twenty years of your life and would hardly be worthwhile. And if you simply gave up, moved on, what could you say you'd been living for?

Sometimes in the middle of the night I woke to the sound of your playing in the parlor. It was always the same little song, notes in a minor key, ascending and then descending and then ascending again, like a leaf blowing in the wind. It was the loneliest song I'd ever heard.

It was only after I'd given up on Malinda that—in accordance with one of those immutable laws that seem to dictate the universe—she showed up. One night, while I was mopping the kitchen floor at the end of my shift, one of the cooks went out through the swinging door into the lobby, and in the gust of sound that came into the room I heard Malinda's laugh. I knew it anywhere. It was brash and forced, and it cut through the noise of any room—it carried longer and louder than every other voice. The door swung open and closed, open and closed, and I stood leaning against the mop handle, listening, a hot twisting in my chest. In place of the excitement I'd expected to feel when I found Malinda there was a nervousness, and with it something else, something akin to anger. Malinda was here, alive and well, and with something to laugh about. Suddenly I saw all of the stories I'd told myself about her—the troubled circumstances she was in, the reasons she couldn't manage to get in touch with me—as delusions, the pathetic fantasies of a desperate person.

I finished mopping, letting my heart settle. Then I went out into the lobby and stood at the entrance to the bar. You were playing music from *Brigadoon,* and there was a small crowd still lingering around your piano. In the opposite corner of the bar the waitstaff sat around as they always did at the end of the night—counting and straightening the cash they'd made, making plans for the rest of the evening—and at the center of them all was Malinda. I hardly recognized her. She had bobbed her hair and dyed it a bright, flaming pink, and she had tattoos running up both of her arms, extending onto her chest and neck. She wore a black sleeveless dress wrapped around her like a bath towel. Sitting next to Malinda was a red-haired man in a green tracksuit. He had an unfinished, embryonic quality—he had a weak chin and a clipped, fleshless nose. In a hoarse shout he was telling a story about hitting a policeman in a construction zone. He spoke of himself in the third person. "So Scotty's going real slow, trying not to hit those orange cones, and the next thing you know Scotty's side view mirror clips a cop by the belt and spins him around like a fucking top."

People laughed.

"So what do you think Scotty does?"

"Take off, man," someone said. "Take the fuck off."

"Nope," he said. "What Scotty does, he pulls over and gets out and offers various solicitous ministrations." He waggled his eyebrows. He was apparently one of those people who took pleasure in using words he considered to be rare and lofty. "I give him my card, my license and registration, I offer him all kinds of compensation. And you know what happens? He says he's fine, he just lets Scotty go. And Scotty just drives on, my friend, with enough in the trunk to send me up for twenty years."

The whole time Scotty was talking he had his arm around Malinda, and she stared up at him adoringly. By all appearances Malinda was happy, but the sight of her under the spell of such a repulsive person turned my stomach. I stood and stared at her. Whoever this was—this pink-haired, exuberant person—it wasn't Malinda.

Finally Malinda's eye fell on me, and all of the mirth drained from her face. She sat frozen, and we stared at each other for a moment. Then, as if with the flick of a switch, she leapt up and squealed. "My little sister!" she cried. "My little fucking sister!" She crossed the room and hugged me. She smelled of some kind of sweet liquor. Brandy, rum. She was so thin I could have snapped her.

"Oh my God," she said, "what are you doing here?"

"I was looking for you," I said.

"Oh my God." She jumped up and down, pulled me over to her table. "Everybody, this is Mary." She introduced me to the waiters and waitresses, as if I hadn't already met them. "This is Pete, and Nick, and Jeff."

"I know," I said. "We've met." It occurred to me then that the waiters might as well have been meeting me for the first time. After the initial curiosity on my arrival, they had entirely forgotten about my existence—they had failed to even mention me to Malinda.

"This is so great," she said. "We're gonna have so much fun."

She sat down and pulled me next to her. "Scotty," she said, "this is my sister Mary."

"What's up, man?" Scotty said. He raised his hand in the air. "Five me," he said.

I fived him.

"That was halfhearted," he said. "Five me again."

I stared at him with hatred. I had a vivid image of punching him in the face. But I fived him again.

"Now that was hearty!" he said. "That was a five with some heart!"

Malinda kept her arm around me while she talked with everyone, and I felt myself sinking into the watchful silence I'd always lived in when we were growing up. On the surface it was no different from my usual silence, but the feeling was different. Instead of the detachment and anxiety I'd felt all through college, there was comfort. I felt relaxed for the first time in five years.

When your last customers left you came over to join us. Malinda made the same fuss over you that she'd made over everyone else. She threw her arms around you and kissed your face, your neck, your ears. You flushed under her attention. *Please,* you said, *get ahold of yourself.*

"You were so right about New York," she told you, "it's the only place in the world worth living. Oh, my God. I had no idea."

I told you, you said, a wistful look in your eye.

"We've been there all summer," she said. "I didn't want to leave. You should come back with us! This place is dead, it's over. You should come back to New York."

A dark mood seemed to pass over you. Your eyes wandered about the room, and you were distracted in your conversation. You made it through a few pleasantries, asking about the places Malinda had been that winter. But when she asked you about yourself, you were vague. *I've been incredibly busy,* you said. *I couldn't possibly begin to describe it.* As soon as someone else—a waitress named Mitzi—claimed Malinda's attention you slipped off. You nodded to me on the way out. It seemed to me that you wore the pinched, bitter expression of a person who had been upstaged.

Malinda started talking about a party, and Scotty started rounding up people. He was the only person I'd ever met who carried a cell phone, and he kept punching numbers into it and shouting at the people who answered. "Scotty!" he said, as a salutation. And I wondered what kind of person would shout his own name, with such exuberance, into a phone. "Major party down at Moody," he said. And though this was nothing more than an idea, a bit of whimsy that had just struck Malinda, word spread quickly and by the time we got to the beach there was, indeed, a party. Groups of people were standing around drinking beer, listening to music, talking and shouting and laughing. Someone had lit a fire in a trash can. Though it was the middle of summer it was still cold by the water at night, and people stood huddled in pairs. I watched Malinda as she approached them, and she seemed pleased by the gathering, like a queen surveying her subjects. She had thought of something, and Scotty had made it happen.

I stood on the edge of the party and watched Malinda drift around between the people she knew. They greeted her with great cries of affection and astonishment. It was a long time before she drifted over and sat down next to me. "Wow," she said. "It's been, like, five years or something."

"I know," I said.

"So what's new? What you been up to?"

"There's nothing at all new with me," I said. "Not a single

thing has happened since you left." At home I'd always affected a deadpan sarcasm, to balance out the hysterics of my mother and Malinda, and I'd slipped into it again. And yet on one level it seemed to me that what I'd said was perfectly true. Since Malinda had left nothing much had happened—I'd simply marked time until finding her again.

"I forgot," she said, "what a bitch you can be." She moved closer to me. She picked up a strand of my hair and let it fall. Again, and then again. "You look weird," she said. "It's like you haven't changed since you were twelve."

"Something's different about you," I said, surveying her hair and tattoos—a red dragon rose up along each of her arms, their necks curling onto her shoulders, their heads turned sideways, extending onto her chest, bright flames emanating from their mouths, meeting over her heart. "But I can't quite put my finger on it."

"So me and Scotty are gonna be here awhile," she said. "Scotty has business all over the place up here. We can catch up. Maybe have lunch tomorrow or something."

"What kind of business?" I said.

"Mostly weed," she said. "And pills. But some other stuff too. He's real busy this time of year. He's really stressed out. He's got, you know, all these clients calling him all the time, and he can't always get what they want and he knocks himself out running all over the place."

It pained me to hear her talk. It occurred to me that if I'd met her on a bus and she started talking to me, I'd take out a book and start reading. "I really want to spend some time together," I said. "I really missed you."

"Me too," she said. "I was gonna call. But I've been bouncing all around and I haven't ever had, like, a single place to stay or a phone or anything like that. I keep meaning to stop home and see what's going on, I just haven't, you know, had much time, with work and everything."

We sat for a moment looking at the water. I felt the topic of our mother hovering between us. And indeed the next thing Malinda said was, "So how's the bitch? Lemme guess. Married again."

"For the fifth time," I said.

She snorted. "Figures."

Then I told her the latest, the most absurd of all the absurdities in our family history. "She had," I said, "some kind of religious crisis."

"Oh Christ," said Malinda. She rolled her eyes, flopped dramatically back on the sand. "Please!" she cackled. "Give me a fucking break!"

"She moved to Atlanta," I said.

"What?"

"She married a televangelist. She runs a day care center at her husband's church—she takes care of all these kids off the street. I think they send a van around and cart them in by the dozen."

"What?" she said again. She sat up at attention. "Are you fucking kidding me?" She clutched her head. "That bitch!" she said.

"If it makes any difference," I said, "she says she prays for you all the time."

"Oh please," she said, "I think I'm going to puke." She stood up and staggered toward the water. I watched her stand at its edge, playing in the water with one of her feet in a distracted, rueful way. It occurred to me that all of the problems that had grown up between us, all the distance, were connected with my mother. Somehow Malinda saw me as my mother's agent, her emissary, and she'd turned against me, too. I stood up and started walking toward her, but before I got to the water she was off again, squealing, throwing her arms around someone else she hadn't seen in a year. "Oh my God!" she cried. "I missed you so much!"

When I returned to my spot on the beach a boy was sitting there. He had a mess of curly blond hair, already receding at the temples—he looked like a young Art Garfunkel. "Mind if I sit here?" he asked.

"Fine with me," I said. I sat down next to him.

"I live over there," he said. He pointed to a house behind us. "That one. With the hexagonal windows." The house was three stories tall, lit up against the night sky, brilliant.

"Oh," I said. I tried to sound unimpressed.

"I heard everybody and came out to see what was happening. None of my friends are up for the summer and I've been kind of lonely."

"That's a sad story," I said.

"I just graduated from Yale," he said. "And everybody I know is, you know, scattered all over the place, starting new jobs and stuff."

"I feel really bad for you," I said, "all alone in your beachfront property. With nothing but a Yale degree."

"You're a pain in the ass, I can tell," he said. "I'll just have to ply you with wine." He had a picnic basket settled beside him, and he opened it up and produced a bottle and two glasses. The whole scene struck me as suspicious, and I looked around for a camera crew.

We drank a bottle of wine, talking about college and what it felt like to be out, what we were going to do with ourselves in the future. The boy was about to embark on a trip around the world. Mauritania, he said. Indonesia, the Seychelles. He'd spent the whole summer taking sailing lessons. "It's just gonna be me," he said. "And my dad's boat. All around the whole fucking world." As he talked about the ports he planned to visit, I kept an eye on Malinda, who was flitting about, smoking and laughing and dancing. I heard snatches of her conversation. "We were so wasted," she said. "Remember that random guy, with the cowboy hat?"

"So what do you think?" the boy asked.

I looked at him. His face was round and plump, and he wore an expression of hopefulness. It was a face that appeared to be unfamiliar with hardship and disappointment of any kind. "I wouldn't want to say," I told him.

"Come on," he said.

"Well," I said, "I think you'll probably get blown over in a storm, or captured by pirates, or robbed and stranded somewhere. I hope you don't. But that's what I think."

"I meant," he said, "what do you think, as in, do you wanna come with me?" I looked him in the eye, expecting an expression of sarcasm, or irony, but he was serious. "Put off grad school for a year," he said. "Have an adventure."

I was quiet for a minute and watched the party playing out in front of us. It had reached its last phase, wherein people made reckless and impulsive stabs at entertaining themselves. Couples chased each other around the beach. The boys caught the girls and heaved them onto their shoulders and ran with them into the water. Everyone collapsed in the surf, screaming.

"Give me one reason," he said, "you can't go."

I didn't answer him. I watched as Scotty threw Malinda into the water. She got to her knees and pulled him down by the ankle. "Scotty's down!" he cried out. "He's hurt!" They laughed and laughed.

"I can't think of a single reason," I said.

This is the last clear memory I have of the evening. The boy and I split another bottle of wine. We hatched plans. We started talking about practical things, like passports and vaccinations, and I began to believe that I was actually going. "There's a guy in town who can get you all the shots you need," the boy said. "And we can expedite your passport. I know a guy who does that. I can't believe you're a French major and you don't even have a passport."

"We'll have to stop there too," I said. "France."

"Of course," he said. "You're gonna need all your personal documents. Your birth certificate and all that. Who knows," he said, "we might even get married." We were lying on our backs now, looking up at the stars, and in such a position, at that time of night, everything seemed possible, glimmering right in front of us, ready for the taking.

Then I passed out.

I woke at the first purplish light breaking over the horizon. My head was still spinning, my skin was sticky with salt and sand, there was a film in my mouth. Art Garfunkel was passed out next to me, with his mouth open. In a flash all of his plans came back to me. I remembered how I'd been swept up in them. But in the light of day they seemed absurd, as beautiful and weightless as dreams. He looked very young, and I felt quite certain then that whatever he set out to do, wherever he went, he was doomed, that he'd be eaten alive. "Good luck," I said, and left him to his fate. I went around looking at the bodies passed out on the beach. People lay about in tortured positions, flung on their backs with their limbs spread wide, like the crew of *The Raft of the Medusa*. I was looking for Malinda, but of course she was gone.

I dragged myself back to the Bavarian, playing out the evening's events in my mind. I knew that Malinda had arrived in town at last, that we had gone to the beach, that I'd had too much to drink and fallen asleep there, and yet the whole evening struck me as a hallucination. I'd spent the summer on pills, and part of me wondered if it had at last caught up with me—if I'd finally lost my mind. It was only when I climbed the porch steps of the Bavarian, and collapsed into the rocking chair next to yours (by then it was fully light, and you were sitting out with your newspaper), that the question was settled.

And where's Malinda? you said, without looking up from your paper.

"I don't know," I said.

You scoffed. *Let me guess. You woke up alone in a strange place.*

"Pretty much. I guess she took off with that fetus of a boyfriend."

That fetus, you said, *has a very impressive stock portfolio. He owns several properties in the area.*

"You know him?"

I've known him for years, you said. *You might say we've had a bit of a professional relationship. I should have known Malinda had hitched herself up to him. He could make life very easy for her.*

"She'll be back later," I said. "She said she's coming for lunch."

Of course, you said. *Of course she is.*

Your tone was peevish, sarcastic, and I hoped Malinda would prove you wrong. But she failed to show up. In the following days you seemed to make a sport of my suffering. A car would pull up to the Bavarian and I'd go to the window to see who it was. *Oh,* you'd say, *it's Malinda this time, I can feel it!* But it was never Malinda, nor was it anyone who intended to stay at the Bavarian. The only people who pulled into the driveway were people who had realized they were going the wrong way, and were stopping to turn around. *You should have seen your face,* you'd say when I returned to my seat on the couch. You'd smile manically, like Jerry Lewis.

"I don't think," I'd say, "that's exactly the expression I was making."

You're right, you'd say. *It was even worse.*

Every year, on July 30, Mrs. Strauss threw a birthday party for her father. *Vaterfest,* you called it. It was your least favorite day of the year. *To see someone so caught up in delusion,* you said. *Pining away like that. It's tolerable most of the time, but this is too much altogether.*

Mrs. Strauss made all of her father's favorite foods—

schnitzel, bratwurst, sauerbraten—and set them on the coffee table in the living room, along with several framed pictures of him. We sat in the living room, on Mrs. Strauss's antique furniture, facing a wall of cuckoo clocks, eight of them in all different shapes and sizes, some simple wooden houses, others elaborate chalets. Outside these houses stood small figures in lederhosen, men chopping wood, women carrying pails—as well as an assortment of wildlife: rabbits, foxes, deer. Normally Mrs. Strauss silenced the clocks, but on special occasions she turned them on to their full, clamoring capacity. She'd set the clocks to sound at four, the hour of her father's birth.

The centerpiece of Vaterfest was a homemade liqueur that Mrs. Strauss unveiled exclusively for the occasion. She served it three fingers high in a crystal tumbler. "My father's recipe," she said. "Everyone back home used to come to him for it, just everyone, because his spirits were the best." I took a sip and choked, tears sprang to my eyes. You laughed, high and trilling, and across Mrs. Strauss's face came a look of delight. "Exactly!" she said. "This is exactly what a girl like you needs for your health."

"Father," she said, "drank a glass of this every morning with breakfast and every night with dinner, and you've never seen anyone in such spectacular health. He had a chest like a tree trunk." Here she looked off and started sculpting the air with her hands. "And arms like barrels. Once at a carnival he wrestled a bear down to the ground. Every morning, no matter the weather, he woke and showered outside in the freezing cold, and he sang the whole while. He was absolutely pink when he came back into the house. Absolutely pink, I tell you!" She turned to me suddenly. "Drink!" she said.

I kept drinking as Mrs. Strauss talked of her father. Once, just to amuse her, he'd bent an iron pipe in half; during one Oktoberfest he'd swung the sledgehammer so hard against the platform he'd lifted the weight all the way to the top, ringing the little bell, which was impossible, those games were impossible to win, don't you know. In a blizzard he carried, she said, her dying mother across the village and up to the cottage of a doctor who lived in the hills, three miles uphill he'd carried her, and she was no waif, she was a big German woman, even taller than he was. When he came home, still carrying her, a layer of ice had formed over his hat and jacket and mustache, even his eyelashes had frozen. In just a short while I was a raw, burning kind of drunk, a warmth was going through me, I was absolutely pink.

Through all of this talk, which you'd no doubt heard countless times before, you were bored senseless. You yawned, sighed, yawned again. Your motions were exaggerated as those of a mime. When you yawned you tapped your fingers to your mouth, your eyelids fluttered.

"Once he was run over by a wagon," said Mrs. Strauss. "The wheels went right over him, and he was hardly the worse for wear. You've never met such a man! It made you happy to be alive, just to look at him!" She paused for breath. And in the pocket of silence you attempted to turn the conversation toward yourself.

I never knew my father, you said, *and I can count on one hand the number of days I've spent with my mother. On a single hand.* You sat back casually in your chair, as if a guest on *Dick Cavett.* Your legs were crossed, and you circled your foot around and around.

Right after she had me she went off to Hollywood. Thought she was a big star just waiting to be born. The closest she got was being an extra. You can see her dancing in a group, in Brigadoon, *behind Gene Kelly.*

"I always preferred Fred Astaire," said Mrs. Strauss. "I used to pretend I was Ginger Rogers." She rose to her feet and went about the room, moving in long, gliding gestures.

You look, you said, *like you're running a vacuum cleaner.*

"I do not!" said Mrs. Strauss. "I had wonderful dancing lessons."

Were they from your father? you asked, in the perfectly earnest voice you used when you were being sarcastic.

"Why, yes," she said.

Mother was bad even as an extra, you said. *She kept turning her face toward the camera, like some producer would notice and call her up.*

"How exciting!" said Mrs. Strauss. "To be dancing in a movie!" She had abandoned her gliding and was now twirling around the room.

It must have been very exciting, you said. *Apparently in her excitement she could hardly pick up the phone.*

"Is she dead?" I asked, surprised at myself.

I don't know, you said. *But she should be.*

"It's almost time," said Mrs. Strauss, and pointed to the clocks. We all sat staring at the pendulums, which swung frantically. I was mesmerized by them, exactly as people in movies were entranced by the swinging chains of hypnotists.

"My brother Karl," said Mrs. Strauss, "made each and every one of those clocks himself. Of course he ended up in a mental hospital. He had predilections he couldn't cure himself of. Obsessions. He'd do nothing but carve little figures all day for months at a time. He became afraid of germs and refused to walk anywhere, he didn't want his feet dirtied. He drew illustrations from the fairy tales he was always reading, all over the walls of the house. He became afraid of the characters in his books, the witches and goblins, and refused to go outside. We had to take him away."

There was nothing to say to this.

"His clocks, they are all facing east," said Mrs. Strauss. "Looking toward home. They want to be back home."

You couldn't pay me enough, you said.

Suddenly I had theories swirling around my head. Could it be, I said, that this was home, this right here, for all of us? For wasn't home, I said, less of a place than a means of connecting with people? The problem was that we just didn't see it. The problem was that the world was made out of fabric, and it surrounded us so completely that we couldn't see beyond it, it was a prison but it was thin, I was sure of this, and behind what we could see was more—infinitely more, I said—finer things, other realms in which our spirits were free, without bodies, in which we were like floating balls of light or gas, and what we were supposed to do was offer brightness to each other, commingle and make new colors, pass through one another gently, instead of what we were doing now, which was passing one another by and hiding in separate corners. And you had to wonder—I held my finger in the air, here—you had to wonder if the horrible, drifting life we were all living now was all the result of the thinnest fabric. It was only the surface and it didn't matter and we could break through it quite easily if we wanted, if only we tried, to what was beyond, togetherness, *this* mattered, we were all going around making the mistake of thinking that we were alone, and we just needed to stop and pay attention, we could all break through if we tried, our hearts were beating in unison, all of our sorrows and fears were the same, if we stopped and realized it, if we all just stopped for a moment and really looked at it, saw through it, the world would be better, it would come together, it would heal. The barriers between us are as thin as the air we breathe, I said. We're all living at the same time, and right next to each other, but there are different worlds and they don't intersect, they're parallel and discrete, but they needn't be. What matters, I said, is people. What matters is home, that we look at each other, really look at each other, and say to each other, You are what matters to me, you are home.

You stared at me for a second, then burst out laughing. As always you made a show of it, holding your stomach, pitching yourself forward. You sounded like someone instructing foreigners to laugh. *Ha-ha-ha! Oh, ho, ho! Hee-hee-hee!* Then one of the clocks struck the hour, and another, and another, until all of the cuckoos were bursting forth from their doors, then retreating, then bursting forth again. When the birds finished calling, each clock played a little song, and they swirled together in an awful clashing of chimes. As the clocks sounded I saw everything I'd just been talking about—which I'd been entirely convinced of, which was so real to me that I could see it glimmering in front of me—disappear, I could actually see it evaporating from the air. I was crushed.

When it was time to leave for work I was so drunk that it was an effort for me to see or to walk. I spent great concentration putting one foot in front of the other. I was under the impression that I was moving very fluidly, with an uncommon grace, but you said, "My God, look at you. Pull yourself together."

"I'm okay," I said, and looked at you very solemnly. "I'm just a little out of my elephant."

Later that night, on the walk home, you told me more about Mrs. Strauss. That her father and brother had been deported by the Nazis, had wasted away in a concentration camp and had finally been killed, that she was only alive because her father had sent her abroad to school with the money he'd saved from brewing liquor. As a young woman Mrs. Strauss had been very beautiful and had married a rich American. On their honeymoon they'd returned to her girlhood village, but it was changed beyond recognition, and the house she had grown up in had been demolished. After that Mrs. Strauss had slowly lost her mind. As a consolation her husband had built the Bavarian as a summer home. Each year when the time came to close up the house for the winter Mrs. Strauss cried for weeks on end, and eventually couldn't bear to leave at all. For many years they lived apart, Mr. Strauss in New York and Mrs. Strauss in Maine. She started taking in boarders. When her husband died, two years after you'd arrived, Mrs. Strauss had disappeared completely into her own mind.

The Bavarian, you told me, was a nearly exact replica of Mrs. Strauss's childhood home. *In her mind,* you said, *she's sleeping in her father's room. And you're sleeping in hers. And I'm sleeping in Karl's.*

You were telling me this, you said, as a kind of warning. *Fam-*

ily is a fine idea, you said. *Love is a fine idea. But in the end they're not worth it. Do you think Malinda would sit around waiting for you?* you asked. You said that the Bavarian was a house of convalescence, a resort of last resort, a place for people with nowhere left to go. And though you had no trouble believing, you said, that I would eventually end up in a place quite like it, it wasn't my time. I was too young.

"What about you?" I said. "Why is it the place for you? You're still young, there's still lots of things you can do. You still have time to make a change for yourself. You could find your mother, for one thing. You could finish your symphony, build a new life for yourself, fall in love again. You could do anything you want."

You rolled your eyes, and used the phrase you'd used with Mark and Addison. *Oh, honey,* you said, *I'm retired.*

In the days following Vaterfest you grew even more distant, and we began to treat each other with the awkwardness of ex-lovers. If you spoke to me at work, it was only a quip. I'd be mopping the floor and you'd pass by on your way out for a cigarette. *How's that floor coming?* you'd say.

"Fine," I said. "It's coming along fine, I think."

Your parents must be very proud.

After work, and on our walks home, you were surprisingly quiet. "What are you thinking?" I'd say.

Oh, nothing, you'd say.

"Well let me know if you want to talk," I'd say.

You'd sigh dramatically. *I can't think of a single thing left I haven't already told you.*

"Well if you do, I'm right here. Ready and waiting. Right here."

August came and still I didn't leave. In the afternoons I sat in the parlor with Mrs. Strauss, who was teaching me how to crochet. I undertook the making of a bedspread, whose pattern was so complicated that I had to keep undoing my work and starting over. At the rate I was progressing, it would have taken me several years to finish. *I certainly hope,* you said one day, *you're working on a handkerchief.*

I was happy when, one night at work, you invited me to join you and Houston on your break. We sat outside by the dumpster, passing a joint around. You were strangely quiet—you simply sat picking lint off your trousers—and so Houston took up the task of filling the silence. "This is it," he said, "my last year. Can't keep doing this forever, no I can't." Like most of the people I'd met at the restaurant, Houston talked almost exclusively of the plans he was making to change his life, to leave restaurant work and pursue his fortune. In October, he said, he planned to go to school to be a realtor. "Sell a few houses," he said, "one, two houses a month, you're set." He stared at the ground as he spoke. "Take it from me," he said to me, "you better start saving up and thinking about what you gonna do next. You need a plan. You got any plans?"

"I don't really have any plans," I said, "because I think plans are kind of dangerous. I think they take you away from the here and now." I had no idea what I was saying—what came out of my mouth was a surprise even to me.

Houston looked at me in disgust. "That's the damned point," he said. "What's so damned special about here and now?"

I looked around. I was on break from washing dishes, smoking a joint with a failed prodigy and an angry ex-wrestler. I was sitting on a crate of rotten lettuce. "I don't know," I said.

"You kids with your here and now," he said. "Y'all a bunch of lazy motherfuckers is what you are. You'll see one day, you get to my age, you'll be wishing you had some plans going on. Bunch of hippie-ass shit," he said, "makes me tired."

"But don't you think that desire," I said, "is a dangerous thing? It's a game that goes on and on. The satisfaction of a desire is the death of that desire, and so we just keep forming new ones and satisfying them, and then watching them die, and forming new ones, on and on, and we're never happy. It's better to be in the moment."

"Sounds like a bunch of college bullshit," Houston said. And I had to admit it was something I'd heard in a philosophy class. "You been to college?" he said. I nodded. "Then what the hell are you doing here?" He stood up and tossed the joint in the dumpster. "Jesus H. Christ," he said. He shook his head. "You dumbass kids. I had about all the fraternizing I can stand."

A few days later, as I was tying on my apron at the beginning of my shift, Houston and the restaurant's owner approached me. "We have reason to believe," said the owner, "that there has been drug abuse here in the workplace." He never actually looked at anyone when he spoke, only stared off to the side, like he was reading from a set of cue cards.

"Gee," I said. "Really?"

"We're testing a random sample of workers," he said.

"There's a nurse in the restroom who will help you through the process."

I stood there. "That won't be necessary. I'm not a drug user."

"Of course not," said the owner. "But under the terms of your employment, you're subject to random testing."

I looked at Houston, but he wouldn't meet my eye. "I have a political problem with that," I said.

"Understood," the owner said. "But it's policy."

"It's not that I'm saying I'm guilty," I said. "It's just a matter of principle."

"Well, looks like you're fired, then," said Houston, still staring at the floor.

"Are you kidding me?" I said.

"You better get along."

"Fine," I said. "Fine!" It was only when I'd stepped outside, by the dumpster, that I could string a sentence together. "Go ahead and keep your stupid job!" I cried. "Like I need to wash your stupid dishes, anyway!"

I walked home, kicking a stone the whole way, my eyes burning, like the kid from "Araby." Far worse than the loss of whatever idea I'd been harboring—that I'd stay at the Bavarian through the winter, perhaps forever—was the fact that I'd ever believed in it in the first place.

Back at the Bavarian Mrs. Strauss stood in the living room, ironing a tablecloth. It was the kind of scene I'd always imagined coming home to as a kid. There was someone waiting there, putting things in order, for the inevitable hour at which I returned home a failure, heartbroken.

"Home so early?" said Mrs. Strauss.

"I guess I dropped too many dishes," I said. "I got fired."

"What?" she said. "But what fools they are! To fire a nice girl like you! What fools!"

"You'll find something better," she said. "There are plenty of places in town who would be happy to have a girl like you."

"I don't know," I said. "I guess I should be leaving."

"But of course," said Mrs. Strauss. She went into the kitchen and a few minutes later appeared with a tray on which trembled two glass mugs, filled with brilliant amber liquid. "Drink this," she said. "Whenever Karl used to get upset, this would always calm him down. I tried to tell the nurses in the hospital what to make him when he got upset, but they didn't allow spirits."

I cupped my hands around the drink and let its steam rise to my face.

"You should have seen Karl," she said. "What a delicate soul he was. No bigger than you are. The world just ate him up."

We sat together sipping the drink that her crazy brother had loved, that had calmed him in his moments of despair. We sat in silence for a long time. It was bitter. And it was sweet.

The next morning I looked to you for sympathy, but you were all sarcasm. *That's a sad story,* you said. *You had a bright career ahead of you.*

"It's just not fair," I said.

Like my grandmother used to say, if dishwashing doesn't work out, at least there's graduate school to fall back on.

"Well, I guess I'm leaving," I said.

Toodles, you said. You didn't even look up from your newspaper. "Toodles?" I said. "All I get is Toodles?"

Oh, excuse me, you said, still immersed in your paper. *Toodle-oo.*

Sometime later, when I was a few hundred miles south and going through my glove compartment for a napkin, I found that you'd snuck a bottle of pills into the car. Inside was a note, written in your impeccable, looping script. *I thought this might help you get through school.* It was only then that I realized you'd arranged to have me fired.

In graduate school I was almost completely alone. I lived in a small curved room, in a third-floor turret of an old Victorian. Technically the room was classified as an apartment. It had a kitchen (just a sink and a refrigerator) in one corner and a bathroom walled off in another. The only light in the apartment was from a small frosted window that faced the street. This was the kind of place people lived in when there was something wrong with them. There was, I often supposed, something wrong with me.

I had trouble making friends. A few times I got together with my fellow French students, who sat around eating Brie and drinking Cognac, rolling cigarettes and wearing little berets and disparaging our country's political and social and educational systems, putting particular emphasis on the Midwest. "Fat cows!" they said. "Dumb fucks!" There was nothing at all wrong with this, except that each of them had lawyers and doctors and corporate tycoons for parents, and each of them received a sizable check in the mail each month—spoils of the systems they despised. True dissatisfaction with the state of the world, I thought, true disgust—I was on its cutting edge. I separated myself from them and lived with the silent rigor of a monk. I read Camus, Sartre. I developed a steely indifference toward human relationships. What did I care about Malinda? Or my mother, for that matter? What the fuck did I care?

I spent my time writing a thesis on a book called *Winter Nights*, an obscure French novel I'd found in the library. The book concerned a boy named Marcel who lived in Lille, an industrial city in the north of France. Marcel spent his days at the textile mill and his nights wandering around the city, listening to stories told to him by homeless and crazy people. Every night an irresistible urge came over him to walk the streets. Because he was a mere boy, people were comfortable unburdening themselves to him. Though the boy never said anything in return, he was happy—wandering about at night gave him a feeling of purpose and connection. But in the last chapter Marcel was turned on by one of the crazy men he'd befriended. The man suspected Marcel of being a spy from the police force, or an emissary from the mental hospital sent to lock him away, and the man attacked him. On the final page the boy's skull was crushed underneath the old man's boot. It wasn't until the last sentence that the author revealed that Marcel was deaf, that the connection he'd felt to people, and they'd felt to him, had nothing to do with language, it was something unseen, finer. I liked to think that if I had written a book, it would be something like this.

My thesis developed into a musing on lost connections, on effort and failure, on meaning and interpretation. I wrote long passages and then crossed them out and wrote even longer passages arguing against what I'd just written. I wrote that there was beauty in Marcel, in the effort he made to connect with people. Then I crossed that out and wrote that Marcel was a fool. "There is no understanding between people," I wrote, "and one cannot rely on others to make meaning of life. One has only oneself. When Marcel's false hopes are justly dashed, the novel teaches us to live for ourselves."

In the practice of writing the thesis I was enacting its theme— the difficulty of communication, the risk of believing in it—and this, I thought, was something unprecedented, something no one else had ever thought to do. I turned in all the pages I'd written, with the lines stricken out and then rewritten, so that people would be able to see, and appreciate, all of the efforts that had gone to waste, all of the words that had fallen to the floor. But my advisor told me that I was full of shit and I had to rewrite it. "I don't want any miscommunications," I said, "I want people to understand not just what I have to say, but what isn't being said, that when one thing is said its opposite lurks just behind it, as a kind of shadow." My advisor looked at me over the top of her half glasses and told me not to worry. "I assure you," she said, "absolutely no one is going to read this."

Toward the end of graduate school I signed on to teach French at my old high school, whose graduation rate had dropped even further in the years I'd been gone. The city schools had lost their accreditation, and everyone who could possibly afford it had moved to the suburbs, or sent their kids to private schools. The high school kept losing its teachers to other, better systems, or to personal crises like cancer and suicide. The previous French teacher, whose job I was assuming, had checked herself into a mental hospital. Nonetheless I was convinced that teaching there, working with the kinds of kids I'd grown up with, would be good for me, the first useful thing I'd ever done.

Back home, my thoughts turned to Malinda again. Everywhere I looked there was some reminder of her. The apartments we'd lived in, the schools we'd attended, the shops and playgrounds we'd frequented. From the bedroom window of my apartment, I could see the street corner where she'd once fallen on her bike and scraped her arm into a bloody pulp. She'd stood crying, right in the middle of the street, while traffic was stopped all around her, and she wouldn't be consoled, she wouldn't move. She had always been a champion crier. She wailed, her face turned red, her whole body shook. Even later in life, after she'd affected a callous indifference to just about everything, she would often break down fully, desperately, spectacularly. There was a crack running through her, and the smallest thing would open it up, turn her inside out. She seemed to suffer more than other people, to bruise more easily. Sometimes I sat looking out the window, at that street corner, and thought of her. Wherever she was now, I was sure she was hurting, I was sure she needed me.

When school let out for break in December I started wandering around the city, going to all the places Malinda used to go. I told myself that my interest was casual, that I didn't really care one way or the other whether I found her, that I wasn't even really looking. But one day, overcome with loneliness, I found myself driving north to Ogunquit. The day was cold, but even still I rolled down the window when I approached the shore, to hear the ocean in the distance, to smell the salt in the air. All through town, I didn't see a single person walking about. A light snow was falling. Everything was closed up, gray and shapeless, as though covered with a sheet for the season.

I showed up at the Bavarian expecting everything to be just as I'd left it. I had learned already, several times, that this kind of assumption was absurd. But still, it was one I couldn't do without.

Mrs. Strauss, in fact, had not changed at all. She was happy to see me and sat me down at the dining room table and began feeding me, as was her custom. When I asked for you, she informed me that you were napping, and I passed the afternoon catching up with her. Her stories changed with the seasons, and she talked of the feats her father and brother had accomplished in cold weather—the felling of trees and their swift dismemberment into firewood; the hunting of snow hares, foxes, deer; the death-defying turns they took on the ski slopes. "When they came in from the cold," she told me, "I used to warm their shoes in the oven."

Then I heard you on the stairs. *Well hello, my dear,* you said. *I'd completely forgotten about you. What a delightful little surprise.*

When I turned toward you I saw instantly that you were a dying man. You were so wasted, so pale, so skeletal, it didn't seem possible that you were upright and moving around. It all made sense to me then—your resignation, your effective retirement. In fact it was a wonder to me I hadn't guessed before.

We spent the next several days together, during which time we never left the house. You said you hadn't seen Malinda, or heard word of her whereabouts. By now she was just one of those people who had passed through town, then disappeared. This was the nature of seasonal work—there was no loyalty, no memory. Even though you'd been at the Oasis for twenty years, the same would happen to you. You'd taken the past season off, and by the next, you said, no one would even remember your name. *No matter,* you said. *I never cared for those people. And I'll be dead anyway.*

You declined to name your illness. In fact you hardly spoke of it, except to say that the previous winter you'd twice been in the hospital with pneumonia, and didn't expect to make it through the current season. You had taken up the role of invalid in the most stylish fashion. You wore a silk dressing gown and walked with the aid of a polished black walking stick. Your slippers were of black velvet. When you coughed, it was into a silk handkerchief.

You slept much of the day, but we stayed up late into the evenings. You stretched out on the couch and told all the stories of your life again. They were essentially the same as before, though less exaggerated. It seemed important to you, finally, to get things right. Often you paused in your recollections to think, to make sure you had the right names and dates. You had me write them all down in a notebook. *You've shown up at just the right time,* you said. *I've been wanting to leave a record of some kind, but I've never liked writing things down. Yes, you're just the solution I was looking for.*

All of your stories stopped when you left graduate school, when you'd moved to Maine. If you mentioned the Bavarian, or the Oasis, it was only in passing, as a means of comparison to something from your childhood, and so the whole last twenty years of your life seemed little more than a trip you'd taken once, long ago, and could hardly remember.

You didn't mention your symphony. On the last night of my stay, I asked if you had finished it, and you stared off as though you hadn't heard me. You paused for so long that I began to wonder if I had actually posed the question to you aloud, or merely thought it. But finally you spoke. *Failure,* you said, *is an art form we are all engaged in whether we know it or not. And I suppose I've finally accepted it, I suppose I've made it my own.*

You stood up and motioned for me to follow you. As you climbed the stairs one of your hairs, which had come loose from the impeccable order of the rest, stood on end and waved about, this way and that, though what current was stirring it I couldn't tell—you moved so slowly that it took us several minutes to ascend the steps.

Your room was just as sparse as my room had been. There was only a bed and dresser, a nightstand. Aside from your toiletries, which you kept on a mirrored tray, you seemed to have no personal effects whatsoever.

You opened the door of your closet, in which hung your suits and shirts—the very same your grandmother had purchased for you before you left Arkansas. Stacked on the floor of the closet were several crates, which held your composition notebooks. *My life's work,* you said. *An exercise in failure.* You picked up one of the notebooks, flipped through it, squinted, frowned, as if you couldn't imagine what had captivated you for all that time. *Take them,* you said, *they mean nothing to me. I don't quite have the strength to destroy them myself, but I'd be glad*

to know they were gone, I'd be glad to know they were in the hands of
someone educated.

A week later I called the Bavarian to see how you were. When
Mrs. Strauss answered the phone it was a voice even more manic
that usual—"Hallo!" she said—and I sensed right away that you
were gone. "We've lost our James," she told me. "Just after your
visit, my dear." She said that you had taken too many pills, that
your pain was so great you'd accidentally ingested an excess of
sedatives. "It's the delicate souls," she said, "that get eaten up." I
was touched by her naïvete, which I'd always suspected covered
up a deep, terrible understanding of the nature of things.

In the evenings that followed I made a habit of sitting down
with your notebooks. On the front page of each book you had
written your name (which you signed in long, slashing letters,
as though you were carving it with a sword) and the date, and
so it was possible to get a sense of their progression over time.
At first glance the books were overwhelming. On each page
there were ten staffs stacked on top of one another, all of them
sounding at once, and it was almost impossible for me to hold
all of the notes in my mind. The kind of mind it would take to
understand that music was very rare, and to have such a mind, I
imagined, must have made it difficult to live in the flat, shallow
territory of ordinary life.

There were a good many things about the notebooks, however,
that were easy to understand. It was clear that you were fond of
the oboe, for instance—of giving it high, trembling notes that
outlasted the rest of the orchestra. In general the notebooks

displayed a fairly obvious back-and-forth pattern, between the mess of spontaneous creation and the attempt at discipline that followed. There were times when the notes were slashed down, sloppy, and times when they were perfectly formed, each note evenly spaced. During your first years in Maine you produced at a furious rate, going through two or three notebooks a month, but as the years went by you produced less and less. In one year, 1988, you didn't get through a single book. In your final days you'd crossed out nearly everything you'd done. Page after page was marked with slashes so violent you'd in many cases broken through the page with your pencil.

Most valuable to me were the notes you'd made to yourself in the margins. Often you wrote the names of composers and passages from other works—you were fond of Satie, Debussy. You had a particular fascination with Beethoven's Seventh. But in other places you'd made notes about the feelings of the passages, the moods you hoped to evoke. What you hoped to create with your music, it seemed, was a sense of the solitary, the ruminative. You sought to create within the listener the sensations that come upon us in private, withdrawn moments. *Kicking a rock down the street,* you wrote. *Waking to rain in the night; flying in dreams; a neighbor seen through the window; voices in another room; children at play in the distance.*

If your work made one thing clear to me, it was that your life was a battle. Essentially you had withdrawn into your work, into solitude, and yet what was your work but an effort to communicate, to be understood? Even the evocation of loneliness was something undertaken with the purpose of communicating it to someone, who would hear it and perhaps understand

it. What impressed me most was how similar our lives were—
yours, mine, and everyone we knew—and yet how little we'd
noticed the connections. We had all known joy and then lost it,
had blindly sought after it again; we had taken up burdens and
carried them for a time, then stumbled beneath them; we had
made strides and then lapsed; we had taken strange paths that
sometimes delivered us to safety and sometimes led us astray;
we had despaired, tried again, despaired, tried again. Through
it all we had somehow felt ourselves alone, misunderstood. In
the end you believed you had failed; you seemed to have died
in despair.

All through that winter my mind was occupied with the question of whether life was worth living. To have ambitions, to make
plans, to hope, to work, to dream, to enter into friendships and
love affairs—I wondered if there was any point. I went back and
forth. I still had the bottle of pills you'd given me, and sometimes I thought of taking one. I imagined myself—suddenly
made loquacious, vibrant, giddy—going out to join the world,
to seek my fortune, I imagined throwing my hat in the air like
Mary Tyler Moore. But then again it seemed to me that all such
efforts—at least the ones I'd witnessed—led to disaster. In my
darker moments I held that bottle of pills in my hand and stared
at it. I thought of taking them all at once.

One night I went through the notebook you'd been working on the summer I lived at the Bavarian, and I came across
the passage you had played over and over again, the one I had
woken to in the middle of the night, the notes rising and falling,
rising and falling, which had sounded to me like a leaf tossed in
the wind. And suddenly the question I'd been turning around

in my mind—whether two people could ever reach each other, or whether we were all hopelessly alone—found a surprising answer. What convinced me that all was not lost, that there was still hope, that people in fact understood one another, if only in the smallest of ways, and mostly unnoticed—was something you'd written, just above those plaintive notes: *a leaf tumbling to the ground.*

Elegy for

Margaret Murphy Collins
Francis Adams Witherspoon

(1952–2003)

The fifties, and all the world wants is a bit of beauty, the forgetting that comes with it. You are born beautiful in a failing industrial city, and you learn soon enough that to be a thing of beauty in a place like this is to bear a burden, to carry on your shoulders all the desperate hopes of that ashy, crumbling corner of the world, its entire population of failures. "What a doll!" people say, wherever you go. "What a doll you are!" Every day of your life someone crosses a room to touch you, to pinch your cheek, to stroke your hair, as if to touch you would be to take a bit of your beauty for themselves. But what happens is something quite different. What happens is that these people leave, in tiny smudges, traces of their desire on you, their desperation, and it spreads like a tarnish. Soon you are coated in it, desperate in your own way. To be noticed, to be touched. You begin to feel on you, every moment, the gaze of a stranger—even in an empty room you feel it. You tilt your head, you toss your hair, you pout, you blink. Your every movement takes on a posed, anguished quality. Soon you are a doll, with a doll's hardness, you are stiff and heartless as a Tin Man.

You grow up, you do the things that girls do. Grammar school, Girl Scouts, dancing lessons, church. You do as you're told: you sit and you stand, you sing and you dance, you take your marks, perform your tasks. You do everything with the casual, indifferent ease that suggests it is all beneath you, that you are just marking time until you come of age, until you head west to make your name and fortune. "That child is impeccable," people say. "That child should be in pictures."

Even at your father's funeral you are self-possessed, the picture of dignified grief. (Your father dies when you're ten, of cancer, secreted away in your parents' bedroom. In the last stages he is too proud to let you see him, but you sneak into the room once and catch a glimpse of him, purple and bloated beyond recognition.) You stand straight-backed by the casket, receiving the line of mourners, offering your hand just like your mother does. *Thank you,* you say, *it means so much to us.* Meanwhile your sisters are compelled to sit down in another room, they are so crippled with sobbing. "Poise," your mother calls it, lighting a cigarette on the drive home. "Thank you for your poise."

At fourteen you start going around with boys—sneaking off with them in their cars after school lets out. What you want is their desire, the weight of it, on top of you. You are known as a cocktease; you take their dicks in your hand and squeeze. The boys cry out, they cry your name. "You're so beautiful," they tell you, "you should be in the movies." *I know,* you say, sitting up. *I'm going to Hollywood when I finish school.* You have plotted your escape from home, and your ensuing rise to fame, down to the smallest details, and there's nothing you love more than talking about it: the clothes you'll be wearing as you board the Greyhound bus, your first months of struggle working as a coat girl at a country club, the director who spots you as he checks his wife's mink. You talk about the kinds of films you'd like to be in, the actors you'd like to work with. Paul Newman, Marlon Brando. "Hey," the boys say, "what about me? Are you gonna be nice to me? Look at Mr. Happy here, Mr. Happy's getting sad." You turn away, pull your clothes together. *Mr. Happy,* you say, *is sad, all right.* You drive them mad.

When you are seventeen a local talent promoter named Vic DiPilato spots you in a dance recital and recruits you to join a performance troupe he operates—dancers, singers, magicians, even a comic. Every weekend they go around town performing for patients in nursing homes and hospitals. "It's not the big time," Vic tells you, "but it's a start." He is the clichéd small-time promoter (the false teeth and the off-color toupee, the powder blue suits and the alcoholic's swollen nose) and at first you turn him down. But then he gives you a line you can't resist. He has a friend in New York, he says, on Broadway, and it occurs to you that you might not have to strike out for Hollywood after all— you might have already been discovered.

On the weekends Vic drives you around the city, and you

dance the Charleston for people who once danced it themselves, but no longer can. There is something absurd in your performances, you think—your health and beauty paraded around in front of cripples, as if to remind them of what they've lost—but people seem to enjoy you. They clap, they cheer, they beg for more. Other members of the troupe grow jealous, spiteful, one of them even quits. But this kind of resentment, Vic tells you, is a good sign—the first sign of a star.

One day Vic picks you up and tells you you'll be performing at the state mental hospital, a Gothic fortress whose tolling clock tower has always filled you with a sense of sublime dread. *I don't know about this,* you tell him, as you pull into the parking lot. *I have a bad feeling. I feel kind of sick.*

"This is show business," he says. "You gotta take every audience you get."

An orderly leads you and the other performers through a series of long hallways. The orderly has a key ring with the circumference of a grapefruit, and he has to stop every fifty yards to unlock a heavy metal door. You lose your bearings. The hallways wind around and around, and you seem to be going in a circle, but it's hard to tell. Everyone in the troupe is dressed in some version of holiday cheer. You wear a red leotard with white fur trim, and the comic—a short kid named Mickey—wears the costume of an elf. There are little bells on the curved tips of his shoes. He looks ridiculous—you want to laugh, just looking at him—but on his face is an expression of such intense suffering that all the fun goes out of it. This place is a horror, a chamber of horrors, and you are wearing the same expression.

Finally you arrive in the women's ward. The patients sit in a horseshoe around you, sunk in their chairs. They wear pajamas and seem to have been wearing them for many years. Though they are of various ages—some not much older than you, some in their senior years—they all look the same. Their bodies are limp and slack, they are ghostly pale, their hair is disheveled, their teeth yellow and crooked. Common to each of them is a spooky thousand-yard stare. As Mickey goes through his act (So a pirate walks into a bar . . .), they seem to be looking straight through him.

When it is your turn, Vic starts up on the piano—"Have a Holly, Jolly Christmas"—and you do your best to dance with an enthusiasm that suggests there is nothing wrong with the hospital or the people in it. But the patients are unaffected—many of them seem not to notice you. It is the first time your beauty has failed, the first time an audience regards you with indifference. Just when you're thinking of giving up, of simply stopping and walking off, one of the older women (her hair is long and white, with streaks of yellow, and her eyes, you notice, are the same pale blue as yours) leaps from her chair with a swiftness you would have never guessed was possible. Suddenly she is on top of you, she has knocked you down on the floor. "Fucking bitch," she yells. "You fucking bitch!" She has a fistful of your hair and pulls your head up, then smashes it against the tile. You stare at her the whole time, too shocked to resist. There is a great commotion, the guards pulling at her, but before they get her off you she opens her mouth—you see her teeth, jagged and rotten—and bites you in the neck. You feel her teeth break the skin, you feel a lump of flesh ripped away. When they pull the woman off of you, her mouth is bloodied.

You are taken to the hospital, then sent home with a concussion and with eight stitches in your neck. For two whole weeks you are sullen and listless, you won't get out of bed, you won't eat. You open your Christmas presents with stoic detachment. "Snap out of it," your mother says, and shakes you by the shoulders. "What the hell is wrong with you?" She doesn't understand that something is broken, something is desperately wrong. Whenever you close your eyes you see the crazy woman's face, the rage she turned on you. You see the way the guards pressed her to the floor—one of the men pressing his boot against her neck. How wild she was, how she fought and screamed.

In January you return to school, but things aren't the same. Nothing interests you like it used to. You don't go out with your friends on the weekends. You quit the performance troupe and even give up your plan of moving to Hollywood. You enroll in Miss LaVonna's Secretarial Academy ("Since 1923, Turning Young Women into Right-Hand Ladies!"), which is the fate of nearly all the girls in your neighborhood. You can't explain what is happening, except to say that it is as though the crazy woman has infected you. The scars on your neck are still tender—you can still feel them throbbing with each heartbeat. Fucking bitch. You fucking bitch.

When the time comes, you don't even want to attend the senior prom. Your date is Mike Murphy, who has been in love with you since kindergarten. He is the handsomest boy in your class, captain of all he pursues: football, basketball, baseball. His father owns a plumbing business and after graduation Mike Murphy will become his partner. In your dying city, this is considered a good prospect ("A business owner," people say. "An entrepreneur") and you are supposed to be pleased to be his girlfriend. But he has always bored you—he talks of nothing but sports, he doesn't like to sit through movies. Prom night, when he shows up at the door (you can see him from your bedroom window, in his blue tuxedo, carrying a blue corsage) you are still in your bathrobe. Your mother calls you but you decline to come down. She barges into your room, hissing. "We bought this dress, and you're going." She takes the rollers out of your hair and brushes it, she sweeps eye shadow across your lids, zips up your dress. "Beautiful!" she says.

Hours later, drunk, you're just another stupid girl with her legs spread in the back of a Buick, some sweaty jock on top of you, bourbon-breathed, pants around his ankles, ruffled tuxedo shirt still buttoned to the neck. You're not particularly enjoying yourself, in fact you're thinking of the crazy woman again, coming after you, on top of you. This is what you're thinking when Mike Murphy—tight end, point guard, short stop—cries, "Oh God, Oh God, I'm coming." He is lost in it, outside himself, and you are outside of yourself in a different way, you hardly notice what's happening. You finger the scar on your neck— two jagged half-circles that look like birds in flight.

One of the oldest stories in the book. Later that summer, in the middle of Miss LaVonna's typing class (*f,* space, *f,* space, *f, f, f,* space) you keep nodding off, and it occurs to you that you're pregnant. *Shit,* you think. *Oh shit.*

The only person you tell is your stepbrother Mike, not because you want him to know, but because you heard a rumor last year about his girlfriend and some back-alley abortion, and you think he might be able to help you. So you climb onto the rooftop of your parents' house, where the two of you sit smoking after your parents have gone to bed. "Aw, Jesus," he says, shakes his head. "What the fuck, Maggie, you're supposed to be smarter than that. Jesus." He blows smoke out of his nose. "God," he says. "Goddamn." He has always been a bit in love with you, and you with him, and it is as though you have run around behind his back. You work your way around to asking, but he won't help you. "I don't know nothing about that," he says. "That wasn't even mine. No way."

For a while you do nothing. *I just need time to think,* you say to yourself. The days go by, and go by. You graduate from Miss LaVonna's. *I'll think about it tomorrow,* you tell yourself, like Scarlett O'Hara, until so many tomorrows go by that you no longer have much of a choice. *Shit,* you think. *Oh shit.*

Mike Murphy is surprised when you tell him. "No way! Really? Holy shit!" He is pleased with himself, like a child who has just learned to walk—he staggers around the room with a stupid grin. A week later, when he asks you to marry him, you reason that it's nothing that can't be undone. *I'm just doing this for now,* you think, *just for the time being.*

And so you sign on for it, a small church wedding with a reception at the Knights of Columbus hall, the two-day honeymoon at the Cape. You return home to your new one-bedroom apartment and spend a day opening gifts. Supposedly you've been set up with everything you could possibly need in life— plates and silverware, glasses and cups, table linens—but when you finish putting things away you think to yourself, *Is this all there is?* Your new apartment is only two streets over from your parents' house. From your back window it is possible to see Mike sitting on the rooftop, smoking, and you stare at him for long, wistful stretches.

You grow fat, fatter, so fat it seems you will never recover. You endure various agonies. The gas, the heartburn, the swollen feet. The doctor visits and examinations. The hideous dresses, like tablecloths. The touch of strangers, pressing their palms against your stomach. You are no longer yourself—you are a mother now. You have been brought into a fold you didn't want any part of, and you see now that all the world's mothers have been lying in wait for you to join them in their private hell, a place where you yourself are of no concern, a place where all anyone ever talks about is the baby. Older women come charging across the street to offer their advice, they never stop, every day they come after you, you can't so much as go out to get the mail without someone approaching you. "What you do is, you rub its gums with a little brandy. What you do is, you drive the baby around in the car when it won't sleep. Don't pick it up no matter what—let it scream its head off, get yourself a set of earplugs, if you pick it up it's just going to be spoiled." Talking with these women you suffer moments of terror, panic, you break out in sweats. *What you do is*, you think, *you run away. You just run away.*

Mike Murphy begins to drink, to stay out late after work. "Better enjoy myself while I can," he says. "Pretty soon, you know, holy shit." When he comes home you're in bed and he puts his hand on your shoulder, he presses himself against you, but you turn around and slap him. *Like I'm not miserable enough already,* you say. He says, "Jeez. Sorry. Jeez." His breath is sour.

Then finally the baby itself. The long, sweaty labor, the delivery, the ass slap and the phlegmy cry, the baby wrapped in blankets and presented to you. Pink, squirming, with swollen eyes and a misshapen head. You are supposed to feel something here—something besides dread, bitterness, tearful agony—but you don't, you don't, you give the baby away to whoever wants to hold it. *Take her,* you say. *Take her away.*

I think there's something wrong with me, you tell your mother. *I don't want it.*

"It's natural," she tells you, "you'll be fine in a few days." But in a few days you're sitting around the apartment in your nightgown, watching television, and you're not fine, in fact it seems that your life has ended. The baby cries and you heat up formula, feed it, burp it, change its diaper. It spits up on you and falls asleep, you fall asleep, then it wakes crying and you go through the whole thing all over again. How long will you last? Two more days? Three? You carry the baby over to your mother's and hand her over. *I can't do this,* you tell her. *I can't fucking do this.*

"Have a drink," your mother says, and she fixes you a high-ball. Every morning of your life, after your father (and then later, your stepfather) left for work, your mother mixed a drink with which to swallow a sedative, then spent the rest of her day refilling her glass, going around in a dreamy, imperturbable fog. She has always been cool toward you and your sisters, has gone around the house tending to her business as if you weren't there. If she touched you or your sisters it was in the way that one touches an insect in the bathtub—with a quick, dismissive pinch. She's never in your life told you she loves you—she simply isn't that kind of woman—and you've always judged her for this. *Heartless bitch*, you've called her. But you see her side of things now, you see it all quite clearly.

You start drinking at home, but the effect is less predictable for you than it is for your mother. You are relaxed for long stretches. But you also suffer fits in which you cry, sulk, rage. You throw things simply to break them, you leave shards of glass and porcelain on the floor—your wedding gifts, the cups and saucers, the creamer, the gravy boat—for Mike Murphy to sweep up when he gets home, which is later and later, less and less. The baby cries and you leave it. You go out for long walks, you simply leave it.

Sometimes when Mike Murphy gets home from work you are dressed and ready to go out. "There's a bottle in the fridge," you say. "I gotta get out of here." You go out to bars and men buy you drinks. You drink so much that you have to be packed into their cars and driven home. Twice you wake up in a strange apartment, with no recollection of being brought there. More often you are brought to your parents' house—your license still lists their address—and your mother sets you up on the couch. She leaves a large plastic bowl beside you on the coffee table. "Darling," she says, "don't vomit on the chintz."

Just before the baby's first birthday you feel a soft, swift, unmistakable kick in your gut. *Jesus*, you think. *Jesus Christ*. A few months later, when you are showing again, people start punching Mike Murphy good-naturedly in the arm. "You kids," they say, "can't keep your hands off each other."

One night, drunk, Mike Murphy crashes the car into a telephone pole and breaks his nose. He is scraped up, swollen, and he comes home wanting sympathy from his wife. But instead you rail at him. *You fucking asshole, you fucking idiot.* You slap him across his bruised face. *I'm stuck here all day with a kid, and you're out crashing the car? You should be kissing my fucking feet!*

"You think you're so hot? You think you're such a hot catch? You're a miserable fucking bitch is what you are. A spoiled fucking brat."

You limpdick little shit, you say, *you piss-ant son of a bitch.* He turns away, you stab your cigarette into the back of his neck, he turns and smacks you across the face, takes you by the shoulders and shakes you, shoves you to the floor.

Fuck you, you say. *I'm going back to my mother's.*

"Fine," he says. "Be my fucking guest."

And so there you are, twenty years old and divorced, pregnant with your second child, living with your parents. The second baby is born, another girl, and Mike Murphy comes around now and then, wanting to see the children. "I got rights," he says, and you tell him to go fuck himself. Then you change your mind, walk the girls over to his apartment and drop them off. *Here,* you say, *here are your goddamn rights. Enjoy yourself.* The girls cry when you leave. They have no idea where they are. Hours later Mike Murphy brings them back, with a look of terror on his face. Both girls are splashed with vomit. "I can't do this," he says. "I'm sorry but I don't know what to do."

It is as if everything between you and Mike Murphy—the marriage, the children—were some kind of vacation gone bad, and now you want to return to normal life, you want a full refund (*Excuse me, but I would like to return these*). You have never managed to feel for the girls what you suppose you ought to feel. Instead, you regard them as younger siblings whose care

you've been unfairly saddled with. You take them on long, aimless walks, one of them in the carriage and the other toddling
beside you. "What beautiful children," people say to you.

"They're for sale," you tell them. "Two for one."

You always refer to the babies in the plural, as if there were
no difference between them. *It's their bedtime, get them to shut up,
their diapers are shitty, they're sick and they're driving me crazy.* Occasionally one of them does something individually, in which case
you differentiate between them by saying *one* and *the other one*.
*One of them falls down the stairs, and it turns out she's fine, but the
other one starts crying!* They are quite different—one is fat and
one thin, one squalling and the other sullen, one with your fine
symmetrical features and the other warped, like the reflection
of the first in a spoon—but they are joined in your mind, nearly
indistinguishable, they exist only in relationship to one another,
like two sides of a coin. Tweedledee, Tweedledum.

When the younger girl is a year old you take a job as a sec-
retary at a junior high school, and it isn't long before one of
the teachers—a tall, slope-shouldered man named Michael
Collins—starts making advances toward you, which are so innocent and pathetic that you sometimes can't keep yourself from
laughing in his face. After work, he always falls into step with
you on your way to the parking lot, as if by chance. "Look who
it is!" he says. "I almost didn't see you there!" As you approach
your car he leaps ahead of you so that he can open the door
for you. You protest, but he keeps doing it, like some errant
knight compelled to perform useless acts of chivalry. One day

in December he kicks your tires and says that they are low, that they need filling. *I don't know how,* you say. So he accompanies you to the gas station and fills your tires. He checks your oil level, also low, as is your wiper fluid and antifreeze. He fills all of these fluids to the top, then smacks his hands together, satisfied.

Thanks, you say.

"My pleasure," he says. And you get the feeling that it is, it actually is.

Well, you say, *I live just around the corner.*

"Okay," he says, and stands waving as you pull out of the parking lot. Not until the next morning does it occur to you that he had to walk back to his car at the school, over a mile away through the snow.

In your judgment this man is flawed in a number of ways: he is too tall and too thin, too pale and soft-spoken, his nose is crooked and has a bulbous tip, he is weak-natured, boring. Still, he is kinder to you than anyone has ever been, and he worships you in the way that you feel you deserve to be worshiped. He starts taking you to dinner, to movies. He meets the girls, who clasp his nose in their fists. He seems to know what to do with them. He tosses them up in the air and they squeal.

No one in your family has ever been to college, and so there is something of a triumph in this man—a man with a master's degree, a man who wears a tie and a corduroy blazer to work. "An educator," your mother calls him, with a certain amount of reverence, and you like the sound of it. *An educator,* you say, looking at yourself in the mirror. *I'm married to an educator.* For it is only a matter of time before he asks you.

As Mrs. Michael Collins you live a dull, steady life in a three-bedroom ranch home, in a quiet suburban neighborhood. You are with your husband almost all of the time. You drive to work together, drop off and pick up the girls together, go to the grocery store together, dinner on Saturday nights, church on Sundays. This goes on for years, and by all appearances you have settled down. Yet you are not at home here. This is the kind of place, you think, where people go to die, quietly and alone, like elephants. Your house starts to look like a coffin. It gets so that thoughts of escape run more or less constantly through your mind.

One day your neighbor, a stuffy widow named Mrs. Barsotti, knocks on your door to inform you that a black man in a Ford Nova has been driving around the neighborhood. "With no apparent purpose," she says. "I just wanted to warn you that there might be trouble afoot."

You close the door in her face. *Bitch,* you say.

"It's her generation," Michael Collins says. "She doesn't know any better."

Something snaps in you, begins to unravel. You start going out at night, to all the old places you used to go, and once again there are men lined up to buy you drinks. You drink, you drink. One night you come home and find Michael Collins waiting up for you, sitting at the kitchen table with the younger girl, building a model ship, and the sight of him taking care of your child, while you've been out with other men, strikes you as funny.

How's your little boat? you say to him, and laugh. *What a bitty little ship you have. What a junior little schooner.* You start laughing and can't stop. You fall down laughing and he tries to pull you up, off the floor.

Michael Collins says, "Come on. She doesn't need to see you like this."

Like what? you say. *Like this?* You unbutton your dress, step out of it, fling it across the room.

"Maggie," he says, "come on now."

Am I making you nervous? you say. Your mood begins to slide, from playful to angry. *Would it make you feel better if I went outside? Would it?*

"Maggie!" he says, but you're already outside on the front lawn in your bra and underwear. "Hey, Mrs. Barsotti!" you cry. "Quick! Call the cops! A black man stole all my clothes!" And then Michael Collins tackles you with a blanket. But you scramble away from him, screaming, and soon enough Mrs. Barsotti comes outside, clutching her bathrobe together at the neck. "Shall I call the police?" she says. "Oh dear, shall I call the police?"

You quit your job, move into an apartment of your own. The girls are eight and nine that year, and much of your daily routine is harried—it seems you are constantly yelling at them. *Get up,* you say to the girls, *get dressed, brush your teeth, comb your hair, wash your face, put your shoes on, did you put your shoes on? Where are your goddamned shoes? Jesus Christ, how should I know? Get your coat on. Go on, go then, go without a coat, the bus is coming, I can hear it coming, go on, get out of here, get out of here!*

When you get home from work the girls chirp at you like baby birds, chirp about their various needs and ailments (they are bored, one of them has a loose tooth, a stomachache, one of them has to make a shadow box of Abraham Lincoln's child-hood home and needs your help, one of them needs money for a field trip) until you crack. *Get out of my sight,* you say. *Go play outside, would you leave me alone, would you leave me alone for two goddamn minutes?* You come down with headaches and retreat to your bedroom, shut off the lights. But they follow you not five minutes later. "Now?" they say. "Can you help us now?"

It's even worse when they try to help you. They bring glasses of water and bottles of pills. "Here, Mom," they say, "for your headache." You see in their eyes they are afraid of you. As if you'd ever harm them. *Get out of here!* you say, slapping the pills from their hands. *Leave me alone!* They run away crying.

For a while they are malleable. You can send them away and still they love you, still they come running for you when you call their names. For there are times when you love them des-perately. You come out of your bedroom and see them sitting on the floor, playing a board game together, one of them says, "Here's your hotel, ma'am," and the other says, "Why thank you, sir." Their voices are high and earnest. They have not yet fallen into sarcasm. You love them, you love them. You sit on the floor between them and kiss them, you make growling noises and pretend to eat their ears, they squeal, they climb on top of you. You love them so much you want to crush them.

The years go by, they wear you down. The life you've always imagined for yourself—the ease, the luxury, the excitement—seems far away, chimerical. You grow bitter. You believe you have suffered like no one else, that you have been cheated, and you mean to have your revenge in whatever little ways you can find. You park in handicapped spaces, throw trash out the window of your car. You drive recklessly, impulsively—several times you back into parked cars, then speed off without leaving a note. Your rules of order are self-righteous, Darwinian. In apartment buildings, when you share a washing machine with other families, you interrupt another person's cycle and remove their clothes and pile them, sopping wet, on top of the washer so you can start your own load. Once, when a craving for an apple pie seizes you, you put the girls in the car and race to the grocery store, you hustle over to the pastry section to find an old woman examining the last apple pie. She holds it up, inspects it, turns it this way and that. She makes a move to place it back on the shelf but then reconsiders and puts it in her cart, and you stalk her until she wanders away from her cart and you swoop down and steal the pie. *You snooze,* you say, *you lose.*

You are bad with money. You forget to pay the bills and the lights go off, the heat shuts down, you go to turn on the faucet and it shudders, seizes. Then you call up the electric and gas and water companies and give them an earful. *I got kids,* you say. *I got a kid who wants a drink of water here, what the hell am I supposed to tell her?* You are always charging clothes on your Filene's card, wearing them, and then returning them as defective. *I washed this once,* you say to the salesgirl, *just one lousy time, and look, it's all pilly!* Nothing thrills you more than arguing with the employees of the stores you patronize. You bully them until they cry, and when their supervisors appear you do the same. Your voice rises into a shriek, and the other customers dart away. "Lady," the managers say, "please. Please."

You can't keep a job. You are easily bored and impulsive,

and walk out of work every six months. Your boss says something discourteous—"Get your ass in here!" he yells from his office—and you march right into his office and remind him that you are a human being, goddammit, and that every human being deserves to be treated with a minimum level of respect. Then you come home, thrilled with yourself, and re-create these scenes for the girls. They sit on the couch watching you. *"A minimum level of respect," I said. You should have seen his face. I think he shit his pants! And then I stand there at my desk packing up my things, cool as a cucumber, he comes out and says he's sorry—he doesn't want anyone to hear him so he's standing there whispering, but I don't even look at him, I just shut off my typewriter and put on its cover, real slow, and I take all the company pens out of the desk and put them in my purse—you know how I love those pens—and he's standing there telling me not to go, he'll give me a bonus, he's sorry, but I just walk over to the elevator and press the button and wait like nothing's happening, I've got all the time in the world. You should have seen the other girls, the looks on their faces, they never liked me but they like me now, let me tell you, they're singing my praises.* Later, though, when the thrill has worn off and you find yourself, once again, without a job, you sit on the couch and drink, you cry, you hold your head in your hands. *Shit,* you say. *Shit, shit, shit.*

When you are feeling low you walk through department stores and sit down at makeup counters and have yourself made up by the saleswomen. They gather around you, touch your skin with creams and lotions and powders, they make you up like a doll. "Oh, look!" they say to each other. "Oh look how beautiful." These are older ladies with clownish makeup and liver-spotted hands, with thinning hair they tease and spray into little peaks. You should be a movie star, they tell you. *I know,* you say.

The girls get older, they change. They lose interest in you, they grow tired of your moods. One screams at you, the other one stops speaking. When you arrive home from work it is to an empty apartment. The girls are out with friends, or prowling through shops, or at the library, they are God knows where. You sit alone, in the peace you always claimed you wanted, but it is far worse, this quiet, than anything else.

For a time you are seized by an obsession with money. It's the eighties, and there seems to be money everywhere (*Dallas, Dynasty, Falcon Crest*) and you can't for the life of you fathom why some of it isn't yours. One night, in a bar, you meet Bud Francis, sole heir to the fortune that is Francis Housewares and Electronics, and when he takes you to meet his parents you size up their house, a small mansion with pillars flanking its front door—pillars! Someday this will all be Bud's. Someday, you decide, this will all be yours.

Just before you marry Bud you take the girls to meet his parents. *Meet your new grandma and grandpa,* you tell them. You show them around the house. The upstairs bathroom, all marble and granite, is bigger than the girls' bedroom. There are two separate sinks in the vanity, side by side, facing a mirror that runs the length of the wall. The older girl, the beautiful one, stands at the sink, turning its gold-plated handles on and off, on and off, as if in a trance. She starts to cry. "Mom!" she says. "There are two sinks!" To learn that life is like this for other people—

that it has been all along, just not for her—is too much. She stands looking at herself in that wide mirror, blubbering. "It isn't fair!" she says.

Life, you tell her, *isn't fair*. As you say this you sense already that things won't work out with you and Bud—you will never live in this house.

With your next husband, Walter Adams, it is as if you've decided to reverse every instinct and inclination you've ever previously pursued. Initially you don't even consider Walter to be a romantic prospect—he is merely a connection that proves useful. When you first meet him, and learn that he is a mechanic, you tell him that your car (a Buick Skylark, which you've custom-painted a bright flaming red) has been rattling, a mysterious ailment that no other mechanic has been able to treat or even diagnose. He tells you to bring your car by his house, and you do, the very next day.

As he works on your car you look around his house. Everything in this man's life is impeccably ordered. His shoes are polished, his clothes are pressed and neatly hung in the closet, his floors are swept, his books and records alphabetized. Nothing is in confusion or disarray. His keys hang by a hook just inside the front door and you imagine that he hangs them, unfailingly, every time he enters the house—he has probably never misplaced his keys in his life. After Walter finishes with your car (he fixes it!) you smoke a cigarette with him on the front porch, and you are mesmerized by the calm that surrounds him. He moves languidly, purposefully. He even smokes in a way that strikes you as refined. Not hungrily, greedily, like other people you know, but very lightly, letting the paper burn, the ashes collect at the tip for whole minutes, after which he taps them, an inch long, into a cut-glass tray. You want to disappear into Walter's life, this small bungalow with its gleaming floors, its manicured lawn, you want to live in this house the way children want to disappear into fairy tales.

In the following weeks you learn that Walter is a twenty-year veteran of the military, where he worked as a machinist. For ten years he lived in Germany, and he seems to have brought back with him the habits and pacing of the Old World. He spends entire evenings listening to records, reading books, playing chess. He fills a bag with breadcrumbs and takes long walks, stopping here and there to feed the birds. You learn things when you are with him: art, music, history, politics. Suddenly it seems there's another world than the one you've been living in—better, brighter, more intricate—and you want to know its secrets.

When you marry Walter—a simple ceremony at the courthouse—the older girl moves out, moves in with your parents. She is tired of this, she says, tired of moving around, tired of you getting married. The younger girl stays with you but seems unmoored—without her sister she doesn't know what to do. She starts taking long walks, she disappears into books. You trouble yourself, sometimes, with the question of whether you've damaged them, all of this moving back and forth, all of this change, but it is not a question you can afford to think about. You are pregnant again, and you intend to do things right this time.

Then things turn. Cruelly, they turn. Your brother dies, and while you are still thick in the grief of losing him, you deliver your child—another daughter—prematurely. When she dies it is as if the life you were trying for, the simplicity, the beauty, has died with her. Aspersions have been cast on you, on the marriage, on the very idea that such a union might succeed, that happiness was possible. When you leave Walter Adams you don't even have to explain. You simply look at him, and he looks at you. You leave wordlessly, over a number of days. You go back to your old ways.

But now you are approaching forty, and your old ways no longer suit you. You move in with a golf pro, ten years your junior, but instead of making you feel younger, he makes you feel older. You are tired in the mornings—your eyes are puffy and there are circles underneath them. Your skin has begun to loosen. You have gained weight in your hips. You sleep less and less, and finally develop a nearly complete insomnia. You spend two years in almost total sleeplessness. At night you lie on the couch flipping channels, and in your exhaustion you are overcome by desperate urges. You wish to purchase the things you see advertised, you wish to travel to the places you see on screen. You consider moving to a remote location, where no one knows you. You consider swallowing a bottle of sleeping pills.

One night on television you see a preacher pacing around in front of a congregation. His name is Les Witherspoon, and he fairly gleams. He is dressed in a shining silver suit and his hair, which is a bit overgrown, is touched with silver. He has a strong jaw, a sharp nose, a sweeping brow—he has the face of a president, something that could be carved on Mount Rush-

more. You have never seen a man of God in quite this light. You
are used to priests in their shapeless robes, their long, somber,
celibate faces, but this man is virile, this man is ecstatic. "Jesus!"
he cries, and you hear the word as if for the first time. You hear
the word spoken as something other than a curse.

You are about to change the channel—your interest in Les is
nothing more, you think, than the passing curiosity in an attrac-
tive preacher—but just then Les asks a question. "Are you one
of the long-suffering?" he says. He looks into the camera and it
is as if he is looking directly at you. "Are you adrift, aimless, do
you wander from one thing to the next to the next, and every
time you're sure you've figured it out, you're on the path now,
but the path just takes you around in the same old circle?"

Yes, you think. *Yes. Yes.*

"I'm here to tell you," he says, "no more. I'm here to show you
the way. Which is God's way." One of the preacher's more influ-
ential techniques is to ask his audience to imagine themselves
on their deathbeds. "Go on," he says, "someday it's bound to
happen. Go on and think of it now, close your eyes and think of
it. You've lived your whole life through, you're looking back on
it, what do you see?"

You close your eyes.

"I guarantee," says the preacher, "the troubles in front of you
now are not the things you'll be thinking of at the end. No, they
are not. Feel them fading away right before your eyes. Now, I
ask you, once you let all of that go, what do you see?" For a
moment your mind is blank. But then what appears to you, to
your horror, is something you haven't thought of in years: the
white-haired woman in the mental hospital, coming for you,

on top of you, her vicious face, the moment your life was taken from you, the most alive you've ever felt.

"This is the moment God was with you," says Les. "And if you've lost your way since then, it is not too late to go back to the person you wanted to be, to make a new life for yourself. Join me," he says, "join our church and the work that we do every day, to bring true meaning to the lives around us."

Les Witherspoon's church is in Atlanta. A person would have to be crazy, you think, to drive all that way to sit in a church. And yet already you are moving about the dark house, stuffing a bag full of clothes, going through the golf pro's closet and drawers and cabinets, looking for the money he keeps rolled up here and there, in the tips of his shoes, in the toes of his socks, in the pockets of his golf bags. You move about as if you're a marionette, as if compelled by some higher force. You leave the golf pro snoring in his bed—you are gone before sunrise.

At church you sit up front, and Les Witherspoon takes a special interest in you, as you knew he would. Several times during his sermon he looks directly at you. After services he makes his way over to you. He sees the scars on your neck, reaches out to touch them. "Sister," he tells you, "forgive me, but a miracle is happening here." He closes his eyes, trembles, presses his fingers into your flesh. "On the night God first spoke to me I closed my eyes and what I saw were two white birds in flight against a white sky, just like this, and I've seen them ever since whenever I pray, and what God is telling me now is that you are someone special, you are a gift He is delivering to me." He raises his hand in the air.

One of your more bizarre characteristics is an ability to

mimic, in tone and diction and accent, the speech of other people, and when you open your mouth to speak to the preacher what comes out is a sermon similar to his. *I was led here,* you say, raising your hand and pressing it against his. *It was a higher power that drew me here, that spoke to me, and I didn't even know what I was doing or where I was going, but the force of it led me here to you, and the moment it touched me it lifted me up out of my despair and since then there has been nothing but light.*

"My brothers and sisters!" Les says, addressing the church, "you are witnessing here God's work, God's bringing together of two people and two destinies, and making one!"

You are married within a month. You move into Les's home, which is the home you have always imagined in your dreams. A stately Colonial on a large lot, with a circular drive out front, in which Les parks his long white Cadillac. Inside everything is white—the carpet, the walls, the sofa, the linens. It is a place of such light, such dazzling beauty, that it manages to obliterate all memory of your previous suffering. Suddenly it seems to you that your life has been driving all along toward a happy ending, but you simply failed to see it until now, you simply didn't have faith. The past twenty years have been a terrible detour, but now all of your troubles are gone and you have been delivered, you have been delivered. You develop the habit of fingering the scar on your neck, dreamily. Nothing can touch you now.

Mother, this was your life. Full of turmoil and heartache, desperate striving, bitter failure, triumph, tragedy, redemption. A role any actress would kill for. And indeed it often seemed to me that you were acting. You laughed, you cried, you raged, you trembled, but none of it seemed quite real—all of your emotions seemed rehearsed. Over the years I came to suspect that you weren't really living your life, but making your way through a series of scenes, playing different parts, changing husbands and homes and jobs like costumes. The life around us had the thin, flimsy quality of a stage set, the walls and furniture and props made of the cheapest, lightest materials. We lived a life whose only certainty was that it would change—just when we'd settled in, just when we'd gotten comfortable, the lights would go down and the scene would be cleared away.

For years I thought of myself as your assistant, your understudy, someone standing on the sidelines with a clipboard, some category of employee who existed for the sole purpose of cataloging your every gesture. In your dealings with other people—your family, coworkers, authority figures—you always presented different versions of yourself, and you relied on me to keep everything straight. *What did I tell the landlord?* you'd ask me. *Did I tell him I was sick or did I tell him I got laid off?*

"Neither," I'd say. "You told him me and Malinda were in the hospital."

Oh, you'd say. *Right.* And then, a minute later, *I said that? That was stupid. He could have just stopped by and figured out you were home.*

"I know," I said. "I told you that."

You did?

I nodded.

Well, don't let me do that again.

One of your favorite phrases was, *Take notes.* You weren't the kind of mother who believed in protecting her children from life's difficulties. You talked all the time, and in great detail, about the stupid mistakes that had brought you to your present fate, and you spared no details. *Birth control,* you always told us, long before we had any idea what it was. *Always use birth control.* You'd look at us gravely. *Are you taking notes?* you'd say.

I had been taking notes. All those years, I liked to think that I knew you better than anyone else, better than you knew yourself. I knew when you came home late you'd need a glass of water and two pills by your bedside. I knew when you were about to quit a job, and started circling the classifieds. With men, I knew when you were working up to leaving, and started preparing for another move. In one case, with Bud Francis, I never even completely unpacked my bags.

When you joined Les's church, I assumed that your conversion would last no more than a year or two, that it was just another role you were playing. It wasn't a part I particularly cared for. After your *spiritual rebirth,* as you called it, your voice took on a spooky calm, a lightness that I found unsettling. You had also adopted a preposterous southern accent. *What a beautiful day the Lord has made,* you'd say when I called to talk.

"Would you knock it off?" I said. "It's me. You don't have to pretend around me."

I don't know what you mean, you said. *I'm disappointed in your attitude.*

"Are you fucking kidding me with this accent? You sound like Minnie fucking Pearl!"

I'm sorry you're so angry, you said. *You should really come join the church and learn how to live in God's love.*

When I called to tell you about my search for Malinda—that I'd found her, and she'd slipped away again, right between my fingers—you barely registered surprise or even interest. *I'm sure you'll find her again soon,* you said. *The Lord works in mysterious ways.*

"Well the Lord," I said, "seems to be on a cigarette break."

Mary, you said, *sarcasm is the defense of the weak.*

Mary, you said, *silence is a way of closing God out of your heart.*

I told myself that it was just a phase, that it couldn't possibly last. You'd come out of it soon enough. And when you did, you'd find me.

I went off to graduate school without even telling you where I was going, and for two whole years we didn't speak. The only connection I had left in our hometown was Walter Adams. For years Walter and I had been playing chess by mail, our letters going back and forth every week, the pace so glacially slow that it took us years to finish a game. Along with his moves (he was fond of traps—Lasker, Monticelli) Walter always wrote a line or two about what he was reading and listening to, just a few phrases dashed off. But in the winter of my second year of graduate school Walter sent a long letter about the sorry state of our city. It had changed drastically in the time since I'd left for college—several of its major employers had failed or relocated—and now it seemed that every third house or business was boarded up, abandoned. The schools were a particular problem. The kids in our city were stuck in a failing system. There was a desperate need for good teachers. Walter's son Reggie, whom I'd never gotten to know very well but whom I'd always admired for his cool reserve, had already worked his way up to assistant principal at our old high school, and there was a position for me there, if I wished to take it. "You might find other useful things to do with your life," Walter wrote, "but you will find nothing more useful than this."

And so I moved back to town, partly with the idea of teaching but also because, much to my surprise, I found myself unable to live anywhere else. The towns I'd lived in since leaving home had presented to me landscapes, versions of life, which I acknowledged to be superior in all ways to the life I'd known, and yet those beautiful college towns also struck me as deluded. I lived in them only partly, I walked through them the way one walks in dreams, with a weightless ease one is startled by, but which one also understands, on some deep level, to be false.

My old high school had taken on the feel of a prison. One was obliged to enter through a metal detector, to surrender one's bag for inspection. There were security guards walking the hallways, with fat clubs attached to their belts. The walls were gray, fluorescent tube lighting flickered overhead. Years prior the hallways had been outfitted with corkboards, to display artwork and announcements, but now these were empty. One of the boards had a heading that read COMING EVENTS, but there was nothing underneath it—just dozens of old staples embedded in the cork and the tiny corners of bright paper from old flyers, announcing events long past.

Most of the students at the school were there because they were required by law to be there. If statistics held up, almost half of them would drop out as soon as they were old enough. In the meantime they cut class and forgot their books, they made their test sheets into paper airplanes and launched them at me, they talked during class, listened to headphones, fell asleep. The only way to get them to display the slightest interest in learning was to teach them foul language and insulting sentences they might one day find useful. "Do you want to learn how to tell someone to go screw themselves?" I asked.

"Hell yeah," they said.

"Let's conjugate," I said. "I screw, you screw, he, she, it screws."

"You're tricking us," they said. "You're trying to trick us into learning something."

"We screw," I said, "you plural screw, they screw."

"Just tell us how to say it," they said.

"And the command form would be?" I asked. "Anyone want to guess? To screw yourself? Anyone?"

Reggie had explained to me that, in a school like this, every teacher had to find what he called a "coping mechanism." Each teacher had developed his or her own style, and so long as that style fell short of criminal liability, it was something to be encouraged. Some teachers walked around the classroom with wooden sticks, which they crashed down on a student's desk when they suspected that student wasn't paying attention. One teacher carried a lighter which she called "the flame of knowledge," and which she liked to ignite casually, as she walked between the rows of seats. When she caught someone misbehaving she ignited the flame very close to his ear. "Are you listening to me?" she said.

"The thing is," Reggie said, "when you start something, you have to see it all the way through, or else they know they got you. Don't go changing your coping mechanism halfway through the class, or even halfway through the year. You pick it, you marry it, you stick with it, even if it kills you."

I'd chosen a bad coping mechanism. I'd start a lesson and the class would be under control for the first ten minutes or so. Then the students would grow restless and start talking, mouthing off, and I'd turn off the lights and sit in the dark staring at them blankly. Sometimes when I did this they settled down, but more often they didn't, and they spent the rest of the class talking and chasing each other around the room like three-year-olds.

The only hope I had in the classroom were the immigrants (a large number of kids had moved to our city from India, and a few from Africa) whose Old World manners prevented them from making a mockery of their teachers. They were a quiet, mournful group who—despite being teenagers—looked and dressed and conducted themselves with the soberness of undertakers. Because of the pressure their families put on them, these kids were the only ones who routinely did their homework and remembered to bring their books. They were the only ones to volunteer in class. But their participation was often disheartening. Their lives, the ways they'd suffered, made my life look like a sock hop. Even the most benign subjects—the kinds of things people talk about when they are learning a new language—had a way of turning disastrous.

"Tell me about the house you grew up in," I'd say.

"It wasn't so much of a house as a tent, with additional rooms made from cardboard. It burned down."

"Well, tell me about your family, then."

"My mother is dead," they'd say. "My father is dead also. My uncle brought me here but he works three jobs and I never see him."

I'd shift gears, desperately. "What do you like most about living in the United States?"

"Nothing," they said. "We dislike it here."

"Nothing at all? You don't like even one little thing?"

"We dislike the houses, the way everyone is shut away in small compartments and there is no community. We dislike the way everyone goes around in cars. The loneliness."

"If you had to," I said, "if there were a gun pointed to your head, could you name something you don't mind so much?"

"There are guns?" they said. "We were told there wouldn't be any guns in the schools here."

"Of course not," I said. "I was only using an expression."

"What kind of expression is this?"

"Let's move on," I said. "What do you want to do in the future?"

"Return home," they said. "Leave here and return home."

I spent half of my time worrying I'd be fired, and the other half relaxed in the sad knowledge that I couldn't be let go—the school was understaffed to begin with. I considered calling in sick to work on a regular basis, like all of the other teachers. If you wanted to last at a job like that, they told me, you had to pace yourself, and pacing yourself meant calling in sick to school every thirteen days. We had enough sick and personal days in our contract, they said, to do that, and only a fool would let those days go by unused. "Take the day off," they said. "Take yourself to a movie."

Most days after school I returned to my apartment and collapsed on the couch. Being around other people had always taxed me, and the climate at school was a particular strain. All afternoon I'd drift in and out of sleep. Then the sun would go down and the apartment would grow dark, and I'd get up and make myself something to eat, turn on the television and sit in its glow. Amidst its chatter I'd start preparing for the next day. Every night I told myself that I'd do better the following day—things were bound to turn, I believed—but by February I'd begun having my doubts. When I sat down to correct quizzes they were more often than not left blank, but for desperate little notes at the top. "Dear Ms. Murphy," they said, "I did not study for this 'cuz I got in a wicked bad fight with my boyfriend. Sorry." Or, "My friend was trying to kill himself and I was up all night trying to get him not to do it. Sorry." Or sometimes, "Dear Miz Murphy, I don't feel like doing this test, sorry but sometimes you just gotta say fuck it. Excuse my French." I gave them all zeros, then wondered how many zeroes I could reasonably give out. Would I keep on failing everyone? Could I fail the whole class? At a certain point, wasn't their failure my fault?

Those days I was too much alone. I'd gone on a couple of dates, but they hadn't worked out. Once I went to a Chinese restaurant with a cardigan-wearing graduate student who seemed perfectly normal (he was studying to be a civil engineer) until he revealed that he kept three pet snakes at home and enjoyed feeding them mice. With a dumpling he illustrated the snakes' manner of devouring mice—he opened his mouth wide and inhaled the dumpling right off the table. But he wasn't really doing it justice, he said. To get the full effect, I'd have to see it in person. Did I want to come home with him and feed the snakes, did I want to do it right now?

For a few weeks I dated an art teacher from the elementary school. Each time we met he wore a blue sweatshirt with its hood pulled up and cinched around his face. I couldn't see his hair, his neck, his ears, the shape of his head. It had been snowing when we'd met, and the hood had made sense, but by the third date it had begun to bother me. "What's your hair like?" I asked. And he informed me that he never took off his sweatshirt in front of another person. Ever.

Sometimes in the evenings I watched Les Witherspoon's cable program, *All God's Children*. It was a habit I was ashamed of—something I likened to watching pornography—and each time I did it, I swore I'd never do it again. But I couldn't seem to stop myself. Les was very compelling, very theatrical. He had a habit of raising his fist in the air and throwing his head back in agony or ecstasy, as the case dictated. He liked to describe, at great length, the suffering all around us—after which he named God as the simple and universal solution. "The babies crying with their hungry bellies and no mother to feed them," he cried, "and the children being pushed around by the devil who's taken over their parents, and the teenagers lost to drugs, and pregnancy, and the factory workers hurting after a long day on the job, making their way to a second job, and the elderly folks suffering in their failing bodies, to all of you I say that God is with you, He is with you, lo, He is with you always." I had to admit that Les was appealing. I'd try to tune him out but I couldn't, entirely, so resounding was his grief. He could have played Hamlet in a community theater.

Les's business was the end of the world, and business was good. "It is coming," he always said, "it is coming. And in preparation one must dedicate oneself in mind, body, and spirit to the second coming of the Lord and the end of life as we know it. One must be prepared for the long journey that stands between this life and the next. One must, in particular, invest in one's church, for the church will be what saves you in the end. Our church," Les said, "has bought a hundred acres of land on the outskirts of town, on a high hill, our church is making preparations to break ground for a newer, bigger church, one that will have the capacity to house all of its members through the great trial. This new church is in the works, it is being designed and conceived at this very moment, just as soon as the money is raised we will break ground and believe me, brothers and sisters, will you ever be glad you were smart for once, you took the time to prepare in advance . . . this church will be a fortress . . . the mind can hardly conceive of the planning that's being undertaken . . . the food and water . . . the heaters, coolers, the medicine, the water purification system, the skilled laborers. It is the poor," Les says, "that are hit hardest and fall first in times of trial, and so it is the poor who must take pains now, who must prepare, and what better corner of the world than this one, this one right here, what better time than now . . ."

After Les's sermon you hosted a short segment entitled "Margaret's Moment." From the church's day care center, you interviewed a small child about the changes the church had brought to his life.

This is Timmy, you said in your new southern drawl. *And he's four years old. Say hello, Timmy.*

And Timmy would wave shyly.

Can you tell people about what you used to do during the day, before you came to school with us?

"Watch TV," said Timmy.

And was there someone to take care of you, if you needed something?

"No," he said. "My mom had to work."

So you were alone all day? you said.

Timmy nodded.

Then you'd turn to the camera. *Now, through our ministries, Timmy receives the loving care that all of God's children deserve. Education, nutrition, and good old-fashioned TLC.* You encouraged viewers to send money, to volunteer, to pray for the children. You were made for the camera—yours was the kind of perfect beauty that made people believe in God's goodness. People called in record numbers to support "Margaret's Moment" and the church made almost twice as much as it had before. Your lifelong dream of being on screen had finally been fulfilled. You had found your calling.

When people called to donate you spoke to them on the air. They always told you how beautiful you were, what an inspiration, how you'd changed their outlook on life. You were modest in your replies. *Oh, it's not me,* you said. *It's just the good Lord working through me.*

Sometimes I amused myself by playing out little scenes in my mind. I imagined calling in to pledge a large sum, and being put on the air. "Why hello, Margaret," I'd say. And your brow would wrinkle, a crack would form in your beatific demeanor. "I'm just calling to support your work with children," I'd say. "It's nice to see someone care so selflessly for children. It is. I've never seen anything like it in my life."

You sound familiar, you'd say. *Are you a church member? Do I know you?*

"No," I'd say. "We've never met."

The longer we went without speaking, the stranger you appeared to me. At times, you didn't seem like my mother at all. At times it was as if the real and the imaginary had been crossed—it seemed to me that Margaret Witherspoon, the southern philanthropist, was and always had been the real you. The mother I'd known—the life we'd lived together with Malinda— had begun to seem like something imagined, some television program I'd grown up watching, long since canceled.

What a surprise it was, then, when the next summer Malinda showed up at my door holding a baby on her hip. "Can I crash here?" she said casually. As if she hadn't been missing for years, as if appearing out of nowhere with a baby was an everyday event. I stood in the doorway, stunned, looking back and forth between Malinda and the child. Malinda had grown her hair out, and it was black again—she looked like her old self. The child she held—a boy in overalls with nothing beneath them—was fat, with an enormous round face and big brown eyes. His curly hair stood out from his head as if he'd been shocked. In his arms he clutched a stuffed dog with a missing ear.

"Who's this?" I said.

"This is Michael."

I stood staring at him. In all the time I'd imagined Malinda— where she was, what she was doing—I had never once imagined her with a child. "Here," she said, handing him to me. "You have a nephew. Congratulations."

I had never held a baby before so I held him away from me, at eye level. We stared at each other. "He's not a bomb," Malinda said. I held him against me and looked at his face, searching for traces of anyone in our family. But he looked nothing like us. He looked robust, hearty, tranquil—something like Buddha. He didn't look like the kind of person who would want anything to do with us.

"Where's his father?" I asked.

"OD'd," she said, like it was the most common of fates. She brushed past me and started walking all around the apartment. She opened every door, every drawer, every cupboard. She opened the refrigerator and stood inspecting it. "Is this it?" she said. "This is your whole place? Is this all you got?"

"I wasn't expecting company," I said. I was still staring at Michael, and he was still staring at me. Neither one of us seemed quite convinced of the other's existence.

"God, what a shithole," she said. She walked back into the living room and sat on the couch. "How can you live in a shithole like this?"

"It's not so bad," I said. "For one person."

"Well it's gonna get worse," she said. "I need a place to stay for a while."

In the following days I tried to find out where Malinda had been, but she was vague. "I just had to get out of this fucking city for a while," she said. "You know?" It seemed that she had no sense of how long she'd been gone. When I asked her what she was doing now, about her plans for the future, she was evasive.

"I gotta get some stuff figured out," she said. "I gotta get cleaned up. I can't keep doing what I'm doing. I need a real job, more of a career-type thing. Maybe massage school. Or hairdressing."

"That's good," I'd say. "That's a good idea."

"Fuck you," she said, "You're always mocking me."

"I wasn't mocking you!" I said.

Malinda spent much of her time on the phone. She was trying to settle an argument she'd had with a boyfriend, someone named Zeke who lived in upstate New York. They were fighting about child services, and which of Zeke's friends or relatives might or might not have called the New York State authorities to report Malinda for neglect. "I make one little mistake," she kept saying, "one tiny little fucking mistake, and I've got a social worker up my ass." She kept calling Zeke and fighting, then hanging up, then calling him back not a minute later. Then he'd hang up on her, and she'd announce that she didn't need Zeke anymore, she was going to start a new life for herself. Until she called him again.

It took Malinda two days to mention you, during which we both pretended that the subject had merely slipped our minds. But finally, after Michael had gone to sleep, she asked how you were. "Don't tell me she's still married to that preacher," she said.

"I think this is her longest marriage yet," I said. "Sometime you can see her on television, raising money for the church. She's always got all these kids around her. It's weird."

"That bitch," she said, "never even met her own grandson."

"To be fair," I said, "she doesn't know she has a grandson."

"Well she should," Malinda said. "If she ever tried to find me she'd know." She sniffed sharply, her eyes wet.

Malinda had always been erratic, moody, unreliable. But she was far worse now. She couldn't keep a conversation going and had a number of nervous tics that grew worse as the day went on. She bit her fingernails, the inside of her mouth. She paced the room, drummed her fingers against the table. She smoked constantly. Sometimes she rocked herself as she sat in her chair. "I gotta get out of here," she said, whenever we got a conversation started. "Can you watch Michael for a few minutes? I'll be right back." She'd be gone for hours.

I watched Michael while she was gone. He was almost two years old, and went about doing the kinds of things that two-year-olds do, which was to say that he was always making a mess. He pulled drawers out of the dresser and emptied them, flinging their contents across the room, he placed his dog inside the drawer and draped a blanket across it. He made leashes out of belts and strings and tied his dog to chair legs, he scribbled on paper with crayon, he sat tearing pages out of books, tearing them down to confetti.

I had always been uncomfortable around kids. When I was with them I felt vaguely nervous, vaguely threatened, like I did when I considered that there were nuclear weapons in the world. But gradually I came to appreciate Michael's company. We went on long walks around the city, during which I told him stories about our family. "Your mother and I used to live there," I'd say, pointing to an apartment building. "Your grandmother, that is, your mother's mother, liked to move around a lot. We lived in all kinds of different places. When we lived here, our uncle lived with us for a while," I said. "Do you know what an uncle is? He lived with us for a while, and he took care of me and your mom sometimes. He was our favorite person for a long time. And so I think it's safe to say," I told him, "that you're named after him. You're his namesake, they call it. You look nothing like him, of course. But that doesn't matter. You might be like him in other ways. You might have his voice, for instance. He really liked music," I said. "Do you like music?"

I wasn't sure if Michael understood anything I said. When I asked him a question, he simply turned his face to me with a curious look. I remembered the time I'd spent with Uncle Mike, listening to his stories, looking up at him, giving him the same look. I began to think that Michael and I were suited to one another.

"Maybe you're quiet like me," I said. "Normally I don't talk so much."

One night, when she had been in town for two weeks, Malinda woke screaming and shaking, her cries so desperate and loud they woke up everyone in my apartment building. With the help of two of my neighbors I had to carry her, raging, to the car. We had to check her into the hospital, into detox.

While Malinda was in rehab I called to tell you that I'd found her. You weren't home, and I had to leave a message with your housekeeper. "Tell her her daughter called," I said.

The housekeeper was confused. "What's that now?" she said.

"Her daughter. Mary. Tell her I called."

"Oh," she said. She was silent for a moment. "Oh, I'm sorry. I wasn't aware Miss Margaret had a daughter."

You called back that evening. "Surprise," I told you. "You have a grandchild. It's a boy. His name's Michael."

I know, you said. *The good Lord told me I did. He told me in a dream.*

"He's Malinda's," I said, "not mine. I found her. Or she found me."

I know, you said. *I knew God would bring her back.*

"Well maybe you should come up and see them," I said. "I think Malinda would really like to see you. She's not doing so well."

Maybe you all should come here, you said. *It's better here, you belong here with the church, you belong here with our family.*

"I have a job here," I said. "I can't just pick up and leave."

You come here, you said. *I have so many responsibilities here, I can't get away, you come here.*

A vein started throbbing in my left temple. There was a long silence.

Can you hear me? you said. *Hello?*

"Yes," I said. "Can you hear me?"

Yes.

"Because I want to tell you something," I said. "It's important." I was speaking through clenched teeth.

Go ahead, darling, you said. *I can hear you loud and clear.*

"Go fuck yourself," I said. I hung up. I didn't think I would ever speak to you again.

When Malinda came back, she was shaky and distant, ashen, like someone whose brain had been damaged by shock therapy.

It took her an hour to eat a bowl of cereal, she'd sit staring at it until the cereal decomposed and the milk turned warm. She slept much of the time, watched television. Eventually she started going out, to AA meetings, or to look for a job, but she started coming home later and later, after Michael was asleep. One night she came home smelling like a bar, and we fought bitterly. "You can't do this," I said. "You have a kid. You need to take better care of him."

"Gimme a break," she said. "Can't I have any fun? You want everyone to end up like you? What do you want from me?"

"I want you to clean up. Take care of Michael," I said. I tried to keep my voice down. He was asleep in the next room. "I want you to do a better job. The school year's coming, and I won't be around to help as much."

"I'm doing the best I can!" she said. She sat on the floor and cried, which had always been her strategy in arguments. "I didn't ask for this!" she said. "I didn't ask to inherit this."

I thought of our father, who had made drunken appearances on our doorstep, once or twice a year throughout our childhood. As we grew older I eventually came to liken his visits to the airing of Christmas specials, or the Thanksgiving Day parade, in that the thrill of his arrival was soon outweighed by the fact that it wasn't as much fun as I'd remembered, what had once struck me as magical was now very plainly a cheap illusion. Eventually, as he stood shaking before us, I could only regard him with embarrassment, with pity.

"You think you're so great?" Malinda said. "You think you're better than me? You just got lucky."

Given our family's history, it wasn't hard to guess what would happen next. One day, while I took Michael out for ice cream, Malinda left town, leaving behind nothing but a short note. *Can you watch Michael for a couple days?* I knew Malinda. I knew it wasn't going to be a couple of days.

In fact it was two years before she returned—sober, for the time being—to see Michael. By then he didn't remember her ("That lady," he said, "has blue hair"), and I had long since stopped seeing myself as a person burdened with the care of someone else's kid—I had come to love him, and had put through the papers to adopt him. Malinda stayed with us for a while, crying almost constantly. Whenever Michael said or did something her eyes welled with tears. He was still at an age when things were new to him—every day he encountered something he'd never seen before—and it was delightful to watch someone respond to the world, its sights and its sounds, as if it were new. I was afraid that Malinda would want him back. But in the end she had only wanted to see him, to make sure that he was okay. "I just can't do it," she told me one night. "I'm sorry, but I just can't do it. I know it's a lot to ask, but you're the best person I could think of, and I just can't fucking do it."

The years went by. Michael grew into a boy. He was quiet and thoughtful, reserved, and I sometimes worried that he was damaged—that the turmoil of his earlier life had inclined him toward fear and melancholy. For a while he was intrigued by an imaginary character called Invisible Mailman. Whenever something went missing in the house, whenever something broke, whenever a room was dark and Michael didn't want to enter it, he blamed it on Invisible Mailman. I didn't really know how to be a mother—I was just making it up as I went along—and I worried about what kind of job I was doing. Michael often stared out the car window in a mournful way, and in moments like this I'd become convinced that there was something wrong with him, that I was messing him up. But whenever I asked him what he was thinking, it was something harmless. "I was imagining if a fox was running next to our car, how fast he would have to run to keep up with us."

"I think I see him," I said. "I think I just saw the tip of his tail."

My days were long, and tiring, and I never felt quite sure of myself. I wondered whether Michael was eating enough, making friends at school, developing the right skills. But then again there were moments of great joy and lightness. Michael would do something funny, he'd imitate something he'd seen on television ("Hey, baby," he said, cocking his head and winking, after he'd seen a clip of Elvis), and we'd laugh, we'd fall over laughing, and I'd know, if only briefly, that everything was going to be okay. Everything was working out just fine.

Even my teaching had improved. After Malinda had left the first time I'd fallen into a dark, devastated mood that even my students—who had trouble seeing me as a human being, with problems and feelings of my own—couldn't help but notice.

"What's wrong with you?" they'd said. Right in the middle of class.

"What may or may not be wrong with me," I said, "is none of your business."

"*Oooooooooooh,*" they said, "Miss Murphy's in a bad mood!"

One student, a skinny redheaded kid who was always cracking jokes, took the brunt of it.

"Give me *être*," I said to him. "In the future tense."

"I don't feel like it, Mary." He'd been calling me Mary all year.

"It's Ms. Murphy," I said. "To be. In the future tense. Let's hear it."

"I'm not feeling it today, Mary," he said. He always won himself a little round of laughter whenever he defied me. "How come I gotta conjugate a verb?"

"It's Ms. Murphy," I said. "And you do it because you can. To be."

"How about NOT to be?" he said, laughing at his own little joke. "Mary."

Before I knew it I had stormed over to his desk and turned it over. His books and papers went flying and he sat, stunned, with his hands held in the air. For a long moment the room was absolutely silent.

"It's cool," he said, his voice high. "It's cool, Ms. Murphy."

To my surprise the students were better after that. They started conjugating verbs aloud, they started turning in their homework. I changed my coping mechanism from benign neglect to intermittent bursts of petulance—I threw my book across the room, I evicted them from class. What they responded to, as it turned out, wasn't some idea of bettering themselves for the future, some notion of the benefits they might gain from learning a language. What they responded to—what we all responded to, I realized—was the idea that someone was watching them, the idea that someone, somewhere, cared one way or another what they did, or failed to do. Over the years I developed a reputation. "Don't take French," I heard one student tell another in the hallway, "unless you're ready to work. Miss Murphy makes everybody work, every damn day, no exceptions. She's a bitch. But she gives a shit."

On Sunday evenings I took Michael over to Walter's. We ate a meal together, then listened to music, played cards. Walter taught Michael to play checkers. And at the end of the evening Michael would watch as Walter and I played a game of chess. When there were just a few pieces left on the board Walter would ask about you, whether I'd settled my affairs with you. "Family's important, you know," he said. "It's best to keep up with family."

"I know," I told him. "I have a family." Every time I said this, I'd realize with surprise that it was true.

The rest of our evening's conversation, though it supposedly centered around the game in front of us, would take on a painfully obvious symbolic quality. "Let's see something," Walter said. "Let's see you move first, for once."

"Oh, I'm working up a plan," I'd say.

"I'm waiting."

"You're never going to see it coming, I'm just wearing you down."

"I'm about worn out," he said, "waiting for you to do something."

"You're weakening," I said. "You're falling into my trap."

Then he'd capture one of my pieces, knocking it over with his own. "Too late," he'd say.

For the most part I gave very little thought to you, no more than I gave to a nagging unfinished errand, like an overdue library book. You crossed my mind occasionally. Every few months, flipping through channels after Michael fell asleep, I watched Les Witherspoon. Sometimes I stayed through to the end, to see you in "Margaret's Moment." And sometimes I didn't.

It was on a summer night, during one of Les Witherspoon's sermons, that I first heard you were ill. Les was talking in a vague way about the devil, using the language of espionage— he spoke of infiltration, subterfuge, betrayal. Finally he came to the point: that the devil himself had found his way into his home, that he had chosen as his victim the thing Les treasured most. "The devil," he said, "is coming after me, because he knows I'm his enemy, he knows I'm working against him. And so he figures he'll come after me in the worst way he can—he'll come after my beautiful wife." I'd been in a trance, half listening, but at this my head snapped up.

"As many of you know," Les said, "our beautiful Margaret has fallen ill with cancer. The devil has seen fit to steal himself away in her body, to spread his cancer through her, but I tell you as sure as I'm standing here he won't get away with it, we won't let him, no we won't."

The next morning I woke Michael early and put him in the car. I hadn't talked much about you, or even Malinda, and he was full of questions. Why didn't he know about you? Why didn't you live where we lived?

"She married someone who lives somewhere else," I said.

Well, why didn't you come to where we live?

"I don't know," I said.

Why didn't we live there, with you?

"I don't know."

What kind of mother were you? he asked. What kind of mother were you?

Somewhere around Virginia I considered that I might be making a fool of myself—cancer meant a lot of things, and yours might be of the minor sort. But when I finally pulled up to the house, just before midnight, I saw that all the lights were on, and there were several cars parked in the driveway. A bad sign, I thought. I rang the doorbell, whose chime was so resounding that it could be not only heard, but felt, from outside. A woman answered the door and I had to explain to her who I was. "I'm Margaret's daughter," I said.

"What now?" she said.

"Margaret Witherspoon, I'm her daughter."

"Oh!" she said. Her brow wrinkled. "Oh! Excuse me!"

The woman led me through the house, and Michael tagged along. There were groups of people milling around the living room and kitchen. I began to worry that you had died—that these people had gathered together for your funeral. But then the woman led me into a large room, where you were lying with Les on an enormous bed, watching *Leave It to Beaver.* He had his arm around you, and his fingers played in your hair.

"Les," the woman said, "someone here says she's Margaret's daughter."

You turned and saw me. *Hi, baby,* you said very casually, as if we'd spoken just moments before, as if you'd been expecting me. And in fact you had been. *We knew you were coming. Les and I prayed for it and we knew you'd come any day now, we could feel it.*

Les got up and spread his arms. "Thank the good Lord you're home," he said. "We just knew you were coming home, we just knew it." He walked toward me and enclosed me in a hug so crushing I couldn't breathe. He smelled strongly of pine, a woodsy cologne. "The devil," he said, still holding me tight, "is trying to make his way into this house, what we're doing is filling it up with people, with warriors, we're filling it up with God's love, we've got a constant vigil going here, the lights are always on, people are staying up and keeping watch, we're not going to let him in. You're going to be a part of it, a crucial part of it. Your mother's own flesh and blood. We've been praying for your arrival, and now that you're here, we've got the advantage, we've got the upper hand, the devil can't possibly stay in this house with you here." One of Les's habits, I realized, was to treat complete strangers as if he had known them all their lives, as if he'd been waiting for them to return to him, as if he'd long been missing their company.

I watched you from the stifling confines of Les's embrace. You nodded your head whenever he spoke. You smiled peacefully, knowingly. I had never seen you in such harmony with anyone. Finally Les let go of me and led me over to the bed. I sat beside you. You were still beautiful—you were always beautiful—but it was clear that you were very sick. Your cheeks were sunken, and your skin had a grayish cast to it. And there was something about your eyes I'd seen before only in the dying—a wistful quality, as if you were looking back on the present moment from a great distance. You placed your hand on mine. "I knew you'd see the light," you said. "I knew you'd come join us in our trial."

"You're home now," Les said. "You're finally home."

Then you noticed Michael, who had been lurking in the doorway. He was a reserved boy and it was his custom to stand apart from people, watching them, until someone spoke to him. When you saw him you flinched. For the briefest flash you fell out of character. A pained, desperate look came across your face, and your eyes welled with tears. But then you recovered. *Well hello there, darling,* you said. *I've been waiting a long time to meet you. Welcome home.*

I wasn't at all at home in that house, but for the next month I more or less moved in, wandering about like an explorer who had stumbled upon a new civilization. There were always a great many people there, their cars lining the driveway and spilling out into the street. They milled around, conducting the business of the church, which seemed more like a corporation, or a political campaign, than a spiritual undertaking. You and Les had set up a kind of headquarters in the bedroom, and all day long people came in and out with questions and requests. There were recordings that Les had to review and approve, sermons and speeches to be prepared, bills to be paid, money to be invested, study groups and camps to be coordinated, staffing and promotion of the day care center. Most of the time Les waved these questions away, saying that they weren't important, but you insisted he deal with them. *The church,* you said, *is more important than either one of us.* For years I had wondered how you could have changed so entirely, how you could have forgotten your old life so completely, but with all the commotion going on around you, I understood.

The motto of Les's team was "Make it happen." People were always shouting it to one another—they answered their phones this way. Les and his followers seemed to be under the impression that they could make you well, that your cancer was some kind of trial whose outcome was under their control, that it was simply a matter of faith. Now and then, when an idea struck him, Les would clap his hands together and rub them. "Here's what we're going to do," he'd say. "We're gonna find someone who knows something about herbs. Someone who's lived in the rainforest. A medicine man." Sometime prior to my arrival, Les had declared that talking about your illness only gave it strength, and so people were forbidden to speak of it. The only people who mentioned your pending death were your doctors, who spoke of it in vague terms. "With cases like this," they said, "it can take weeks, sometimes months, for the cancer to overtake the body."

"With the exception of miracles," Les would say.

"Of course, of course!" the doctors would say, flustered. "Miracles."

You had a full-time nurse named Quiz. She was a short, squat woman with the rasping voice of a lifelong smoker. She wore the same thing every day—maroon-colored scrubs and white tennis shoes—and she gave off an air of no-nonsense practicality. Her attitude toward you was pitiless and pragmatic. She moved around constantly. She changed your sheets, did your laundry, washed your hair, vacuumed your room, monitored your vitals and distributed your medications, bathed you, massaged your legs. When I offered to help with your care, Quiz wouldn't hear of it. "I'm paid till five," she said, "and that's how long I work." She hardly ever took the breaks she was entitled to. For her meals she liked bologna sandwiches with mustard on white bread, which she could make in under a minute, and eat in just a little more. "No fuss, no muss," she said. She drank diet soda all day straight out of aluminum cans, and when she was finished she crushed them in her hand as though they'd done her a personal injury. Every two hours she stepped outside on the front porch for a cigarette, which she smoked as if she were in some kind of race.

It was during one of these cigarette breaks that I learned about the nature and history of your cancer—no one else in the house would speak of it. Not long ago, Quiz said, you had suspected you were pregnant—your womanly cycles, as she called them, had stopped, and your stomach was swollen. But you'd taken a test and it had come up negative. For a few months, busy with work, you did nothing. Weight gain, you thought. Menopause. But then you grew tired, and you were overtaken with sharp pains. When the doctors cut you open, they saw that the cancer was everywhere, and they simply closed you back up. The only care that your doctors could recommend was palliative. "Which is me," Quiz said, draining a Tab. "Twenty years I've been doing this. The same thing every time. But it never gets any easier."

"How long does she have left?" I asked her.

"Week," she said. "Ten days. It's hard to tell."

I asked you why you hadn't called Nana and Pop, who had retired to Florida and were only a short drive away, and you said it was because you weren't dying—that God was merely putting you through a trial. So I called them myself, and they drove up to see you. They visited you every day but didn't stay long. They were always wearing the same thing (Pop in his bus driver's jacket and Nana in her Senior Ladies Bowling League windbreaker, with its clever slogan across the back: "Dolls with Balls") and as with other people whose clothes never changed— waiters, soldiers—they seemed less like people than functionaries, people fulfilling a duty. Nana had drunk herself nearly into a stupor. All she could do was press your hand and give you a sad half-smile. Pop simply patted your shoulder and said, "You look good today. You look good." Theirs was an uncommunicative generation. Pop had been held for five months as a prisoner of war in a German camp and had been starved to the brink of death, but he'd never once spoken about it. And so your premature death wasn't about to start him talking. "Well," Pop said after twenty minutes, "we don't want to wear you out."

They declined to stay in the house, and continued to live in their mobile home, parked outside on the street. In the evenings they invited me and Michael into their miniature world, where the beds and tables folded down from the walls. They drank highballs and watched game shows—*Wheel of Fortune, Jeopardy!* Each of them had developed a tremor that caused their heads to nod in perpetual agreement with everything. They were in their eighties now, and their lives had come to this, this tiny coffin-shaped pocket of the world.

What a family. Whatever instinct it was that brought normal families together, that bound them to one another, we lacked entirely. We only came together in times of crisis, and even then we couldn't get it right. We didn't even know where Malinda was, and she didn't know you were dying. She was out there somewhere, probably alone, probably struggling. You hardly mentioned her, except to say that you knew she was safe, that God was looking after her. *Everything's going to be just fine,* you kept saying. You still spoke of being saved, of the miracle that would be visited upon you. All you had to do, you said, was wait for it, all you had to do was believe. I wanted to shake you. Your faith seemed to me like a way of letting go of whatever brutalities you didn't wish to think about. I wanted a glimpse of the mother I'd always known—savvy, sarcastic, brutal—instead of the regal, beatific creature you'd become since joining the church. The ways in which we'd lived, and failed each other—I wanted to face them. But you only faced me, as you faced everything those days, with a calm, vacuous smile.

In the last days you grew weaker, you had trouble breathing. The cancer had spread to your spine and even the smallest movement was painful. Your doctor ordered a morphine drip. You and Les stopped talking as if you were going to survive— you talked instead of meeting in the hereafter, of God's plan, which was mysterious at the moment but which you had no choice but to believe in.

You slept much of the time. When you woke it was always from a vivid dream, a memory from your life which you felt compelled to relate. You believed that certain long-lost memories were returning to you for a reason, that God was speaking to you.

On one of your last lucid days you told me a story about myself I'd never heard before. *You were born on a spring day,* you said. *It was sunny and warm, I went to the hospital in a sundress, two days later when it's time to take you home there's a snowstorm, and Pop has to put chains on the tires. Nana and Pop are in the front seat with Malinda, I'm in the back holding you, we're making our way home, the car's sliding around. We're almost home, we're stopped at a red light, and suddenly the back door of the car opens and some lunatic gets in—he's escaped from the mental hospital in his pajamas, you can tell right away his mind isn't right. His feet are wrapped in white trash bags. He has this long, ugly face, he's missing his front teeth, his hair is all over the place.*

And the crazy man says he wants to go to New York, he needs to get back there to finish a painting, he has a paying client waiting for it, millions of dollars. He starts telling us all about this conspiracy against him, these demons underground are trying to suck his talent out through his feet, the hospital is run by them and they're trying to trap him and make him powerless, they took away his pencils and paper and the only way he could draw was to scratch on the walls with his nails. He says he's the most talented artist in the world. Pop, he just turns around and acts perfectly normal. I guess he was used to this kind of thing from driving a bus all those years. "We'll get you to New York right away," he says. We drive around for a while and I'm holding on to you for dear life. Then Pop pulls over in the parking lot of a grocery store and says, "Here we are, New York City." And the crazy man looks out the window and nods. Before he gets out he leans over and takes a long look at you. He takes his finger—this skinny finger with a long, dirty fingernail—and he strokes your forehead with it, back and forth, back and forth, and I start crying, I thought he was going to take you, or hurt you. He could have hurt you very easily. But he didn't. He just got out of the car and shut the door. He waved to us as we pulled away. I can still see him standing there in his pajamas, in the snow.

These were the kinds of things that happened, you said, when you grew up across the street from a mental hospital. It wasn't that unusual. In the old days, they used to let the patients out on weekend furloughs, and they'd walk the streets all day. Sometimes the doorbell would ring and one of them would be standing there with a broom, asking if they could sweep the steps or the driveway. It was just a part of life. What was unusual, you said, wasn't the episode itself, but the ways in which it now reminded you of your own misfortune with the crazy lady. *I see now that he put a mark on you, the same way a mark was put on me. I used to think it was a curse,* you said. *But now I know it means something good. God's trying to give me comfort about you. He wants me to know that our souls are joined, we'll always be together.*

The last coherent thing you ever said had to do with time. You woke one morning and said that time was nothing like we thought it was. *There's no past,* you said, *and no future. Everything's happening all at once, it's like everybody's life is this hallway with a million rooms, white rooms, and in every room something is happening, it's all happening at once.* You said that the past felt very distant to us, but this wasn't really the case. We were young and old at the same time, all the scenes of our lives were unfolding all around us in a sort of perpetual present. If we looked carefully—if we really looked—we could see the past and the future, all around us. If we tried, we could feel it.

When we die, you said, *it's not really the end, because all the moments you ever lived you just keep on living. And so we'll never be apart.*

Whenever you spoke of these visions Les closed his eyes, he took your hand in his and raised it in the air, he trembled. "Dear God," he said, "thank you for giving us your wisdom. Thank you for bringing us peace." Tears ran down his face. I sat staring at him, at you. How certain you both were in your faith. How easy it was for you to believe. Everything made sense to you. Every trial had its purpose, every mistake was redeemed, every wound was justified.

I wanted to believe, too. I wanted to reconcile with you in some way. But I was too distant from you. In raising Michael I'd come to believe that what joined two people wasn't blood, or fate, or signals granted from on high—what joined people together were the small actions they performed for each other each day. I made Michael breakfast, I took him to school, I picked him up and took him to the park, we had dinner together, did his homework, played a game, I read him a story and put him to bed. What joined two people together wasn't always exciting. The cooking, the cleaning, the laundry, the maintenance of the home and car, all the mundane things you never wanted to be bothered with—this, I believed, was what bound people together. At the end I gave you my hand, I nodded as if I agreed, because this was what people did when they loved each other. But as far as our souls were concerned—whether they were joined together for all eternity—I couldn't quite feel it.

Still, I missed you when you were gone. After you died I thought about you more than I ever had before. I spent long hours conjuring you, trying to remember everything that had ever happened between us—every gesture, every word, every color and shape and texture and sound and scent. I wrote down every scene that came to mind. As if by doing so I could bring you back to life. If what you said was true, then the dead were still with us, the dead weren't really gone. Every moment that had ever passed between us was still alive in rooms all around me, and if I tried hard enough, I could break into them. I supposed that, sitting there putting words on a page, this was what I was trying to do. I thought of Uncle Mike, of the friends I'd known and lost, I thought of you. Somewhere unseen, but very close, you were young again, and I was newly born. You sat holding me in the backseat of Pop's car, the snow fell, the tires slipped on the road, a door opened and a stranger got in, he rode with us for a time, he leaned toward us, he extended his finger and moved to touch my forehead, you held me tight, there was no distance between us, nothing had gone wrong yet, we hadn't yet lost each other. Even now the stranger was touching his finger to my forehead, he was moving it back and forth, he was leaving his mark, his blessing, and if I believed, if I only believed, I could feel it, I could be with you again, I could almost feel it.

Acknowledgments

I am grateful to the following people for their friendship: Grace Patenaude (your loveliness increases . . .), Bart Patenaude, John and Doreen Hodgen, Janice and John Lucena, Lillian St. Onge, Michael Holko, Jenni Frangos, Marly Swick, Michelle Boisseau, Kim Palmer, Leslie Koffler, Clancy and Rebecca Martin, Christine Sneed, Aisha Ginwalla, John Hildebidle, Tony Ardizzone, and Jenny Greene.

I would also like to thank the people who encouraged this book in its early stages: Jill Meyers and Stacey Swann at *American Short Fiction*, Jeanne Leiby at *The Southern Review*, Kit Ward, and all at W. W. Norton & Company, especially my editor, Amy Cherry, Denise Scarfi, and the incomparable Carol Houck Smith.